Kelli Hawkins writes novels for adults and children as well as reports for a private investigator. Over the years she's travelled whenever possible and worked all kinds of jobs: she's been a political journalist, a graphic designer, a mystery shopper – even a staple remover. Her debut novel, *Other People's Houses*, was a top 10 bestseller.

Also by Kelli Hawkins

Other People's Houses
All She Wants
Apartment 303

KELLI HAWKINS

THE MILLER WOMEN

HarperCollins*Publishers*

HarperCollins*Publishers*
Australia • Brazil • Canada • France • Germany • Holland • India
Italy • Japan • Mexico • New Zealand • Poland • Spain • Sweden
Switzerland • United Kingdom • United States of America

HarperCollins acknowledges the Traditional Custodians
of the lands upon which we live and work, and pays respect
to Elders past and present.

First published on Gadigal Country in Australia in 2024
by HarperCollins*Publishers* Australia Pty Limited
ABN 36 009 913 517
harpercollins.com.au

A catalogue record for this book is available from the National Library of Australia

ISBN 978 1 4607 6334 6 (paperback)
ISBN 978 1 4607 1578 9 (ebook)
ISBN 978 1 4607 3712 5 (audiobook)

Cover design by Louisa Maggio, HarperCollins Design Studio
Cover images © Magdalena Russocka / Trevillion Images
Author photograph by Jennifer Blau
Typeset in Bembo Std by Kirby Jones
Printed and bound in Australia by McPherson's Printing Group

MIX
Paper from
responsible sources
FSC
www.fsc.org   FSC® C001695

To my mother and my daughter,
neither of whom are murderers.

Everything was black and white.

The sky above an inky, never-ending deep black; billions of stars obscured by clouds like dusty smudges on a chalkboard.

The snow under her bare feet so white, glittering like crushed diamonds. Falling snowflakes dissolving the instant they touched the heat of her skin.

I am white-hot, she thought. Ice and fire.

Snow blew into her eyes. She heard the thump-thump of a dance tune. Everything else was silent; muffled by snow.

Ahead, the man stood, his back to her. Oblivious.

The weight of the pocketknife in her hand was satisfying; the blade flicked open, ready.

She stepped forward.

PART I

AFTER

NICOLA

I hitch the shopping basket to a more comfortable position on my forearm, searching the shelves for the foreign, and hence impossible to find, biscuits Abby insists are necessary for the cheesecake she plans to make this evening.

There!

I reach up and grab several packets and drop them into my basket, striding off as fast as I'm able given the supermarket is busy with other unorganised, after-work shoppers exactly like me.

Towards the end of the aisle, an elderly man squints at the ingredient list on a packet of choc-chip biscuits. His trolley blocks the way, so I hover, fighting the urge to tell him to just get the biscuits. Surely there is some sort of rule that says once you hit eighty you can give up calorie-counting. I shuffle into his line of sight and he jerks around, seemingly stunned to find another person in the supermarket.

'Sorry, love,' he says with a confused smile. 'My wife told me to get double choc-chip biscuits, but I'm buggered if I know what that means. These ones?' He holds the packet towards me.

My expression softens. 'You want these ones.' I reach over and pluck a different packet from the shelf.

'Oh, I see,' he says, examining the picture. I shelve the others as he nods, looking relieved. 'Thank you, dear. She'll enjoy one of these with a cuppa tonight.' He moves his trolley to one side, and I find my mood buoyed by the five-second encounter.

I examine the shopping list on my phone as I reach the end of the aisle. *Cream cheese.* I'm looking down when a male voice calls out – a surprised 'Ah!' – and I slam face-first into a brick wall. Not an actual brick wall as it turns out, just a man, shaped like one.

A firm hand grasps my bicep and I stay upright, but there's the sound of plastic crackling as something hits the floor.

'Nic?'

I steady myself and look more closely at the brick wall. 'Hudson! Fancy running into you here!' I smile. 'And I mean *literally* running into you.'

Hudson grins, then bends over and picks up a packet of pasta. His other hand holds the biggest tin of tuna I've ever seen.

'Sorry,' I say, 'I wasn't watching where I was going.'

'No shit.' He gestures to my gym clothes. 'You been working out without me?'

Hudson is my oldest friend. We went to school together, back when he was a skinny closet gay and I was a nerdy book lover – a far cry from the gym junkies we are now.

'Tonight's my boxing class. Women only, remember? I told you about it.' I've been training more often lately. I always do when I'm stressed.

'Oh, right. Girls only.' He makes a face. 'You should come box with me.'

'No thanks, you'd take my head off.'

Hudson moves out of the way for a woman who purposefully bumped him with her trolley from behind. She gives me a snooty look as she heads past me up the aisle. I know her. Her son is in Abby's year, and we went to school together. Though together is pushing it, we were hardly in the same universe back then.

'Is that Stephanie Lowe?' Hudson whispers, and I shush him – his deep voice is much louder than he realises.

Stephanie is in workout gear too. But whereas mine is sweat-stained, hers is matching pastel lululemon. Bone dry. Her high ponytail swings as perfectly as it did twenty years ago.

She glances back our way then stops in front of the health food section, which is – rather oddly – opposite the biscuits.

'Stephanie Sutton now,' I whisper back. 'She married Richard Sutton, the accountant.'

Hudson grunts.

Stephanie plucks a jar from the shelf, frowning at it, though her lack of wrinkles suggests she's started making the more than three-hour trip to one of the cosmetic clinics in Byron Bay.

I turn back to Hudson. 'So, are you planning on having a little bit of pasta with your tuna tonight?'

'Yeah, I'm making a tuna bake. Jeff's request.'

'He's not sick of your fancy-schmancy food, is he?' I ask in mock horror.

'No, no, nothing like that. I'm just a very supportive boyfriend.'

'I must be a supportive mother.' I hold my basket towards him. 'Sushi, Abby's favourite. And assorted baking goods. She's making a cheesecake tonight. You know how she gets.' I roll my eyes and Hudson's expression tightens.

'She's heard what happened then? It's really thrown Jeff for six.'

'Heard what?' My heart stops beating for a moment, then I realise he can't be talking about my problem – he doesn't know about it. No one does. Well, almost no one.

His eyes widen. 'Cara Ross is missing.'

Fear fizzes through me. As usual, my first thought is for my daughter.

'Oh, Nicky! You didn't hear?' Stephanie has magically reappeared, inserting herself between Hudson and me. Most people are aware I hate being called Nicky and I'm pretty sure Stephanie Sutton is one of them. She lays a manicured hand on my arm. 'She was reported missing this morning. She's Abby's friend, isn't she?' she asks, her inflection telling me she's fishing for gossip.

I set my basket on the floor, needing a few seconds to gather myself.

'Cara?' I reply, glancing at Hudson who regards me with concern. 'They know one another. She's not a close friend, though.'

A beat passes as I look from Stephanie to Hudson. *How does everyone know about this except me?* 'What happened to her?' My brain races through the possibilities while I try to remember the last time I saw Cara.

More importantly, when had Abby last seen her?

'No one knows.' For a moment it seems Stephanie is answering my unasked question. 'I thought Lee might have mentioned it.'

'Lee doesn't talk about police matters. He's a stickler for the rules.' Which, unfortunately, is true.

'Rumour has it she's run away.' Stephanie moves closer as a twenty-something couple zoom past. She smells amazing, like frangipani. The fact that she smells so good annoys me immensely. 'It's very sad. She's such a lovely girl. Smart, and in the first hockey and netball teams too. We were only saying at the last P and C meeting what a wonderful scholarship recipient Cara has proven to be. A credit to the college.'

Cara had started at Arundel Christian College this year. The school doesn't normally offer scholarships for the final year of school, but her ATAR estimate from her last school was over ninety-nine per cent, and the board jumped at the chance to bring her in. She'd lift the school's average – and prospective parents were always lured in by the very high achievers.

Stephanie pauses, raising her eyebrows. 'Her parents are a bit churchy though …' She leaves the sentence hanging, as if I know what she means.

I do, of course.

'Even for a Christian school like ours,' she says after the meaningful break, then sighs. 'And teenage girls can be tricky. I'm lucky to have three boys – I mean, the house smells of footy socks most of the time and they need constant feeding – but I don't fear for my boys in the same way you must for your daughter. Girls are such a worry. Especially ones like Abby, she's so pretty.' She gives a mock shudder. 'It's terrifying, thinking about the depraved people out there.' Her hand waves to take in the entire world, presumably, but seems to indicate the packets of biscuits lining the shelves. '*Predators*.'

A memory slams into me. Blindingly white snow. My favourite cable-knit jumper, smoky from the open fire and soft against my skin. The smell of spilt beer and a blast of freezing air from the open balcony door.

I blink the scene away, thudding back to Arundel and the overheated supermarket. A flash of rage rushes in.

Teach your fucking sons, I want to tell Stephanie. *And stop blaming our daughters.*

Before I can open my mouth, Hudson speaks. 'Well, Stephanie, you'd better be getting back to Dicky and your boys. They must be hungry for that ...' He glances at the jar in her hand. 'Hulled tahini.'

Stephanie gives Hudson a look that tells him she's not impressed by his muscles, his managerial position at the VW dealership in town or his baby-faced good looks.

I stiffen my spine. 'Yes, it's good to see you, Stephanie, but I'd better get home too. Dinner won't prepare itself.' Though it almost has. It's sushi on a plate after all.

'Of course, Nicky. Say hi to Abby. And tell that policeman of yours to contact me or Richard –' she flashes a look at Hudson '– if he needs anything. Anything at all.'

I nod, wondering what use the police might have for a part-time interior designer and her accountant husband as they search for a missing teenager.

'What a bitch,' Hudson mutters as Stephanie saunters away, and this time I don't shush him. He takes my hand. His fingers are cool and smooth; mine are on fire. 'Honey, don't let Stephanie get to you. Abby will be fine. More than fine. She's smart and she's tough. And I'm sure Cara will be home soon.'

I want to believe Hudson, but the worry is there.

It's always there.

He catches my eye. 'Things have been good between Abby and Cara, haven't they? Not like, you know, *before*?'

'I've got to get home, Hudson.' His eyes are on me as I make myself walk calmly towards the checkout.

I need to get home and make sure Abby is safe.

More than that, I need to look into my daughter's eyes.

I have to find out what Abby knows about Cara's disappearance.

*

I dash to the car in the dark, the air cold enough to catch in my throat. On the main street, several restaurants are open, their interiors glowing dimly, doors closed against the cold. It's a weeknight so there aren't many customers, most of them probably tourists in town for a romantic, if chilly, break.

It takes a few turns of the key to get my old Subaru started and I vow for the hundredth time to look at buying a new one.

The trip home is quick, the wide streets quiet. In winter, locals hunker down at home. Arundel isn't a typical Australian blue-green, grey-gum town of olives and khakis and browns. Our 'Englishness' is our main drawcard. Sitting on top of a tableland, we have colder temperatures than neighbouring areas — snow even settles on the ground a couple of times a year. On quiet frosty mornings when my footsteps crunch over the grass, or in spring, when Mum brews tea and we sit out the back at Hillcrest, breathing in the scent of her roses as the sun sets over fruit trees, Arundel's appeal is obvious.

At other times, the town feels as fake as the Loch Ness monster and as insular as the British royal family.

But it's home. Other than one short escape attempt I made way back when, it's always been home.

Ten minutes later I pull up outside our house and use the remote to open the garage.

Lee's not back yet, which isn't surprising, given the news about Cara. Tracking down a missing teenager will keep him – the whole station – busy.

I'd noticed Lili's hatchback out front so Abby must be here too. I grab the grocery bags from the passenger seat, my mind racing with all the terrible things that might have befallen Cara.

Calm down, Nicola. She's probably off somewhere with some friends.

I know from experience that teenagers can be oblivious – even careless – about their parents' worries. It's only as they get older that they come to understand and fear what's out there; who's out there. I catch an echo of Stephanie's comments in my thoughts and tamp them down.

'Abby!' I call, opening the door to the kitchen. Heat hits me and I dump the bags on the bench then lower the temperature on the control panel before heading for the stairs. I take them two at a time, hearing voices, then laughter from Abby's room.

'Abby!' I call again from outside her closed door, then knock. The laughter stops.

'Come in!'

Abby and Lili are perched at opposite ends of Abby's bed, both with phones in their hands. I examine my daughter's eyes for clues to her state of mind, but she gives away nothing, so I smile at Lili.

Lili is as blonde as my daughter, the two of them sporting decidedly Stephanie-circa-2001 ponytails. They wear corduroy jeans and cropped knitted jumpers, stylish even in casual clothes. It makes me aware of my messy, sweaty appearance.

Abby's friends are lovely, but it's always me who feels like a gawky teenager in their presence.

'Hi Mum.'

'Hi hon. How are you girls going?'

'Good thanks, Mrs Miller,' Lili replies. Arundel Christian College places great value on politeness.

'How was the movie marathon?'

'Yeah, fun,' Abby says. 'We watched old horror movies. *Scream. A Nightmare on Elm Street. Carrie.*'

'That sounds terrible!'

'No, it was hilarious, Mrs M,' Lili says, smiling. 'Abby's the bravest. She didn't even react to the jump scares.'

'Huh. Well, she certainly doesn't get that from me.'

The trial HSC exams finished this morning. Abby and her friends had spent the rest of the day celebrating at Lili's house, which is five minutes' walk from us, on an acreage at the edge of town with a turquoise infinity pool overlooking the rolling countryside. Lili's parents own several service stations and her mother definitely visits Byron Bay for her Botox, but I like them well enough.

'Did Abby offer you something to eat? Fruit? Toast?'

They give one another a look at that, and I realise it was the wrong suggestion. Seventeen-year-old girls don't eat toast, at least not in front of one another.

'We weren't hungry,' Abby says. 'We had salads at Nature's Café between movies.'

'Lucas didn't even charge us!' Lili says, glancing at Abby, whose expression remains neutral. 'He never charges Abby. Or Cara.' She looks downcast and I sigh internally, vowing to talk to Lucas. He's a lovely guy, recently moved here from Sydney for a 'tree change', but he's in his late twenties and far too old to be crushing on seventeen-year-old girls. I'll pay for the salads and tell him to back off. I glance at Abby. She's all legs and hair and cheekbones, and I'm not sure she understands the effect she has on men yet.

Or does she?

My daughter is so effortlessly beautiful that sometimes I stop what I'm doing to look at her, wondering how I could have made something so perfect. And when she wants to be, Abby is as charming as she is gorgeous. She doesn't get either of those things from me. I'm attractive enough, in a shorter, darker, more boyish way, and my greatest charm lies in my awkwardness, or so someone once told me.

'How are you girls holding up?' I ask, bringing the conversation around to what I need to find out. 'I heard about Cara going missing.'

Something unspoken passes between them.

'It's all anyone is talking about on their socials,' Lili says.

'She wasn't at the Ancient exam this morning, which was weird,' Abby offers. 'I figured she must have been sick.'

'Isn't she boarding at the school? Surely she couldn't have left without anyone noticing?'

'She moved home with her parents for the trials.'

'She was in Calder Head when she disappeared?'

The sleepy beach town where Cara's parents live is only an hour away from Arundel. You drive down the plateau and head directly east until you hit the coast.

'Yeah, she said it was quieter there for studying,' Lili says. She hesitates, then adds, 'Sergeant Cook and Constable Baker came to my house after lunch today to talk to us.'

'Oh?' I focus on Abby. 'Lee came to see you?'

'Yeah. He wanted to know if we had any idea where Cara might be.'

Is that normal procedure? I wonder, a knot forming in my stomach.

'And did you?'

'No.' Lili sighs. 'I mean, we haven't seen much of her since the trials started.' She flicks a look at my daughter, who is wearing a concerned expression. 'We assumed it was because she was so busy studying.'

'I hope she's all right,' Abby says. 'We all do.'

There's silence.

I'm about to ask if Lee had said anything else, but something in Abby's eyes stops me. Instead, I say, 'Well, I bought sushi. Do you want some?' Sushi seems acceptable, given their muted enthusiasm. 'I'll shower, then give you a shout when it's ready.'

In the shower, the needles of hot water are heaven on my back, yet I can't relax.

Abby's expression had been so hard to read.

Even as a kid she'd been inscrutable.

On her first day of kindergarten Abby had been quiet. Nerves, I supposed. Then we met her teacher and she'd skipped off without a backwards glance. I'd watched her blonde pigtails bobbing as she hung her bag on a hook in the hallway and lined up at the door, my heart breaking at how comfortable she was. Not a tear in sight, unlike most other kids, who gripped their mother's hands or clung to their legs. Before I turned to leave, Abby ran back over and hugged me with her skinny little arms. 'See you later,' she'd said, her hot breath on my cheek, smelling of toothpaste. I swear that she was trying to cheer *me* up.

I've always been in awe of Abby. The way she forges through life, the high achiever I'd always wished I'd been. Where I struggled – not quite smart enough, not quite brave enough, certainly never confident enough – Abby excelled. In sport, at schoolwork, at being popular.

After that very first day in kindergarten, she never looked back.

*

When I wake, it's light. I lie still for a few seconds before I remember.

Cara Ross is missing.

Lee's side of the bed is empty, the flung-back doona the only sign he slept here. After several hours of tossing and turning I must have dozed off because I didn't hear him come to bed.

Lili stayed later than expected, leaving about 9.30 pm. I'd considered bailing Abby up when she came inside after waving Lili off, but at the sight of her slumped shoulders I chickened out, telling myself that my baby needed sleep, that I'd talk to her in the morning. I kissed her goodnight, her cheek so warm under my lips I worried she might be coming down with something.

Now the clank of the pipes tells me the shower down the hall is on.

Oh yes, Abby had squad this morning. She'll be showering before school.

There's a familiar creak as our door opens and I freeze.

'Hey there.'

My breath huffs out as I roll towards the voice.

'Lee.'

He's leaning against the door jamb, dressed in chinos and a white shirt, a tie loose around his neck. An ex-rugby player, he's broad, still muscular, not run to fat as big sportsmen often do.

'I thought you'd left for work.'

'Still here, as you can see.' He walks over and sits on the bed, brushing the hair from my face before kissing me. He tastes of Vegemite and coffee. Today, something about that is reassuring. Comforting.

'Come back to bed?' I raise my eyebrows suggestively and run a hand over his stomach, as flat as it was when we first met, even if his six-pack has disappeared. Lee groans.

'I wish,' he says, sitting up and turning away to knot his tie. I feel a pang at being rejected, though I can't deny partly making the offer because I doubted he'd be able to take me up on it.

Usually I *was* up for it. Just a few days ago Lee had taken me out for a lovely dinner, we'd even had drinks afterwards at the pub, dancing to a dodgy DJ's nineties music. Lee had requested the Silverchair song that we bonded over the very first time we met, and we slow danced as the guitars roared around us. We'd had great sex that night.

It's only natural that, after five years together, things are a little more unexciting, the early morning sex a little rarer. Lee's head is shaved now, which he was quick to do when he started thinning on top, but other than that he wears his age – thirty-nine – better than most. His eyes are still as clear and blue as ever, and the laugh lines around them suit him.

'I heard about Cara,' I say.

'I bet. Everyone knows everything in this town.' Lee sighs and rubs his short beard. The skin around his eyes looks bruised from tiredness. They're bloodshot too.

'When was she last seen?'

'Saturday night. August tenth.' The night of our dinner. 'The parents were both at church all day organising some event the father was running that night. The mother said Cara went to bed early and that's the last time she saw her.'

'But they didn't report her missing till Monday?'

'They assumed she was still in bed when they left for church on Sunday morning. They'd given her the day off to study for the Ancient History trial exam. And then the father was busy with sermons, socialising, talking to parishioners –' Lee shakes his head '– whatever they do in churches.'

'Pray, sing, listen.' I shrug. Like me, Lee had never been a churchgoer. But, unlike Lee, I'd gone to a Christian high school. He'd attended a public high school.

'Yeah, whatever. The Orange Dawn Church is one of those modern happy-clappy churches.'

'When did they get home?'

'Late. Cara's door was shut, so they assumed she'd gone to bed.' His gaze becomes distant. 'It wasn't until they went to wake her yesterday that they realised something was up.'

'So she could have left anytime on Sunday then? Or even Saturday night, if she snuck out?'

'Yeah. My main worry is that Cara's wallet and phone were found in her room. If she'd left of her own accord, she would have taken them with her.'

'You'd think so.'

'Shit, I shouldn't be telling you this.' He gives a wry smile. 'I've always said you could be a police officer with your interrogation skills. You're wasted at that paper.'

I have to admit it is surprising to hear him talk so freely. Lee is normally tight-lipped about work stuff.

'This case feels close to home, doesn't it?'

Lee isn't Abby's biological father, though we've been together since she was twelve, and they get on well. Really well, thank God. You hear horror stories about stepfathers and daughters.

He looks at me. 'So, Cara hasn't visited Abby for, what? A month now?'

'More like a couple of weeks.'

'Did something happen between them?'

'Didn't you ask Abby that?'

'Yeah. She said Cara's been busy studying. That she wants to get into medicine. I didn't realise she was so smart.' He blinks rapidly, looking pained enough to cry. 'Sorry.'

'Don't be sorry.' I rub his forearm.

'You met her, didn't you?' I ask, yet of course I know the answer. I'd tried to stop them meeting, wanting to keep my police officer partner far away from Cara Ross.

He nods.

'The night of the school dance.' His expression is pinched when he looks at me. 'I'm hopeful we'll have her home soon.' One of Lee's best qualities is his unflappability so my stomach flutters to see him look worried. Could something bad have happened to Cara? 'The parents insist she wouldn't have run away, but I've heard how strict they are.' He shakes his head. 'I've got to brush my teeth then get back to it. I need to talk to the Missing Persons unit, make some more calls.'

'Should we be worried?'

He removes his arm from my hand. 'I've already said too much.'

'Of course,' I say, piqued that he's pulling me up when he's the one who started blabbing. 'The girls said you and Mitch Baker interviewed them at the Camerons' house. You don't think the girls are involved, do you?' He shoots me a look. 'Fine, fine. You can't say. But I'm *assuming* you just wanted to find out if they'd seen her in the past couple of days.'

He stands up. 'Nicola—' he says, a warning in his voice.

'It's Abby we're talking about here. And her—' I go to say friend, then change it to, 'someone she knows. A vulnerable teenage girl. I worry—'

'As I said, I'm hopeful we'll find her soon. And Abby is fine,' he says softly. He's unaware exactly why I'm so overprotective of Abby, though he must have guessed, at least in part. I've never told him about her father. I can't. And that's Lee's other superpower: his compassion. He would never push me to tell him something I'm uncomfortable with.

I haven't even told Hudson, who, to his credit, has also never pressed me for details. Only one person in this world knows about Abby's father, and they found out through blind luck.

Occasionally I feel guilty about keeping things from Lee. He's such a good man.

He sighs and kisses my forehead. 'I've gotta go, babe. See you tonight. I'll try to make it in time for dinner, it's just with all that's going on—'

'It's fine. Text me later and tell me your ETA.'

My phone buzzes across the bedside table.

'Here.' Lee passes it to me without checking who's calling. 'I'd better be off. Love you.' I hardly hear him as I look at the screen. It's Mum.

'Mother dearest,' I say into the phone as Lee enters the bathroom. The tap whooshes on.

'Daughter.' I can hear the smile in her voice. Birds chirp in the background. She's probably already started gardening. The garden at Hillcrest needs constant care, though that's not why she does it. The garden is her happy place. 'I didn't wake you, did I?'

'No. I'm still in bed, though.'

'Lazy girl,' she says in mock disapproval. 'You don't take after your mother.' I hear a snip as she prunes an errant branch. 'I might come over today. I have some kale for you. And pears. You don't work Tuesdays, do you?'

'My days are very flexible. That would be great,' I say. Lee emerges from the bathroom and waves as he leaves. After I'm sure he's gone I blurt out, 'Have you heard that Cara's missing?'

'Yes.' *Snip.* 'Since the weekend apparently. She's probably run off with a boy.'

I wonder how my mother heard about it, though on reflection it's obvious. My mother – Joyce Miller, secretary of the golf club, CWA treasurer, lady who lunches, Meals-on-Wheels volunteer, Rotarian, ex-nurse at the local hospital – knows everything about everything in this town. Sometimes I find it funny, sometimes useful.

Mostly it's annoying.

'Do you honestly believe that? I was worried when she first started at the school, given her and Abby's history, but they've become friends.' The anger in Abby's eyes as she'd glared at Cara in the coffee shop last week pops into my mind before I shove the memory aside. 'She seems sensible. Not the type to get into trouble with a boy.'

There's a pause as I realise what I've said. I redden, speaking rapidly to fill the silence. 'How did you hear about it?'

'Maree's daughter, Cassie, works with Lee. She's in administration. And she isn't as circumspect as your Lee.' *Snip.*

'So, I'll come around for morning tea, shall I? I'd like to see my granddaughter if she'll be around.'

'The trials are over so she's back at school today. Come for afternoon tea instead?'

'Fine. I'll see you both then. Is four too late?'

'Perfect.'

I'm about to say goodbye when Mum continues. 'Darling.' Her voice is so confident it makes me feel both better and worse. 'Please don't stress. Everything will be fine.'

'You don't know that, Mum,' I mutter. This is a common exchange between us. Me, the worrying daughter; Mum, who can fix just about anything.

Just about anything.

*

I switch on the morning news.

Cara's disappearance is mentioned briefly, with her school photo and a phone number to call if you have any information about her whereabouts. I watch until the end of the bulletin, my heart pounding, but that's it.

Twenty minutes later Abby and I head for my car. Abby has her Ps and we often fight over who will drive, probably because we're both control freaks. Today I reach the driver's seat first.

'So, honey, how are you feeling about this whole Cara thing?' I ask when I'm merging onto the main road. I prefer to question her while I'm ferrying her around – it's harder for her to avoid me.

'Fine. Everyone reckons she'll be home soon.'

'Is that what you think?' I keep my eyes on the road but sense she's watching me.

'I guess.'

'You haven't been hanging out much lately. I thought she was part of your group now?'

'She was. She is. She's been busy with study.'

'Oh, okay.' I hesitate, then add, 'Darling, if something happened between the two of you, you'd tell me, wouldn't you?'

She doesn't answer at first and I glance over at her. Her expression is unreadable. 'What are you trying to say, Mum?'

'Nothing.' I hesitate, then bite the bullet. 'It's only ... I saw you arguing at the café the other day.'

'And you – what? You think I did something to her? *Hurt* her?'

'Of course not, Abby.' *What* do *you think, Nicola?* 'I'm concerned, that's all. What was the argument about?'

There's a stony silence. When she speaks, it's like the words are being dragged from her. 'If you must know, it was about Taj. She's been flirting with him.'

'Oh.' I'm not sure what I'd expected; not that. Abby and Taj are an item, but I hadn't realised it was serious. Abby's always been fairly uninterested in boys; in relationships. She could have any boy she wanted, which is half the problem. It's too easy for her.

'Anyway, it's nothing. We had words and she promised to back off. That's all.'

'And what does Taj have to say about all this?'

'God knows,' she mutters. 'He's probably stoked to have us both fighting over him. Anyway, it's over between us.' *She's broken up with Taj?* 'What exactly is it you think I've done, Mum?' She's angry rather than upset. 'Cara's just run away, hasn't she?'

I think about the wallet and phone left behind in Cara's room. 'Yes, probably.'

'Besides,' Abby says, looking at me, 'do you really want to talk about the day you saw us arguing?'

The breath is sucked from me. *Is that a threat?*

'Let's drop it,' I say, my voice croaky. 'I'm sure she'll be home in no time.'

'I should've bought a car of my own,' Abby grumbles, looking out the window. 'This is why I want to go overseas. To get away.'

'Sydney is away.'

'Not far enough.'

I swallow against the sudden tears that threaten.

We sit in silence.

'If anyone's done something to Cara, it'll be someone in her family,' Abby finally says, grumpily, though with perhaps a touch of remorse in her voice. 'Her dad's a religious nutter. He's *obsessed* with her. And her mother is so overprotective she makes *you* look relaxed.'

I don't answer, but my daughter's words make me think.

Cara's been lovely since she's come back into our lives. At first I decided that if I got to know her it would help me protect Abby. I couldn't let history repeat itself. But my fears seemed unfounded. Cara came over every Thursday to study – until recently. She was interested in my work, adored hearing stories about what a clever kid Abby was – she even enjoyed listening to Mum drone on about plants. She was quick-witted, older than her years. Good with people.

Cara was fun.

Is, Nicola, is. I give a shake to clear my head.

Is great fun.

She had won me over. Now, though. Now I wonder if Cara Ross fooled me.

I change lanes, admitting that Abby has a point about Mike. I never knew Mike and Donna well, though we met several times after the incident, six years ago now. We'd all been keen to ensure the police and Isabella's parents knew that it had been an accident. To brush it under the carpet. And after that, I kept well away from Calder Head.

Pulling up in the school drop-off area, I recall how Mike had doted on Cara. She was an only child – smart and pretty – and I had always assumed he was merely a proud though concerned parent.

Now I wonder, is Abby right?

Could Mike have hurt Cara?

Abby climbs out of the car, hesitates, then sits back down. She faces me, an apology in her eyes. 'Mum, this has been harder on me than I realised.'

'Oh, Abby, hon, I know.'

I want to gather my daughter to me, to ease the ache in my own chest as well as hers. Instead, I push a lock of hair behind her ear.

'I'm sorry about what I said before. About the argument. And moving away. I'm a bit stressed, probably.' Abby shakes her head. 'But you're right.' She smiles, lighting me up like sunlight. 'Cara has a way of landing on her feet, doesn't she? Sometimes it seems she's one of those people who'll skate blissfully through life, nothing bad ever happening to them.'

'Charmed.'

'Yes.'

A look passes between us. Abby hugs me. Her hair smells of chlorine and coconut. An ache tugs at my heart. It's ever-present now, that twinge of worry for my daughter. She's getting older, pulling away from me.

'We can only hope,' I say, as she lets go.

'Yes. Cara will be fine,' Abby comforts me now, and I'm transported back to that first day of kindergarten.

Then she's gone, striding off with her posse. Four of the five girls are blonde. Abby, Lili, Hayley and Bethan. The fifth girl, Grace, wears her dark hair long and straight, her make-up as flawless as if she was on the cover of *Vogue*. Abby says that's thanks to an obsession with YouTube tutorials. Lili and Grace have been Abby's best friends since she started at Arundel in year seven. The other two girls, Hayley and Bethan, are newer friends.

I watch them walk away, my thoughts returning to Cara.

Where could she be? Has she run away?

If something has happened to Cara, her friends might be in danger too. Which means it's up to me to protect my daughter, any way I can.

*

I'd been backpacking a month, so when the waitress placed the cooked breakfast in front of me, I could have cried.

Bacon, sausages, fried potatoes and eggs. The smell of fatty grease made my stomach rumble out loud and she smiled. 'It tastes as good as it looks, hon. Enjoy.'

'This is the best meal I've seen in ages,' I said apologetically. 'I start job-hunting tomorrow. Thought I'd spend the last of my cash on a decent fry-up.'

'Well, sweetheart, you've gotta keep your strength up if you're gonna get a job.' She bent down until I could see her nametag, which read Wendy. 'You need any more toast or bacon, just holler and I'll bring you some – free of charge,' she whispered, then walked away to seat new customers.

The café was almost full, mostly with tourists, Banff being as busy in winter as it was in summer, especially now on New Year's Eve. Most customers sat in groups or couples, though there was an attractive guy alone at the next table. He had broad shoulders and shaggy blond hair, and his sandy stubble and red-rimmed eyes suggested a hangover. In front of him was a laptop, a coffee at his elbow. He glanced at me and I averted my gaze, focusing instead on my plate. Yolk oozed over the potatoes. I started shovelling food into my mouth while reading from my guidebook. Before I knew it my plate was clean. Wendy appeared immediately. 'Can I get you anything else?' she asked, then winked.

'I'm full – but thank you.'

She took my plate. 'I'll box you up a slice of our famous cherry pie for later.'

Tears threatened. Wendy reminded me of my mum. Looking out for me. I pictured Hillcrest on a summer's day, could almost smell the star jasmine that bloomed at home this time of year.

Get a grip, Nicola. You've been gone less than a month. This is the trip of a lifetime, remember? You can't be homesick already.

'Do you reckon the waitstaff are nice because they want tips or is it because they're Canadian?' It was the hot guy. He grinned at me. He had a cute chin dimple that grew bigger when he smiled. His eyes were an unusually light blue, like the hydrangeas Mum grew along the side of the house.

'Both?' I ventured.

'You're a fellow Aussie, I see. Who'd have guessed it?' He rolled his eyes.

I laughed. Every second person in Banff appeared to be Australian. I should have realised this guy was too, he had that laidback look about him. Moving from hostel to hostel I'd become an expert at telling nationalities apart. The neatly dressed Germans, the red-faced Brits. Blond Swedes. Clichés were clichés for a reason. Australians and New Zealanders were even more casual than most backpackers, disdaining shoes inside. Always a beer in hand.

'Where are you from?' I asked, trying not to redden. I wasn't great at chatting to men I didn't know. Or ones I did know, if it came to that. I'd left Arundel in search of adventure – to really *live life* – as I'd told Hudson. He'd been so proud of me for leaving, heading to the opposite side of the world. Jealous, too. And yet, overcoming my shyness had proved far more difficult than I'd expected. Joining conversations in shared kitchens, asking dormmates if they wanted to grab a drink – none of it had come naturally. Perhaps the bacon grease had gone to my head, as this time it felt easier.

'Sydney,' he answered. 'You?'

'You wouldn't have heard of it.'

'Try me.'

'Arundel, about five hours north-west of Sydney. It's in the middle of nowhere.'

'Arundel ...' He looked thoughtful, then slyly pleased. 'Actually, a guy from my class was from there. Digby Hill.' He raised an eyebrow. 'I don't suppose you know him?'

'Of course, I do! I know everyone in Arundel.'

He appeared surprised, before realising I was taking the

piss. He made a rueful face. 'Sorry, I guess it's not that small a town.'

'It's pretty small,' I admitted. 'And I do know Digby. His family, anyway. I went to primary school with his younger brother, Christian.' This was true. The Hills lived out of town and, like many of the wealthy rural families, sent their kids to board in Sydney for high school. That made the hot guy four years older than me, so twenty-two or twenty-three. 'Arundel's about the same size as Banff, just a lot less pretty.'

'Canada's amazing, isn't it? A little chilly this time of year, though. The guy at the petrol station told me it was going to reach a top of minus six degrees today. Practically summer.' He widened his eyes. 'Apparently it was thirty-four in Sydney yesterday. How are you finding it? I'm Sam, by the way.' He leaned across and gave me his hand, which was warm and smooth and seemed twice the size of mine.

'Nicola,' I said, shaking it. 'I don't mind the cold. Arundel gets snow. Not as much as this, though.' I gestured at his laptop. 'Where do you work?'

Sam looked down as if only now realising it was there. 'Oh. I don't. Not at the moment. I'm out here snowboarding before going back home to work for my dad. I was just checking emails. This place is one of the only cafés in town with decent wi-fi. Plus the coffee's good – for Canada. Shit compared to the cafés at Vaucluse, though,' he said wistfully. 'Dad wants me to take over the business eventually and apparently that means I can't ever have a relaxing holiday.' He rolled his eyes again.

The signs of Sam's wealth were obvious. The brand name puffer jacket hanging over his chair. The chunky watch on his wrist. The faint goggle marks on his tanned face that told of days on the slopes.

'And you're looking for a job, I heard? Sorry, I'm a stickybeak.'

'That's fine. Yeah. Eventually, I want to be a journalist and travel the world – foreign correspondent or investigative journalist, ideally.' Sam gave an impressed nod that made me feel like a fraud, so I added, 'That's the dream, at least. But at the moment I'm just looking for any old job. New year, new job. Today's my last day of freedom.'

'One coffee.' Wendy set a small box in front of me. She jerked a thumb towards Sam. 'Don't let this one distract you, sweetheart. He's a charmer.' But she smiled at him in an affectionate way.

'Don't listen to her! She's the charmer, and for one reason only.' He paused dramatically, rubbing his thumb and index fingers together.

Wendy laughed. 'Lucky you're a good tipper, *mate*.' She tried for an Australian accent and failed. 'Otherwise I'd get Big Kev to kick you out for that comment.' Her expression became serious. 'There's a storm coming in tonight, young Aussies –' she pronounced it *Ussies* '– lots of snow, could be a blizzard. Don't go driving, all right? The roads will be dangerous.'

We nodded and she moved off to another table. Sam typed a few words then sighed and closed his laptop. 'My father wants feedback on a new development in Cronulla, but stuff it! I'm still on holidays. Like *you*, Nicola. Can I …?' He gestured at my table and when I inclined my head, he packed up his gear and moved to sit beside me. Up close he smelled great – like chocolate and sandalwood.

He thumbed through my guidebook. 'What have you seen so far?'

I filled him in on my adventures so far, and made him

laugh when I mentioned the British backpackers I'd travelled some of the way with, who ate Marmite sandwiches nonstop. 'We called in at Jasper,' I continued, 'but we missed Lake Louise as they'd been there before.'

He slapped his hands on the table. 'You missed Lake Louise?'

'Yeah. I was so bummed.'

'Well. That's it then!'

'That's what?'

'That's what we'll do today. My car's outside. I'll take you to Lake Louise.'

'Oh no, you don't have to do that—'

'I do. It's my duty as a fellow Australian and temporary Canadian to show you Lake Louise. You can't miss it!'

I was hesitant. I didn't know this man. But he was Australian. And he knew Digby Hill, so he was hardly a stranger. And I had driven across the Rockies with a bunch of far dodgier British tourists, one of whom constantly tried to get me drunk, presumably so he could sleep with me.

Plus, Sam was gorgeous.

I knew what Hudson would say.

You need to live a little, Nic.

'Come on.' Sam gave me puppy dog eyes. 'The lake's frozen. It's incredibly beautiful. We could hire some ice skates, have a long lunch ...' He leaned forward. 'I'm friends with the maître d' at the chateau's best restaurant. I could call him, get us a table—' He clocked the look on my face. 'My shout, of course. I can afford it. You'll be getting a job cleaning toilets tomorrow. How about one last decadent day?'

He knew I was wavering and called Wendy over. 'Can I get the cheque please, lovely Wendy? Add Nicola's bill to it. And a fifty per cent tip for yourself.'

'Whatever you say.' Wendy grinned. 'You're the boss.'

'You can't—' I started as he pulled out his wallet.

'I can,' he said, determined. 'For your last day of freedom. How about it?'

'I … don't know. Am I dressed well enough?' I had my favourite cable-knit jumper and jeans on, with a puffer jacket and beanie, gloves and scarf on the chair beside me.

'You look gorgeous,' he leered comically. 'Absolutely perfect.'

Even though he was joking, I flushed.

'Come on, I'm not a serial killer, scout's honour.' He put a hand over his heart.

I grinned. 'Okay. I'm in.'

*

Mum arrives exactly on time, as usual.

She kisses my cheek and thrusts a string grocery bag and a bunch of yellow flowers at me. 'Kale, pears and a cauliflower for you, darling. And some daffodils – they've recently started to bloom. Is Abby home yet?'

Mum visits us regularly, and on afternoons when I don't need the car Abby sometimes drives out to Hillcrest – forty-five minutes out of town – and they spend an hour or two in the garden. Mum's garden is a sprawling oasis of roses, peonies, foxglove and lavender, with vibrant green lawn underfoot and fruiting trees, including apples and mulberries, to offer shade. The CWA conducts sold-out tours of Hillcrest's gardens one week every year, for which Mum prepares for months.

'Yes, she's baking.' I exhale. 'Macarons.' I load the word with meaning.

'Ah. That sounds … complicated. Is she okay?'

'As far as I can tell. But if she's baking … She broke up with Taj.'

'Mm. I see.'

There is something in her eyes. 'You knew?'

She purses her lips. 'Yes, darling, I'm sorry. She told me last week.'

'You didn't think to tell me?'

Abby and Mum have always had secrets that exclude me. I try not to be jealous.

'She asked me not to.' That stung. 'And you? How are you?'

Mum gives me a look but I brush it off. 'I'm fine. You know me.'

She nods. 'I'll go and say hello.'

'Mum, wait.'

'Yes?'

'I'm not sure how to tackle this thing with Cara.'

'It'll be fine. The girl will be back home soon.' Mum waves a hand dismissively.

'You think so?' I want so much for Cara to walk back into her parents' house. For her to tell them she was off with a boy or had gone to a festival with friends. For her to be ticked off and grounded, yet safe.

I just don't believe it.

'Certainly. Why wouldn't I?'

'Abby and Cara's history, for one thing,' I say.

'Oh, Nicola. Abby was a child then. They both were. It was a terrible misunderstanding.'

'That's not what you used to believe.'

'Well, it's what I believe now. You don't seriously think Abby could have hurt the girl, do you?'

I hesitate. 'I saw something. A few days before Cara disappeared, she and Abby argued. Abby says it was over Taj.' I grimace. 'I might have confronted her about it this morning.'

'Oh dear. Was that wise? No wonder she's baking.'

I wait a beat. 'Mum. What if Abby is like …'

'She's not.' Mum places a hand firmly on my arm. 'She's not like him.'

'That's not my only worry.' I swallow hard. 'What if she's like me?'

Mum opens her mouth but nothing comes out.

Abby appears at the door to the kitchen. She has flour on her hands and I can see where she's wiped them on her jeans. She frowns at us both.

'Hi, Grandma. Why are you standing out here talking? Have you heard something about Cara?'

'No, darling. We're coming in to see you now.' Mum smiles and hugs Abby, who towers over her. From where I stand, Abby could be her big sister. 'The house smells amazing. Nicola said you were attempting macarons. Strawberry by the smell of them?'

'Raspberry.'

'Don't you get sick of kitchens?'

'All I do at the café is make sandwiches and wraps and heat up muffins in the microwave. It's not baking.' She raises her eyebrows at my mother. 'So, do you want macarons or what? The first batch will be ready in ten minutes.'

'I won't say no.' Mum turns to me. 'Let's put the kettle on.'

*

We sit in the kitchen, trying hard to pretend it's a normal day.

But today is not a normal day.

There's tension between us.

Abby pipes buttercream onto one tray of macaron halves and starts sandwiching them together. She takes a break to pass one to each of us, not meeting my eyes. She hasn't looked at me properly since I dropped her at school this morning.

God, Nicola, why did you have to open your big mouth?

'They're delicious, hon,' I say, biting through the thin crust into the light, chewy biscuit. 'Are you going to try one?'

Abby picks up a tiny macaron and takes a small bite. 'Yeah, not bad. Could be a touch sweeter.' She sets it aside and starts pulling Tupperware containers from the cupboard.

'How's work?' Mum asks me.

'Fine. Petra wanted another article about the new brewery on Scott Street. Anyone would think she has a share in it,' I say dryly.

'I'm not sure she should be allowed to promote her fiancée's business.'

'Oh, it's fine. It's only a follow-up article. And Sadie's doing it tough. It's been quieter than usual this year.'

'I suppose so.' Mum is grudging. 'Tell Petra I want to talk to her about starting a CWA column. And there's a new domestic violence support group that needs publicity.'

Mum seems to have forgotten what happened last time she tried to get me to push her agenda, but I don't bother to argue. 'Will do.'

I love that Mum supports local issues, but she doesn't seem to understand that *Arundel Trails* is a light-hearted read, not a big city newspaper.

God knows I've talked to Petra about pursuing some more worthwhile stories, but she is adamant that, in a free local magazine, people want to read about who won the footy grand final and who had the biggest pumpkin at the show. She's forever saying that people mostly pick us up for the free TV guide – those people, she says, are our market.

It's a small staff at *Arundel Trails*. Petra is the editor, Harry does sales, and I do the writing, subbing, photography – you name it. I'm not the kind of hard-hitting journalist I'd dreamed of being as a teenager, but I enjoy writing and Petra's been good to me over the years.

'And Lee? How's he going?' Mum continues.

'He's very busy, as you can imagine. I've hardly seen him the past couple of days.'

'He must be flat-out.'

'Yeah. He was quite upset this morning. And you know he's normally so calm under pressure.' I sigh and lower my voice so Abby can't hear. 'Don't tell anyone this – I mean it, Mum,' and she opens her eyes wide in a *who me?* gesture. 'Lee said Cara left her phone and wallet behind. That doesn't sound as if she's gone away for a few days, does it?'

'No,' Mum draws out the word and for the first time she sounds worried. 'It doesn't.'

Abby snaps the lid on a large Tupperware container filled with pale pink macarons and pushes it across the bench. 'Take these, Grandma.'

'Ooh, thank you, my dear.'

'Mum!' I berate her. 'Are you still passing Abby's baking off as your own?'

'I most certainly am.' She grins. 'Oh, Nicola, don't be like that! I've got a reputation at the golf meetings for my exquisite baking now.' I shake my head at her. 'This is the one tiny itty-bitty crime I commit. Surely you can forgive me?'

'Hmmm,' I say, smiling. 'So Petra can't help Sadie out, but you can trick the women in town into thinking you're an expert baker?'

She pokes her tongue out at me. 'Fine – I'm a hypocrite!' she says, laughing, then turns to Abby. 'I might ask you to make me something special for the next CWA bake-off too, darling. What they don't know won't hurt them.' She stands up to leave, the container in her hand. 'I'd better dash. Got a CWA meeting tonight actually. These lovely macarons, made by yours truly –' she winks '– will go down a treat.'

Abby kisses her goodbye and I show Mum out. When I come back, Abby has another container of macarons in her hand.

'I forgot to give Grandma this batch. I'll run them out to her.'

'You don't want to keep any?' I ask, but she's already gone.

As the sink fills with water, I take the sheets of baking paper from the trays Abby used and open the bin. Abby's half-bitten macaron sits on top of the eggshells.

After all that, she didn't even eat one.

I close my eyes. Is something bothering Abby again? Even more than usual?

I'm drying the trays with a tea towel when she finally comes back.

'You took your time,' I say lightly.

Abby grabs a glass from the cupboard and fills it with water. She's so far away from me. Angry.

'Yeah, sorry,' she finally responds after gulping half the glass. 'I thought Grandma should know the recipe in case any of those CWA busybodies ask her.'

'You're too nice to her.' I reach an arm out, then freeze, my hand hovering at her shoulder.

'Well, she's a good grandmother,' Abby says and I can't help but read the criticism in what she doesn't say, an ache in my heart.

*

The next morning I'm off to visit a resort that's recently opened on the coast. Petra wants me to do a big fluff piece about their three pools and upmarket restaurant so they'll think about buying advertising space in *Arundel Trails*.

I head to the highway and put my foot down, my car spluttering unhappily. Outside the town, sheep farms dominate the landscape. Arundel is a wealthy place, for many, though there's an underclass of labourers, cleaners and hospitality workers who help keep the local economy afloat. Some of the wealthy landowners spend money in town, but the worst of them buy their LandCruisers, animal feed and farm machinery in Brisbane.

The local radio station soon becomes static, so I switch the music off, thoughts of Cara running through my brain.

Late last night, as Lee slid into bed reeking of stale coffee and sweat, I'd whispered, 'How's the case going?' All he would say is that no one seemed to have any clue what had happened to Cara Ross.

It's as if she's vanished off the face of the earth.

People can *seem* to disappear, but eventually the sun comes out, the snow melts and the flesh, which has been hidden all winter, is exposed.

The resort is as fancy as I had expected and will no doubt bring many more Sydney tourists north this summer. Petra will be pleased with my photos and the quotes I coaxed from the manager. It's not until I leave the resort lobby, a cavernous space that smells of lemongrass, with an armful of brochures and a face stiff from smiling, that I have a brainwave.

Cara's disappearance is a big story. A *news* story.

Obviously, she could return tomorrow, in which case there would be no story. But if she doesn't come back tomorrow; if something has happened to her ...

God forbid, of course.

But, if this is a real story, why can't *I* write it? I know the main players, I live in the town; heck, I'm practically married to the policeman investigating the case.

All I ever get to write at *Arundel Trails* are thinly veiled advertising features, stories about local bake sales, sporting team victories and the occasional missing dog.

Now I've been gifted something important.

I dump the brochures on the passenger seat of my car and settle into the driver's seat, tapping the steering wheel.

Could I write an investigative story about this?

Local Girl Goes Missing.

As a thwarted 'real' journalist the thought excites me. But it is more than that.

If I investigate, I can keep tabs on Cara's case, stay on top of what the police are thinking, find out what happened to her. I can keep control of the situation. Not to mention it will distract me from the other thing.

And, of course, I can protect Abby.

Lee will hate the idea. So maybe I won't tell him – for now. I'll have to come clean at some point because, as the lead detective on the case, his input will be important, but if he sees that I've been fair and done a good job, maybe he'll be fine with it.

I turn the ignition key decisively. I'll go to Calder Head, visit the Rosses. See where my nose leads me. Maybe Mike and Donna will be willing to talk, maybe they'll have some useful information. I picture a disapproving Lee, but I put him out of my mind and reverse from the car park.

It's time to do something for me, for my career.

And for Abby.

*

In Calder Head, I soon find the Ross family's old house, which is across the road from the beach.

It was a rental property, and it looks even more rundown now than it did back then. Paint peels from the walls of the dilapidated Queenslander, though it still has lovely proportions, with a generous veranda and a gable over the front door. Bikes and boxes are overflowing from the veranda, and two surfboards lie in the weed-infested grass of the front lawn. No doubt it'll soon be sold, razed and another giant two-storey house will join the others lining the beach.

At the end of the block is a small supermarket, which appears to have had a makeover, and a café called Mario's, which has been there forever. The beach opposite is gorgeous – white sand and gentle waves on this perfect winter's day. There's not much else to Calder Head, other than the caravan park at the other end of the beach, and the surf club at this end.

The town looks much the same as it did the day I collected Abby from the surf club six years ago, tapping across the scuffed timber floor in my work shoes to where the police had left her in the far corner of the hall. As a kindness, they'd walked the girls over there for interviews instead of taking them to Ramsey Police Station, which was half an hour's drive away. Abby had looked so small sitting on a fold-out chair in her swimmers, with her head bowed and a beach towel wrapped around her shoulders. A sound had made me turn and I'd seen a tiny figure – Cara – seated in the opposite corner. She was birdlike, fragile, looking much younger than Abby. Her doe eyes glistened. When she saw me, she pressed her feet into the floor and her chair jumped back with a shriek that startled her. Two uniformed policemen approached me solemnly. Abby lifted her eyes to meet mine, her tear-streaked face bright with fear.

My step faltered.

Abby looked different. Sharper, somehow. I was overcome with a desperate desire to wind the clock back. To see my old Abby sitting there before me – because I didn't recognise this girl.

I shake the memory away and take the next turn away from the beach, then another left.

I wonder how I'll find Mike and Donna's new place but before I can finish the thought, I have a piece of good luck. In the driveway of a two-storey tan-rendered McMansion there's a shiny black BMW four-wheel drive with an Orange Dawn Church logo on the side.

Thank you, Lord, indeed. I cut the engine. The Ross house is huge, far too big for three people, and new enough that the plants in the garden beds are seedlings, some with labels from the garden centre sticking out of the sandy soil beside them. I guess being the founder of a church pays well.

I've seen Mike's face on a few billboards on the highway. Orange Dawn is, as Lee so accurately described, a happy-clappy church. I'm all for freedom of religion but the main tenets of the Orange Dawn Church — known locally as the Oompa-Loompa Church due to their penchant for using the colour orange in their advertisements, signage and accessories — aren't my cup of tea. Big donations from parishioners are encouraged. They are reticent to support homosexuality and abortion. There haven't been any sex scandals, though, which is one positive. On my way here I drove past a new Orange Dawn building in Ramsey. The modern concrete and glass edifice looked as out of place in the old-fashioned town as I would among the well-groomed ladies on the Arundel golf course.

I dredge up old memories of Donna and Mike. The times after that first meeting in the surf club are a bit of a blur. Then I didn't see them for years, until a parent–teacher night at the end of last term, though we managed to avoid a conversation. The past isn't always worth revisiting.

I'm hard pressed to recall much about Donna, although I do recall her fussing over Cara, who'd had issues with her health, apparently since she was a baby. In my mind Donna remained a worried, dowdy mother. Mike was more memorable; with his mega-watt smile, colourful tattoos — there were numerous crosses and Bible verses among them — and the Jesus-length hair he wore in a man bun. It was a look that made him particularly popular with teenagers and young families.

I'm psyching myself up to approach the house when my phone buzzes with a text.

It's Hudson.

Just checking in. How's Abby?

From the moment Hudson heard that Cara had started at Arundel Christian College he said I should keep her and Abby apart. He thought the girls could be a bad influence on one another. I half agreed, though what could I do? I couldn't remove Abby from the school she'd been at for the past six years, not right before her HSC. How would that help her? And then the girls had become friends again, so it was a moot point.

She's okay, I respond. *Me, less so.*

Stephanie Bitchface didn't get to you, did she? Let's egg her house later.

I can't help smiling.

Ha ha. Good plan. Or maybe some hulled tahini. See you at the gym tomorrow.

I slip my phone into my pocket and walk to the front door.

The doorbell echoes throughout the house. I listen for other noises but it's quiet, the only sound the waves cracking onto the sand a block away. Then there's a muffled shuffling sound, and the door opens.

Mike Ross still has Jesus hair and a man bun, but his mega-watt smile is notably absent, and he hasn't shaved this morning. He's a tall man, well-built, wearing board shorts and a black t-shirt. He has even more tattoos on his arms than I remember. His eyes are red, and he regards me with an expression that's a mix of worry and hope. 'Hello? Can I help you?'

'Mike, hi. I'm Nicola Miller. My partner, Senior Sergeant Lee Cook, is heading up the police investigation into Cara's disappearance. We met a few years ago. You might remember my daughter, Abby … Abigail?' Recognition dawns. 'You must be so worried, and I was over this way for work and thought I'd call in to see if you need anything.'

43

'Thank you,' he says, blinking. It's hard to reconcile this man with the charismatic preacher on billboards. Mike doesn't seem to want to invite me inside, but politeness wins. 'Please, come in.' The house smells of coffee. We walk from the entrance hall into the living room. It's decorated in neutral grey tones, except for a small timber crucifix with a metal Jesus on it hanging on the wall opposite. On the coffee table a modern edition of the Bible sits on top of a pile of books – the spine of one reads *Great Churches of the World*, another is simply titled *Jesus*.

'Who is it, Mike?' a woman calls out, then emerges from a doorway leading to a kitchen and dining area. Through a window behind her, I see a backyard not yet landscaped, still with an old Hills Hoist in the centre of it. Donna is holding a tea towel and she stops when she sees me. Soft rock music comes from the room she emerged from.

Cara's mum is rounded and comforting, with wavy dark hair and deep worry lines between her eyes. She's younger than me, though appears ten years older, thanks mostly to her old-fashioned slacks and loose cardigan. She doesn't look like she belongs with Mike.

'It's Abigail's mother,' Mike says, though it's clear Donna is well aware who I am. 'Sergeant Cook's *wife*?' He makes the word a question, his eyebrows raised.

I shake my head. 'Partner.' I can't remember exactly what his church thinks about shacking up with someone you're not married to.

'Yes, hi, Nicola,' Donna says. Her voice is like slipping on a warm pair of pyjamas. She must be an asset to her husband when he deals with his flock. 'I see Abby at the hospital café sometimes, she's a lovely girl.' Something flashes behind her eyes. Abby had told me Cara's mother volunteers with the hospital auxiliary, selling lollies and crocheted goods to raise money for medical equipment.

'I'm so sorry to hear about Cara,' I say. 'Lee's doing everything he can to find her.'

'Thank you, we appreciate that.' There's an awkward silence.

'I was hoping we could chat?'

'Oh, Nicola, I'm not sure we're up for a chat.' There's a waver in Donna's voice. She wrings the tea towel, her knuckles white. 'I'm finding it difficult to think straight.'

'I'm sorry, I—'

'Is there new information?' Mike asks and my stomach churns to see the hope in his eyes. Whatever I thought I'd find here, it's not going to happen. I can't do this. Suddenly I have a lot more respect for Lee, for dealing with people in these situations on a regular basis.

I clear my throat. 'No. I'm sorry. I thought … I wanted to say I'm sure Cara will be home soon.'

Mike's eyes flash. 'I'm so glad you came by to tell us that,' he says derisively, his top lip curling. The veins on his neck pulse. I'm struck again by how powerfully built he is. He's standing too close to me and I take a step back. 'How useful!' he continues.

'Mike!' Donna chides him. 'She's just being nice!'

Mike turns on her. 'We should never have let Cara go off to that school. Why did you talk me into letting her go? She should have stayed in Calder Head. Arundel *Christian* School.' Mike can't keep the disdain from his voice. 'What a joke. They were responsible for my child.'

'Cara was at home when she went missing, Mike,' Donna says gently. 'It's not the school's fault.' She addresses me.

'I'm sorry, Nicola. My husband has been very upset by our daughter's disappearance. We both have.' She walks over and takes Mike's hand. He visibly calms, taking a deep breath in a way that makes me realise he's soothed himself this way before. After a moment he lifts his head. I blink in surprise to see the change in him. Here is his bright smile. His eyes lock on to mine – I'm the sole focus of his attention. He's Pastor Mike now. It unsettles me how easily he snapped out of his anger. How easily he turned on his charm. Something flutters deep in my belly, a stirring of recognition.

He reminds me of Abby's father.

'Yes, I'm so sorry, Nicola,' he says, his smile softening into an apologetic expression, so natural it makes me shiver. 'That was uncalled for.'

'It's ... that's fine.'

'Donna's right. I'm very worried about my daughter. But Cara has always had a mind of her own. Perhaps my wife is right and she's gone away for a few days. I'm praying that's the case. Anything else doesn't bear thinking about.' His pleasant demeanour falters again. Donna puts her arm around his waist.

'We have to have faith.'

'You're right, of course.' He turns to address me. 'We've been through so much with Cara, you see. She was so frail when she was little. I prayed to God every day to make her well again, and He did, He brought her back to me.' His jaw clenches. 'He won't take her from me now. I have to have faith.'

Donna leans her head against Mike's shoulder.

I shouldn't be here. 'I should go. I'm sorry to intrude.'

Mike's phone buzzes. 'It's the police,' he says. 'Your *partner*, probably.'

'Oh yes.' *Shit.* 'Look, um, Mike, please don't tell Lee I'm here. He might get in trouble if his bosses find out I'm talking to people involved in a case. I wanted to offer my support, but I probably shouldn't have come.'

Mike considers this, then nods as he lifts the phone to his ear. He says hello and leaves the room.

Donna tilts her head, her brow furrowing as she watches him go and I have a weird sense of déjà vu. She turns to me and the moment passes. 'I'll show you out,' she says, and starts walking towards the front door before pausing. 'Does Sergeant Cook know about Cara and Abby and what happened to them back then?'

Happened to them? That's an interesting way to put it.

'No. I haven't told him.'

'I understand. It was so long ago and they were only children. Children who made a mistake.'

I can hear Mike speaking in a low murmur, his words unintelligible. I smile at Donna. 'I have to admit, at first I was worried when Cara started at Arundel. I didn't want Abby to be reminded of the past.'

'I totally understand.' Donna nods. 'Cara wanted to put it behind her too.'

'Well, I appreciate that she didn't divulge details. You've raised a wonderful daughter.'

Tears fill her eyes. 'The past few days have been so difficult. I thought all our worrying about Cara was in the past. And now ...'

'She's a fighter. She'll be back.'

She sighs. 'Yes, you're right.' She walks past me and I smell lavender. When she raises her hand to the doorknob her cardigan falls back from her wrist, exposing several small bruises that mar her delicate skin.

The hair on the back of my neck lifts.

'You and Mike are under a lot of stress at the moment,' I say, trying to keep my words level. 'It must be very difficult. For both of you.'

Donna looks over her shoulder in the direction of her husband's voice, then nods distractedly. 'Yes, he is terrified for Cara.'

'I'm sure he is,' I say carefully, leaving a weighted moment before continuing in a quieter voice. 'But that's no excuse for violence.'

She focuses on me. 'Violence?'

I motion towards her wrist. She lifts it, examining the bruises as if she'd forgotten they were there.

Then she drops her arm, letting the cardigan cover them.

'Oh those!' She gives a nervous laugh. 'They're nothing. I can't even remember how I got them. Perhaps I bumped my arm hanging out the washing.' It's a poor explanation and she realises it, changing the subject. 'Thank you for coming.'

'Donna,' I say in a low tone to ensure my words don't carry through the echoey house, 'if someone has hurt you, you can tell me.'

There's a flash of fear in her eyes.

I knew it!

She opens her mouth, closes it, then tries again. 'Thank you for your concern, Nicola,' she whispers, her voice wavering with an emotion I can't pinpoint. 'But the Lord is all the protection I need.'

*

'That's a moose!' My heart leapt into my mouth.

We'd swept around a bend on the snow-covered four-lane highway about fifteen minutes outside of Banff and there it was, right in the centre of the road.

Sam braked, turning the wheel in what appeared to be a well-practised manoeuvre that caused the pick-up to skate and slide for a dozen terrifying metres before slowing to a standstill.

We ended up a stone's throw from the moose. The animal was taller than the pick-up, which was an oversized American one twice the size of the utes back home. The moose regarded us lazily. His fur was brown and mottled, and he had those distinctive antlers that were so familiar to me from cartoons, though in real life they were much scarier, wickedly spiked, almost as wide as I was tall. I turned from the creature to Sam, open-mouthed.

He was smiling at me. 'You haven't seen one up close yet, have you?'

I shook my head. He wound his window down. The icy air was shocking.

'What are you doing?' I hissed.

'Just saying hi.'

'He could kill us!'

'Hey, moosie,' Sam crooned, the way you'd speak to a skittish horse. 'Perhaps you'd like to wander off the road for us. We have a lunch engagement, and we don't want to be late.'

If he used that voice to call me, I'd come running. But Sam's charm was lost on the animal, which continued to just stare at the car. Eventually it turned and sauntered away into the pine trees.

I watched it go with a heavy heart.

'What a creature, hey?' Sam said. 'A moose like that weighs as much as a car, you know. The Canadians go on about our deadly snakes and spiders, but I reckon moose and bears are much more frightening. It'd be a lot worse to hit one of those guys with a car than a kangaroo, too. We'd have been goners if we ran into him going a hundred k's an hour.'

He was right. The thought was terrifying.

'We'd better move,' he said, turning the key in the ignition. 'We don't want to be rear-ended.'

Driving on the slippery snow and ice in Canada made me nervous, especially since it was combined with the disconcerting feeling of being on the wrong side of the road. Every time Sam turned a corner I flinched, expecting a head-on collision.

The view, however, made up for all that. Mountains surrounded us, more magnificent than I would have believed possible. After a month in Canada, I still wasn't immune to their massive size, their wild beauty. The jagged peaks were white with snow, though here and there patches of grey rock caught the sunlight. It was as if I could reach out the window and touch them. Bright blue glacier ice spoke of a timelessness that made my own life seem inconsequential.

As we approached Lake Louise the clouds closed in and snowflakes drifted down, though the storm wasn't expected until much later that night.

Luckily for me, Sam handled the slick road like a pro, relieving some of my tension. It helped that he was a talker. He told me about his father, who sounded like he was controlling and expected a lot but spoiled his only son too. And his mother, whom he clearly adored.

'How long have you been in Canada?' I asked.

'Since June. I came over after finishing my business degree. I've set up a house as a kind of base camp. I travelled a bit before the snow came. Now me and the boys mostly snowboard.'

'Wow. That's some holiday.'

'The others come when they can get a couple of weeks off work – to let off steam.' It sounded like a party house. 'At the moment there's four of us. Riley was a school mate, and Angus and Jonesy went to uni with me.'

It's hard for me to imagine the kind of life where you can drop everything to go to Canada to party. My mum has plenty of money. After Dad's death she inherited his property – most of which she sold – and his artworks – which she also sold. But she doesn't throw money around; I'd accused her of being tight on more than one occasion. She'd given me the money for my flights, but it was up to me to pay for the rest of my trip. It was character-building, she told me.

'I'm lucky,' Sam said, as if reading my mind. 'My dad picks up all my bills. However, since I head back to Australia next year to repay him with thirty years of corporate drudgery, I don't feel too guilty.' Despite his words he didn't seem worried at the prospect.

There was a beeping noise from the centre console where a mobile phone rested.

'Can you check that?' he asked. 'It might be one of the boys.'

'Cool phone,' I said, flipping it open. It was heavy in my hand, and the keys were backlit in blue. 'Fancy.'

'I picked it up over here. It's the latest model.' He sounded proud. I didn't have a phone, and calling Mum cost a fortune, so we only spoke on Sundays.

'There's a message from Riley.'

'Can you read it to me?'

'The phone's locked.'

'Guess the password.' His eyes shone with glee.

'Your birthday?'

He shook his head. 'Nah, something even more obvious.'

'One, two, three four?'

'Not quite.'

'Four, three, two, one?'

'You got it!'

I rolled my eyes, then tapped the numbers in.

Where are you? Missing some good powder today. Call me before the party tonight.

'You want to pull over and call him?'

'Nah. The boys are fine without me. Every day is powder day over here and the storm will dump more.'

The hotel at Lake Louise was as fabulous as I had heard. We skated on the frozen lake – a new experience for me – and I enjoyed it, despite several falls. Sam skated well, given his size. He even tried to lift me once, much to my terror, though he set me down lightly without mishap. Afterwards we had a late lunch of steaks and beer followed by a chocolate fondue in a prime table overlooking the lake. None of the staff asked my age and they all knew Sam well. Being with him was like being with a celebrity.

A girl could get used to this, I thought, dunking a strawberry into chocolate. Beyond the window, the lake heaved with tourists walking and skating on the ice. Horse-drawn carriages clopped by in a line. Sam said they were for clueless tourists, so we didn't take one and I didn't tell him I thought it looked fun.

By the time the valet brought around Sam's car, I was stuffed full of food and sleepy from the beer.

'Thank you, Sam, this has been awesome.'

'No problem.' Snow was falling a little heavier now and the day-trippers were leaving. Buses queued outside the hotel and people swarmed towards the car park. 'Lake Louise is always a treat.'

'Is it okay to drive in this weather?'

'Absolutely. This monster can handle anything. It's got the best winter tyres money can buy.' Sam took my hand, rubbing it lightly with his thumb. My heart shifted in my chest. 'Do you want to come to our place before you go back to the hostel?' he asked. 'We're having a party. Might be a nice end to your last day of freedom?' He gave me a look.

My nerve endings tingled.

Could this be the day?

Could Sam be the one?

'I'd love to.'

*

I drive to Mario's Café and take a seat inside near the window.

The tables are a little wobbly. Two older couples sit separately, both having Devonshire tea, which is listed on the small blackboard on the wall under 'Specials', along with a curried egg and iceberg lettuce sandwich and a chicken and mushroom crepe with white sauce.

An older gentleman with a grey moustache arrives as I'm stuffing a folded napkin under the table leg, introducing himself as the one and only Mario. I order a salmon sandwich and a pot of tea. Outside, a middle-aged woman throws a stick for a black Labrador on the gorgeous stretch of otherwise empty beach. The dog bounds through the waves and swims out to fetch it with a joy that is infectious.

My fingers fiddle with my knife and fork as I ponder my troubling encounter with Mike and Donna.

Mike had seemed genuinely worried for his daughter, yet he'd become angry so quickly, his emotions turning on a dime. And Donna, a soft woman trying to please her husband, to calm him down. I hadn't mistaken the fear in her eyes when I'd asked her about those bruises.

Did Mike hurt her?

Was he hurting Cara too?

Perhaps things had come to a head while she was home studying for Ancient History on Sunday? Maybe Mike had lashed out. Cara seems like the perfect daughter, though obviously behaving well or badly has nothing to do with the reasons for domestic abuse.

I keep coming back to Mike's noticeable worry for his daughter. Cara often described Mike and Donna as strict parents, so maybe she got into trouble for breaking curfew or seeing a boy, and they'd fought and she'd run away. That would explain Mike's concern. Perhaps he blames himself.

But wouldn't he tell the police if that was the case? Unless, as the head of the church, he worries that would reflect poorly on him?

I don't notice Mario has returned with my food until he asks in a jovial voice, 'One white tea and a salmon sandwich?' He sets down a mug with a teabag tag fluttering over the side, then a small crockery creamer and finally a plate on which sits a white bread sandwich neatly cut into four triangles. The salmon is tinned, not smoked as I'd assumed. The sandwich is surprisingly delicious, with soft, fresh bread, cut very thickly and seasoned perfectly. Outside, the middle-aged woman is now on the footpath, her wet and sandy dog back on the lead. He pulls her along as she smiles indulgently at him. I envy them their simple pleasure.

I pick up a second triangle. Should I mention Donna's bruises to Lee?

Or would he have already noticed them?

Perhaps not. Donna was probably wearing that baggy cardigan for a reason.

I curse under my breath, apparently not quietly enough, as Mario jerks around to stare at me. I take another bite of my sandwich and smile at the same time. His attention returns to the conversation at another table.

There's no way I can tell Lee about Donna's bruises without him finding out I was there. I'll just have to hope Lee does his job.

*

That night Lee makes it home for dinner. I've spent ages cooking lasagne, which is a family favourite, though none of us eat much. I check the news sites too often, but there is nothing.

'How was school?' I ask Abby. 'Any trial marks back yet?'

'No.' She's been answering in monosyllables all afternoon. She glances at me then relents a little. 'I might get Bio back tomorrow.' She spears a piece of spinach from the side salad and puts it in her mouth.

I make a non-committal noise. Is she behaving normally? I can't tell anymore.

I try Lee, keeping my voice light. 'How's the case going? Don't worry, I'm not asking for specifics.'

'We're following up a few leads but we haven't found anything concrete.'

'She's been missing – what – three days now?' I ask.

'Possibly five.'

'Did you investigate her parents?' Abby asks through her spinach. 'They're not normal.'

'We don't know what's happened to Cara yet, Abby.'

'We learned about cults in Religion in year ten,' Abby goes on. 'I reckon the Oompa-Loompa's a cult.'

'It's not a cult,' I say. 'Is it, Lee?'

'No. Not officially. The followers of those sorts of churches are desperately searching for something to believe in. They're lonely. Maybe they don't have family to lean on, like we do.'

Abby tilts her head and looks at Lee.

'My mother was like that,' he continues. I sit up straighter. Lee doesn't talk about his parents much. 'She came from money and fell for a guy who never had any. It didn't help that he gambled it all away. She might have become involved with the Orange Dawn Church, if it had been around then.'

Lee's parents are dead now, but his home life hadn't been great. He told me his mum and dad used to argue a lot, saying it was only football that got him through his teen years. I used to feel bad that Abby didn't have a father, but stories like Lee's made me realise she was lucky. Having a father around isn't always a good thing. Abby had me and my mum, and hopefully that was enough. I've always believed it made us closer.

But, examining Abby now, I wonder how close I really am to my daughter.

Has Abby ever really trusted me?

'There's something about Mike Ross that draws people to him,' Lee says. 'He's got a real charisma. People believe in him.' Lee lifts his gaze to Abby. His words are casual, though his eyes are sharp. 'Have you met Cara's parents, Abby?'

'No,' she says, avoiding my eyes. 'But I've seen her dad on TV and billboards, and I heard the way Cara talked about him.'

I remember that day at the surf club, how Mike and Donna had rushed in as I held Abby in my arms. How Donna had sobbed and Mike had spoken to the police in a low voice. How the police officers had called me over, explaining to the three of us that our daughters had almost killed another girl.

'So you aren't friends with her anymore?' Lee continues.

'No, it's not that. She's been busy studying, I told you.'

'Is there anything about Cara that I should be aware of, Abby? Her likes or dislikes? Anyone you can think of who might have had a reason to hurt her?'

Abby gives him a disappointed look. Then her eyes flash to mine. There's something hidden in there, something I can't decipher. 'No.'

'She's not involved in anything she shouldn't be?'

She glowers at him. 'She's a straight A student, Lee. And she's sporty. Polite. Everyone adores Cara Ross. Everyone.' Abby spears a slice of tomato with her fork and holds it in the air, its juice splattering her plate. 'Who on earth would want to hurt her?'

*

I rise at 5 am and leave without waking Lee.

It's a short drive to the industrial estate that houses Sweat Zone, the gym Hudson and I attend three times a week.

Hudson's top-of-the-line Volkswagen sedan arrives and I wait as he parks next to me.

'Hey gorgeous.' He opens his door and kisses my cheek. He's wearing a new Adidas tracksuit in emerald green. It's fitted and matches his eyes. 'How are you? You look like shit. Also, can you please let me hook you up with a new car? Having my best friend drive an old clanger like this around town reflects badly on me, you know.'

'Yeah, yeah. I love your new outfit, by the way. Understated.' I grin. Hudson adores beautiful things. Clothes. Cars. People. I've long suspected my old royal blue Subaru offends his aesthetic sensibilities. Though I have to admit he's right – the car is a piece of shit.

'You know me, lovely. I always put my best foot forward.' I laugh, and then he pulls a face as he changes the subject. 'This thing with Cara. It's not looking good, is it? Do you think she's run away or do you reckon she's dead?' Hudson's not big on small talk. He grabs his gym bag from the back seat and straightens up, pulling out a banana and peeling it as he watches me.

'I hope she's run away,' I say, 'but I'm not sure.'

'It's this shithole,' Hudson says, his mouth filled with banana. 'It eats people alive.'

Hudson's own escape attempt from Arundel lasted a little longer than mine – three years in Brisbane, to be precise, until his mother, Diana, was diagnosed with early onset dementia. He came home to care for her and she lived for another four years, all of them in her family home. He might have stayed here after that, but he does still bitch about Arundel. A lot.

'Cara went missing from Calder Head,' I point out.

'Whatever. I blame this place. Too much crime. It's getting worse.'

That's a dig at Lee and I bristle, managing not to bite.

'You and Jeff must be due for another Bali trip.'

'Why?'

'When you get bitchy it means you need a break.' Jeff works as the groundsman/handyman at Arundel Christian College. He was a landscape architect in Brisbane but he followed Hudson home when Diana got sick. Jeff never seems to mind that he earns half the money he used to; in fact, he enjoys low-key country life more than Hudson does. Jeff is a quiet guy and we've never become very close, but he adores Hudson. He's solid.

He sighs. 'I miss the city sometimes. Country towns are so urgh!' He pretends to vomit.

Part of me is sad that we never properly made it out of Arundel, though we've both made good lives for ourselves here, and at least I have my best friend by my side.

'I'm thinking of writing something about Cara's disappearance,' I say casually. 'Something freelance, if Petra doesn't want it for the paper. From the perspective of someone who's involved.' I scrunch up my face. 'I went to see Mike and Donna Ross.'

'Really? Does Lee approve of this visit? Of you writing this story?'

'I haven't told him. Not yet, anyway.'

Hudson raises his eyebrows.

'I will, though, of course.'

'Of course,' he says. 'Just remember what happened last time. That story your mum wanted you to write? The domestic violence problem in town. Lee wasn't happy—'

'This is different.'

Hudson looks sceptical.

'I explained that story to him and we're fine now. He thought the article targeted the police because they didn't do enough for victims, when that wasn't the point at all.'

'Well, he wasn't happy.' He shrugs. 'It's probably a good idea to keep this investigation to yourself.'

Hudson and Lee will drink beer together, laugh at one another's jokes, but there's always a hint of friction. I've made it work, though. I just don't do many barbeques when they're both present.

We're early so I fill him in on what's transpired over the past couple of days. He gasps at all the right places (Mike losing his temper, Donna's bruises and her obvious fear when I asked her about them). He also vows to visit Mario's Café when I tell him what a time-warp it is.

'For what it's worth, I think it's great that you want to get back to writing hard-core news. You're very good at it. But be careful. I'd hate to see you get hurt.'

'Course.'

'How's Abby going?' He waves to a couple of others from the class who are heading inside.

'She seems okay. You know Abby, it's hard to tell.'

'I do know her,' Hudson says. 'I've talked to her a few times in the past couple of days. She's amazing, Nicola. She'll come through this like a champion.' Hudson is Abby's godfather, and he adores her. I love that they have a strong bond. Before I met Lee, Hudson was like a dad to Abby. It's the main cause of friction between him and Lee, not that either of them would ever articulate it.

As a kid, Abby wrapped Hudson around her little finger. Mind you, she'd had my number too. She'd ask me why she didn't have a dad when I made her go to bed early, or cry as if the world was ending when I told her to eat her vegetables. I gave in too often. And it wasn't only me. Her year three teacher told me Abby had talked a little boy into eating a sandwich from the bin. She regularly avoided punishment thanks to a quivering lip or a cute smile.

Abby received an invitation to every birthday party, was the first pick for every sports team and if something bad went down, she always came out of it squeaky clean.

Was that normal?

That's why I'd been pleased when she befriended Isabella. Isabella was such a sweetheart. An innocent. Bizarre, given the insane wealth of her parents. I'd thought their relationship would be good for Abby.

It hadn't quite played out the way I'd intended.

More people arrive for class and we follow them into the gym. Hudson bins his banana skin. The instructor cranks up the thumping music that's at least a generation too young for me and we jog around the warehouse to warm up, then I burpee and squat and push-up my way to forgetting about Cara Ross for an hour. There are about twenty-five people in the class. Hudson and I are two of the oldest members, but we're strong and I derive a sneaky pleasure at being fitter than people in their early twenties. And today I go hard. I need this session.

It's not until I'm lying on a towel on the floor, wet with sweat, my legs twisted to one side in a stretch that I notice him, lying on a towel to my right.

Tom Foley, a History teacher from Abby's school. Tom's about forty with a wife and three kids. Slim and great at cardio, not so good with the big weights. An excellent teacher, according to Abby, one of her favourites. Tom faces away from me. The dark curls of the back of his head are damp with sweat. That's when it comes back to me. Tom and Cara. I saw them together. We turn to the other side, then the cool-down is over. There's a smattering of applause and a few thanks for the instructor.

When I sit up and swivel around, there's an empty space where Tom was a minute ago. I spy him putting a towel in a duffel bag and climb to my feet. 'You ready?' I call to Hudson, and he gives me a startled look from where he's stretching on the floor, then stands up. He doesn't ask what's going on, simply grabs his bag and follows me outside. In the car park I see that Tom's joined a small group of people deciding where to go for coffee.

I sidle up.

'You want to come to the Coffee Cart, Nic? Hudson?' The question comes from a slim university student with a towel slung around her neck. The uni students always have time for coffee when most of us are racing off to work.

'Maybe next time, Courtney. Thanks, though,' I say.

The girls wander off and Tom also heads towards his car.

'Tom?'

He turns around to my call. He's an attractive man, with youthful, even features and the sort of stubble that needs shaving every day.

'Can I have a quick word?'

He glances at his watch, then says, 'Sure.'

Hudson is beside me, so I say quietly, 'Give us a minute?' He regards me for a moment, then nods, strolling away.

Tom pulls the edge of his towel free and wipes the sweat from his face. 'How did Abby go with the trials?'

'She didn't tell me much, so good, probably. Look, Tom, I saw you with Cara Ross last week, after class. Last Thursday afternoon. I don't usually come to the gym then, but Hudson wanted to do some extra weights ... anyway, that's not the point. The point is, I saw you talking to her out here.' I take a breath. 'She seemed upset.'

His expression becomes guarded. 'It's terrible that Cara is missing.'

'It is.' I wait and he presses his lips together.

'Look, it's not really any of your business, but Cara wanted another extension on the Ancient History essay she should have handed in before the trial period even started. And we can't allow students extra time without a good reason. She wasn't happy about it. Year twelve is a stressful time for students, sometimes they take it out on us.'

I want to say that it seemed like more than that, but he cuts me off.

'Sorry, I have to go. I've got a staff meeting before school. Say hi to Lee for me.' Tom gets into a maroon four-wheel drive, and I'm left with the memory of him and Cara arguing last week. I can picture them, standing close together, their words urgent yet hushed. It didn't appear to be an argument over a late essay.

I stride over to my car and find Hudson standing beside it. 'What was that about?'

'I'm not sure. Maybe nothing.' I unlock my car. 'I'll talk to you later.' Tom drives past as the Subaru's engine splutters to life. He gives me a curt nod.

I don't nod back.

There's one image from last Thursday that I'm sure I didn't imagine.

Cara was standing stock-still listening to Tom's low words. Then Tom pulled her close, grabbing her arm, his fingers curled around her bicep.

As if he was pleading with her.

*

When we arrived at Sam's house, hidden away in the back streets of Banff, I couldn't help saying in an awed voice, 'Oh *damn.*'

Sam was delighted by my reaction.

Although it was crafted from stone and timber and glass, the house was modern, a luxurious ski retreat perched at the end of a cul-de-sac behind a multi-storey resort only a few minutes from town.

'Come and check it out before it gets dark.' Sam backed the pick-up to one side of the driveway. He shoved the key above the sun visor.

'You're not scared someone will steal it?'

'It's a rental.' He shrugged. 'It's insured.'

We ran to the porch to avoid the snow, which was coming down more heavily by then. He took out a set of keys and opened the front door.

'At least you lock something,' I said as he took my coat and hung it on a peg, stuffing my beanie and gloves into its pockets. My bag remained slung over my shoulder. It had my passport and wallet and a couple of personal things I didn't want to leave at the hostel.

'Well, there's beer in here,' he joked. 'Someone might steal that.' He tilted his head to listen but the house was quiet. 'The guys are probably still on the mountain.'

'In this weather? It'll be dark soon.'

'Either that or they're at the *bar* on the mountain.'

The inside of the house was as impressive as the outside, with more timber and stone. It had appeared to be one level from the front, but the cavernous entryway showed two further levels below, with windows at the back overlooking a ravine. We walked downstairs to the main level, through a lounge room with an open fire and into the kitchen. Unopened piles of red plastic cups and dozens of untouched bottles of spirits sat on the enormous island bench.

Sam examined the bottles. 'It appears a substantial New Year's Eve party has been planned.' He smiled at me. 'We have the house to ourselves for now, though. How does a beer by the fire sound?'

'Um, good, yep.' I tried to perch on a kitchen stool and almost slipped off.

Sam laughed. 'You're so awkward, Nicola.' I blushed. 'No, I mean it in a good way. It's your greatest charm.' He grabbed matches and newspaper and took my hand, leading me back into the lounge room. I stood nearby while he lit the fire, enjoying the smoke; I'd always loved an open fire. The room was homely yet luxurious, exactly how I imagined a fancy hotel to be.

'The house is very tidy considering there are four guys living here.'

'Lucky for us we have a very thorough cleaner. Shereen comes every day, even tomorrow. Otherwise, the place would be a hotbed for disease. If these surfaces could talk.' He made a face.

'Ew!'

'Yeah. You should've seen our uni dorm. Riley's always been a tidy bastard, though, even at school. He nags us to tidy up our shit all the time.' He rolls his eyes. 'But why bother when the cleaner comes every day?'

Once the fire had taken hold, Sam returned to the kitchen for beers. I settled onto the couch, butterflies in my stomach but also feeling loose-limbed and drowsy. The idea of an empty house, after a month in hostels where it was impossible to get a moment's peace, was intoxicating.

'Here you go,' he said a minute later, falling onto the couch beside me and passing me a beer. As I grabbed it, a little slopped out of the bottle onto my jumper.

'Ah, shit,' I said, brushing at it. My jumper would stink of beer for months now. It was lovely soft wool. I wasn't even sure how to wash it.

'Oh, damn, I'm sorry. Are you wet?'

'Not really. I'll be fine.'

'Come upstairs and I'll get you something else to wear while it dries.'

I raised my eyebrows.

'Seriously,' he said with a smile, 'the view from up there is amazing. Come see.'

I set my beer on the coffee table as he took my hand.

Today had been a dream – meeting Sam at breakfast, the skating and lunch at Lake Louise, and now this perfect house. *This* was why I'd come to Canada. Why I'd left Australia. To have experiences like this.

I couldn't wait to tell Hudson about it; it might even be worth an expensive phone call to Australia from the far too public payphone in the hostel tomorrow. With my heart fluttering against my ribs, I had a strong feeling I was about to leave my old self behind.

*

At the office the next morning I cyberstalk Tom Foley.

The office is just a couple of rooms above a bank on Arundel's main street. The stairs creak, the kitchen overlooks an alley where the bank employees gather to smoke, and the carpet is water stained. I'm only in the office three days a week, and even those are flexible. I tell myself regularly that I'm lucky, I'm on a good wicket at *Arundel Trails*.

Petra is on the phone in the small room – her office – when I enter, so I wave, sit down at my computer and start it up. I thrum my fingers on the desk as it loads, then open Facebook to search for Tom Foley. He doesn't post often, though there are a series of shared photos about his son's soccer team at the top of his feed. But his wife, Eva, often posts about their picture-perfect family. I stare at the photos, trying to glean more about their relationship. The family of five camping, fishing rods in hand. The eldest boy in a high-school uniform. Their daughter in a tutu at a ballet concert. A photo of Tom and Eva captioned 'Date Night! #overdue', which shows the two of them grinning at one another in the local tapas restaurant. I recognise Eva. She's in the CWA with Mum – she's one of the youngest members. I text Mum.

Do you know Eva Foley?

Mum replies almost immediately. *Yes.*

What's she like?

She makes very good ANZAC biscuits.

'Not helpful, Mum,' I mutter.

You met her at the golf club xmas party last year.

Oh yes. I remember the event well. Little kids running around, overstimulated with sugary drinks, every surface in the clubhouse sticky. Santa ran late and by the time he came up the ninth hole in a golf buggy, half of the children were in tears, the others screeching as though they were at a rock concert. We were only there because Mum had convinced Lee to do the barbeque. I spent ten minutes asking strangers for Panadol before Eva came to my rescue. I didn't recall much about her except that she had the sort of smile that transformed her pleasant face into someone beautiful.

Thanks, Mum, see you on Sunday. Xx

Harry wanders in, bringing with him a cloud of cologne and three coffees in a cardboard carrier.

'You're a legend, Haz,' I say as he passes me one.

'I know, I know.' Harry grins, then frowns at me. 'I heard your daughter is friends with the girl who went missing.'

I realise I haven't seen Harry since news of Cara's disappearance broke. 'Yeah. They're at the same school.'

'I saw a picture of her on TV and couldn't get over how much she looks like Abby.'

'You think?' I try not to sound offended. Cara is pretty, not beautiful like Abby.

'Yeah, they're like twins.' He sips from his own coffee. 'There are a tonne of Sydney journos loitering outside the police station.'

'I know. Lee said they're allowed to be there. He can't get rid of them.'

'Pack of vultures,' he says mildly. 'Anyhow, I'm sure Lee will find the girl soon,' he adds, then heads into Petra's office to put a coffee on her desk. I angle my computer screen so that he can't see it before he returns and settles into the chair beside mine.

Scrolling further down Tom's page I finally find something useful: a group of teenagers in Arundel Christian College uniforms. In the centre of them stands Tom and another adult I don't recognise. It's an excursion and the photo is taken outside an impressive sandstone building. I enlarge it and examine the students. Cara is beside Tom and faces him rather than the camera, while he smiles straight down the lens. Abby is at the other end of the group, an aloof smile on her face. The photo was shared by another parent to Tom's page three months ago, and they've captioned it, 'Took this amazing bunch of humans to the Greek antiquities exhibition @ausmuseum. Great day!' It was from their history excursion to Sydney. I stare at Cara's face. What's her expression? Adoration? Simple friendliness? Laughter at a joke? I squeeze my eyes together, frustrated.

Tom Foley wouldn't be stupid enough to have an affair with a student, would he? That sort of thing goes on in books and movies, not in Arundel. Examining the photo again I have to admit Harry is right. Cara is beautiful. And charming. I should know, I've been on the receiving end of it. But if she was interested in someone like Tom Foley – a teacher – she wouldn't act on it, surely? If it came out it could ruin her chance at Oxford or Cambridge. And for Tom, well, it would destroy his career, his family.

No, they wouldn't.

'Sugar?' Harry waves a sachet at me.

'No, thanks.' In my head, I compare Cara's smile in the photo to the way she looked at Tom outside the gym last week.

I need to talk to Lee.

*

I wait till it's late.

It's a Friday night and Lee is home early for a change. After takeaway pizzas I pour a white wine and Lee grabs a beer and we move out to the backyard. It's freezing, but we are bundled in hoodies and I've already lit the fire in the cast-iron firepit in the centre of the lawn. It's an ordinary, suburban yard that backs on to the bush, but we love sitting out here. Beyond the fence are several huge eucalypts. Their trunks glow grey in the moonlight and on a cold night such as this, the air is fresh and the leaves rustle, even though the breeze has dropped.

'It's a cold one,' Lee grunts as we settle into the Adirondack chairs near the fire. Abby says she's doing homework, though she's probably texting her friends.

'Sorry I've not been around much this week,' Lee says, reaching for my hand. I grip his, some of my stress falling away at the warmth of it around mine. 'Things have been full-on at work,' he continues. 'I've got detectives from Missing Persons breathing down my neck, acting as if we're small-town hicks who can't tell our arses from our elbows, and we still have no strong leads.' He sighs. 'The buck stops with me, of course. And there are other cases I have to deal with too. There's this damn drug dealer, Seth McFadden. He lives in the Heights –' the fanciest part of town '– and his neighbours are giving me grief about him. There's a dodgy smell coming from the joint; people coming and going at all hours. But his uncle's on the local council and I have to get all my i's dotted and t's crossed before I can search his place.' He shakes his head. 'It's a nightmare, babe.'

'You've got this, Lee.'

He pulls me to him and kisses me on the mouth, tasting of beer, his beard comfortingly scratchy against my skin. As we pull apart, the smoke turns, drifting into my eyes. A memory threatens and I push it aside. Sometimes this happens; on cold nights when Lee chooses beer over whiskey, the smoke and the smell and the goosebumps on my skin – but I refuse to give in to it, tamping it down.

We lean back in our chairs, still holding hands. Despite the distant sound of cars on the highway out of town and the occasional barks of the German shepherd down the street, it's peaceful. Lee's hand loosens around mine. A pang of tenderness strikes me. He's ready to sleep and it's not yet nine o'clock. Lee used to work cases like this in Sydney – and some far worse – but this is different; this is a girl he knows, in a community he's truly a part of. Lee might have only moved to Arundel five years ago, but he's devoted to this town, and people have responded to that. He's well respected and well liked; two things that aren't always easy for a small-town police officer to achieve.

'Lee,' I prod, before he falls asleep.

'Mm.' The beer bottle sits at an angle in his lap, yet it looks safe enough. His expression has softened.

'Lee,' I say again, a little louder.

'Huh?' He jolts and blinks. 'I'm awake.'

'Sure you are.'

He pulls himself upright a little more, grasping his beer more firmly. 'Am now.'

'I need to tell you something.'

Alarm flits across his face, then he focuses on me. 'What is it?'

'It's about the case. About Cara. I saw her a few days before she went missing. I only remembered this morning.' I fill him in on my discussion with Tom Foley at the gym.

'Have I met him?'

'Probably not. You didn't come to the last parent–teacher meeting, and we don't know him socially.'

'Okay. Well, thanks. I'll follow it up tomorrow morning. See what he has to say for himself.'

My shoulders loosen. I'm pleased to get that off my chest. Of course, I hope Cara will reappear happy and healthy. Alive. However, if anything has happened to her, I'd prefer it was Tom Foley than …

No, Nicola, don't think about it.

Lee's awake now and he's regarding me intently. 'How're you holding up?'

'I'm fine.'

'You know Cara. This must be hard for you too.'

'I don't know her that well. But, yeah, it's hard.' I hesitate, then add, 'I'm not sure if she and Abby are even friends anymore. Not really.'

'Do you have any idea why?' He's asked me that before, but I don't remind him.

Instead, I snort. 'Other than the fact that they're teenage girls?'

'Good point.' He takes a mouthful of beer and I sip my wine. It tastes sour and I surreptitiously pour it onto the lawn. The sky above is bright with stars and the trees shiver in the wind. It makes me aware of my smallness in the scheme of things. My unimportance. I take a deep breath. It seems a good time for the truth to come out. All of it. About Abby and Cara and Isabella, about seeing Donna and Mike and the article I plan to write. Maybe even about Canada.

Because soon all those secrets might come out, whether I like it or not.

My mouth opens, but Lee beats me to it.

'I'm off to bed,' he says. 'Big day tomorrow. Again.' He rises with a groan, kisses my cheek and walks across the lawn towards the house.

The moment has passed, and I'm left alone in the darkness.

*

Sam gave me a tour on the way upstairs.

'There are two bedrooms at the front of the house and a couple more on the level below too, but I've got the master,' he said as we climbed the stairs. 'It's up here at the back.' We walked along a corridor and stopped. He opened it with a flourish. 'Ta–da.'

'This is so cool.' The room was large enough for a king bed and a sofa, with a bathroom and wardrobe at one end, along with a television mounted above a console table. Along one whole side, windows overlooked the ravine, though since it was dark my reflection was the only thing peering back at me, my frame slight beside Sam.

'We missed the last of the daylight,' Sam said, disappointed. 'On a clear day you can see over the ravine and across to the mountains.'

He entered the walk-in closet and emerged with a navy t-shirt, throwing it at me. Self-consciously, I went into the bathroom and stripped off my jumper and t-shirt, slipping Sam's on. It was lovely and soft and much too big. In the bedroom I put my bag on the floor near the door then joined him at the window.

He'd switched on an outside light. A balcony ran the length of the windows, a snow-covered table and chairs in the centre of it.

Sam stepped behind me and pulled me into him, his hands on my waist. I rested my head against his chest, his flannel shirt smelling of washing detergent and faintly of his sweat.

He lowered his head and kissed the back of my neck.

I relaxed into it.

His hands moved up my waist, under my t-shirt, over my stomach and ribs until they cupped my breasts. I turned around and he kissed my mouth, harder. My hand pressed against his chest, his heartbeat was fast. His penis was hard against my hip through his jeans. He took his mouth from mine and shuffled me towards the bed.

'Sam,' I said, uncertain now, his grip too strong. 'I'm not sure ...'

'It'll be fine,' he murmured, and his voice sounded different. Husky and raw.

He pressed my shoulders down until the bed was beneath me, then lifted the shirt he'd given me a few minutes earlier up over my head and threw it on the floor. Then he pushed me back against the bed. He kissed me again, insistent now.

I tried to pull away. I didn't want this right now. 'Sam, I ...'

He was heavy now, his bare leg – I didn't even realise he'd taken his jeans off – between mine.

'Sam,' I said again, more sharply. I wanted to end this.

He rolled to one side and I breathed a sigh of relief, thinking he had heard me and would leave me alone. Instead, he moved down to the end of the bed, unbuttoning my jeans and yanking them down in a sure movement, pulling the bedcovers back and climbing on top of me as I tried to scramble back up the bed. 'Sam, I'm not … I haven't …'

'I'll be careful, don't worry. It'll be fine.'

'No, I … Please, stop.'

His hand was on my shoulder, his tongue in my mouth. I shoved at him, but he was stronger than me. I tried to say stop again, but his mouth was pressed against mine, his gaze unfocused.

Without warning he flipped me over, pressing me into the sheets. Alcohol and sweat filled my nostrils.

'No! Sam! Stop!'

He wrenched my underpants down, used his hands to spread my knees apart, then he was inside me. The pain was sharp and surprising. I lay still and prayed for it to be over as he continued to thrust at me. It must have only been a few minutes, though it seemed far longer. Then he grunted and it was done, his body collapsing on mine. I couldn't breathe, from the weight of him on me, or from the shock, maybe. The only sound Sam's harsh panting.

My eyes squeezed shut. Distantly, car doors slammed, voices called to one another. I couldn't imagine ever talking again. Ever getting out of this bed.

A phone buzzed on a hard surface and Sam stirred. He pulled out of me and I was flooded with relief, as well as a strange feeling of loss.

'Sorry I rushed that a bit, babe. I couldn't help myself. You're just too hot,' he murmured, yawning.

I couldn't stop shivering, though the room was warm. This wasn't the way I'd expected to lose my virginity.

*

Two am thoughts.

I'm not sure if everyone does this or if it's just me, but there are times when I should be asleep where I lie awake, my brain ticking over, rehashing moments until things that seemed perfectly normal in the light of day become huge – e-fucking-normous, actually – so magnified that they take on a significance totally out of proportion to the original problem and become all I can think about.

All. I. Can. Think. About.

Sometimes, if it's a particularly bad night, I have heart palpitations. Sometimes I fling back the doona and drink water or read a book or scroll on my phone to distract myself. Sometimes I tell myself whatever I'm thinking about isn't important, but it doesn't work.

By morning, however, it's a different story. While I'm drinking my breakfast smoothie, it becomes painfully clear I had hugely exaggerated the problem. That the mother at the school gate wasn't trying to tell me Abby had bullied her precious daughter at lunchtime, which will lead her down a drug-addled path to prison or a stripper's pole. That the man who passed me in the park with a briefcase, giving me a friendly nod, wasn't following me.

But the concerns I unpacked about Tom Foley during the night linger the next morning.

In fact, all weekend I continue to wonder, could Tom Foley have had something to do with Cara's disappearance?

There's the argument. His evasion when I questioned him about it. The way she looked at him in that photo on Facebook.

On Saturday night Lee tells me that Tom gave him the same story he gave me, almost word for word. That Cara wanted an extension for an overdue History essay.

Sure.

Lee seems to have bought it, at least for now. And Tom has an alibi, if you call being at home with his family all weekend an alibi. Though I'm sure he's bound to have had time to duck out at some point without his wife knowing. Or with her knowing, if she's protecting him.

Plus, if Tom is having sex with a teenage girl, he would lie about it to the police.

We all lie to cover up our crimes. Or our secrets.

You want Tom to be involved, a voice says.

I ignore the voice and, despite my overactive imagination, the weekend passes uneventfully. Lee is at work most of the time. Cara's missing person case and the local drug dealer are taking up all his time. Abby studies – or stays in her room on her computer – except for her brunch on Sunday with my mum. It's a weekly ritual that started when Abby was a baby. Mum would take her out in the pram to give me an extra hour or two to sleep in. Generally, I'm all for it, though sometimes they come back with in-jokes at my expense. Or Mum will let something slip that reveals Abby's told her something she hasn't shared with me. But I'm happy they're great friends.

Honestly.

This week they stay out longer than usual and when Mum drops Abby home she bolts to her room.

'How was she?' I ask Mum as Abby's bedroom door closes.

Mum smiles at me and pats my arm. 'She's good, darling. Really.'

'Good? Her friend is missing and she's "good"?'

'There's no pleasing you with her at the moment, is there? I mean, she's coping quite well. You can trust her, darling.' She says it without judgement, and I feel terrible.

'Mum?' Abby's voice comes from the stairs.

'Yes, hon?'

She sticks her head over the landing. 'Did Grandma tell you about the car we saw?' Her voice is teasing and my heart lifts to hear it. 'We saw this little black SUV parked across the road from Nature's Café.' *Shit, that reminds me I haven't talked to Lucas about those free meals he gave the girls.* 'A Mazda. It was cute. Grandma says if I stay in Australia for uni or take her up on her patisserie offer, she might buy me one.'

'Does she now?' I look pointedly at Mum, half-smiling, then back to Abby. Mum has said she'll help Abby pay to go overseas to uni, though both of us hope she'll stay. Mum's even offered to set her up in her own business, a cake shop they both refer to as a patisserie in exaggerated French accents. 'Does that mean you're thinking of staying?'

'Not really,' she admits and my heart sinks. 'But I'm not *not* thinking about it. It was a pretty nice car. We saw it later on our way home. It was zippy.'

'I'm not sure I want you to get a zippy car. Or one that's better than mine.'

'Every car is better than yours, Mum!'

I make a huffing sound and change the subject. 'Well, the idea of you staying in the country is appealing.'

'Don't get your hopes up. It was just a car.'

After Mum leaves and Abby goes back to her room, I spend the rest of the day organising the kitchen drawers, a job I've put off for ages, but those thoughts from the early hours keep sneaking back into my head.

What should I do about Tom Foley?

There are two options. One, I can do nothing; let Lee and the police do their jobs. That's the sensible option. Or two, I can continue investigating Cara's disappearance and see for myself if he's involved.

Of course, I choose option two.

*

Sam reached across me to get his phone and the touch of his skin against mine made me feel sick. Something sticky trickled down my thigh. When he fell back onto the other side of the bed I was relieved he was no longer near me.

He pressed a button. 'Yeah? Hey, Jonesy. You boys back?'

I heard another voice through the phone, then Sam spoke again.

'Pizzas? Sure. There's cash in the drawer. God, you boys'll have to pay for something one of these days.' He laughed and then spoke in my direction, 'They're back and they're getting pizzas.'

I said nothing.

'Yep, we can hear you.' He laughed. 'Yes, I'm with a *friend.*'

He rolled off the bed and stood up. I heard him walking towards the console table near the television.

'You know me, Jonesy!' He laughed again and my skin crawled. 'One sec, mate. Let me grab a smoke.' He put the phone down and scrabbled around. It sounded as if he was pulling on pants and a shirt. Then there was the unmistakable flare of a cigarette lighter. 'You want one?' he called. I ignored him again. After a couple of seconds he said, 'Fine, I'll take it outside.'

Moments later the door to the balcony opened. Freezing air poured in, reaching me almost immediately. I rolled onto my back and looked down. My underpants were around my ankles. My bra was still in place, though one strap was loose. With shaking hands I plucked it back over my shoulder, then tugged my underpants up, seeing the bright red blood on the sheets. My body was tender and bruised, inside and out.

Moving gingerly, I tugged the bedcovers up to my neck, still shivering, though not from the cold.

'Yeah, I'll bring her down in a bit,' Sam said in a low voice on the balcony. 'Show her off. Yeah, she's a … probably an eight. Maybe a nine.' He guffawed. 'Better than the last one *you* brought home.' He listened. 'Soon, okay? Give her a minute, mate. You know what I'm like …' He trailed off. 'Yeah, I realise I said that last time! Yes, and the time before that. Hey, I can't help it if they can't get enough, can I?'

Sam has done this before. The realisation dawned on me, my throat burning with bile.

He'll do it again.

*

On Monday morning I miss my run and tell Lee I'm coming down with a cold.

Then I call Petra, who is so understanding that I feel bad taking the day off work, promising her and myself I'll make up for it soon.

Abby gets a lift to school with Grace and, just like that, I'm free.

Once alone, I change into plain black gym clothes and drive to the school. I don't know what I'm expecting to discover, as Tom Foley should be at work all day. The whole thing is bound to be a waste of time, but I'm compelled to do it anyway. I take snacks, my laptop and a cap, like the world's dodgiest detective. I tell myself this is what any good investigative journalist would do.

Tom's maroon four-wheel drive is in the car park, so at least he's here. I find a spot with a view of his car and settle in to wait.

By the time the bell goes for recess, I'm a nervous wreck. I've spent the whole morning ducking down or pretending to check my phone every time someone emerges from the school. I've eaten all my food and bitten my nails, a habit I've had under control for years now.

You're a fool, Nicola, I berate myself. *What on earth are you thinking?*

I click my seatbelt on and press the ignition key, and of course it's then that Tom Foley walks out of the office and across the car park. He moves quickly, a scowl on his face. He pauses as he reads a message on his phone, then shakes his head and climbs into his vehicle.

Why is he leaving school in the middle of the day?

For the fiftieth time that morning I pretend to check my phone, dropping my head as his car passes. A couple of beats later I follow him.

Tom drives over the speed limit so it's a struggle to stay close enough not to lose him, yet far enough back that he doesn't recognise my car. It appears he's heading to town, and he is, before continuing on until we're on the road towards the coast. I'm worried he's going to Calder Head or even further. Once Arundel falls behind us the green lawns and manicured hedges disappear, and the landscape changes to eucalypts, rocky outcrops and drought-ravaged fields filled with hungry sheep and cattle. It's been a dry winter and there's little green to see, only shades of brown. It's like driving across an army camouflage uniform.

This is technically a highway, one of the main ways in and out of Arundel. Even so, less than a couple of kilometres from town it becomes a two-laned potholed road with scrub on either side. I'm trying to determine if I should turn back when Tom surprises me, taking an unmarked exit left onto a dirt road. My heart thuds and my hands are sweaty on the wheel as I continue past.

Come on, Nicola. You can't lose him now.

I indicate and brake, letting a couple of cars pass before making a U-turn and heading back to the dirt road. I take the turn, then stop and sit in the car, watching the dust from Tom's recent passing sparkle in the sunlight above the track.

Should I follow him? I tap on my phone's map app, checking my location. The track is ominously named Deadman's Road and appears to be a shortcut through to Coben Road, another of the main approaches to Arundel, this one heading south. Is that where Tom's going? There doesn't appear to be anything else on the track. If Tom reaches Coben Road too soon, I won't see which way he goes, and I'll lose him.

I get moving, driving as fast as I dare on the dirt track, which is only wide enough for about one and a half vehicles. At each corner I'm forced to slow down to watch for oncoming cars. I crest a small hill and descend, spying Coben Road ahead. Near where it intersects with Deadman's Road are several houses — rundown timber cottages. None of them is fenced, except for the first house, which has a new-looking chest-high wire-mesh fence, with timber poles at intervals. Parked out the front is Tom Foley's car.

He's approaching the house as I reach the bottom of the hill. Continuing straight will see me merge with the main road, so instead I turn down past where Tom has parked. Slowing, I catch sight of his back as he disappears inside. Through the closing door I glimpse long blonde hair.

Cara?

My heart thuds. Could she be hiding out here? Or perhaps he's keeping her hidden away against her will?

I stop a few houses down and kill the engine. I grab my keys and phone, tugging my cap on and sticking my earbuds in my ears. Outside, it's quiet – middle-of-nowhere quiet. My feet crunch along the gravel and a car whooshes along the main road. Other than that, nothing.

The houses are the type with car parts littering their front yards and plants in dozens of ancient concrete pots. The kinds of places that house people with gun licences and pig dogs – the sort of people who don't welcome strangers.

I walk with purpose along the street back towards Tom's car, trying to seem as if I'm exercising and hoping that people do that out here. Fifty metres past the house Tom Foley entered, I backtrack. There are a couple of derelict cars on this side of the house and I duck down behind them, hoping no rats or snakes will come scurrying or slithering from underneath. I pretend to tie my shoelace.

Crouching in the dust, I wonder if Tom plans to stay inside for hours – or even overnight. But after five minutes, the door creaks open. Dogs start barking from somewhere inside.

'Thank you so much. Josie's going to be thrilled,' Tom's voice is clear.

'No worries.' It's a woman, too old to be Cara, her accent broader. 'I'm sure he'll be very happy with your family. Just remember to transfer the ownership when the paperwork comes through.'

'I will. And thanks again for seeing me at short notice. Eva was keen to come herself, but she had a last-minute booking she didn't want to turn away. Not that I mind, it means more time with this little guy. Luckily I have a few spare periods today.'

I peer over the top of the car wreck. Tom is visible in the front yard with a pet carrier.

Shit, it's a puppy. He's getting a dog for his daughter.

It appears to be a golden retriever. Tom talks to the woman as he straps the carrier into the back seat of his car, asking about pet food and toilet training before saying his goodbyes. I move further around the cars to avoid being spotted and watch him drive away in a cloud of dust. He slows as he reaches my car and then stops.

Bloody hell. He recognises it. Why wouldn't he? He saw me in it just a couple of days earlier and it's distinctive.

I hold my breath as Tom's car crawls past and then he speeds off. After he's gone I stand up and walk back. I'm momentarily startled by the woman, who hasn't returned inside and is instead weeding her garden. She's older than I expected, and her bottle-blonde, brassy, lank hair is nothing at all like Cara's. She blinks in surprise at the sight of me.

'Morning!' I call, starting to jog. She doesn't respond, instead stares at me through narrowed eyes.

Once safely in my car I make a U-turn, averting my gaze from the still-watching woman, then join Coben Road and head back towards Arundel.

*

Forking tuna onto bread at the kitchen bench, I decide I'm not ready to throw in the towel yet. Tom Foley might not have been keeping Cara prisoner in a backwater settlement, but I still don't trust him. It's not yet clear why he'd met with her outside the gym, or why he'd grabbed her arm so urgently, but I'm sure it had nothing to do with a History essay.

My sandwich remains untouched as I open Tom's Facebook page. No puppy pics yet, though if the dog is a surprise gift for his daughter he won't want to risk spoiling that with Facebook updates. There is nothing new on his wife's profile either. She has 786 friends and we have seventeen mutual friends. Most of them acquaintances, other than Mum.

The About section reveals that Eva went to the University of Newcastle and to high school in Orange. Her employment details show her working at Eva Foley Physiotherapy. There's an address and, even better, a website. Eva Foley Physiotherapy has a soothing sage-and-white website with images of happy families galivanting about in the great outdoors, presumably pain-free thanks to her ministrations.

My finger hovers over the rectangular 'Book Now' button. I click it.

There's an option for the next available appointment. *Click.*

It comes up as Wednesday at 10 am. Two days' time.

Entering my details, I have no idea what I'll say to Eva about Cara and her husband.

You don't have to say anything, Nicola. You can have a massage and leave it at that.

I'm pretty sure I won't do that.

*

That Sam had done to other women what he'd just done to me made me feel nauseous. I wanted to sink into the mattress, to have it swallow me whole.

Music started up downstairs, a throbbing dance song that vibrated through the bed.

Sam gave a low chuckle in response to something too muffled to hear. He lowered his voice. 'This one? But there'll be girls at the party … can't you …' With an effort I lifted my head. Sam was still on the balcony, one hand resting on the snow-covered railing. With the other hand, he ashed his cigarette into the darkness. He wore Ugg boots along with his jeans and t-shirt. He'd noticed me move and regarded my curled-up form with detachment, then shrugged and said, 'Fine, if you really want to, Gus.' He turned his blank gaze from me. 'Don't say I don't share!' His words were light. 'Yeah, yeah … sure … text you in a bit.'

He sat his phone on the snowy table and took another drag of his cigarette, stretching his back and flexing his neck from side to side.

My earlier numbness had vanished. What was that about? What was Sam planning to do with me? Fear was rising in me like a bushfire.

Carefully, keeping my eyes on him, I shuffled to the edge of the bed, lowering my legs to the floor. My thighs were sticky and as I stood up liquid trickled down my legs again. I was still only wearing my underwear but I didn't feel the chill. I didn't feel anything other than terror and a blinding white heat that filled me. Woke me up. I stumbled over to the door and scooped up my bag, dumping it on the bed. A scan of the balcony showed me Sam still smoking, his back to me. Inside the bag, my hands scrabbled, finally landing on Dad's old Swiss army knife. The knife fitted easily into the palm of my hand and had a satisfying and familiar heft. It was the one memento of my father I had, and it made me feel safer to have it with me while I was backpacking. Plus, it was useful in emergencies. My eyes were on Sam as I prised the blade out with shaking hands while walking towards the open door.

I didn't even feel the cold snow under my feet. Sam took another drag and threw the cigarette out into the void, then turned around.

His blue eyes widened as the blade sunk into his stomach. It made no sound; he made no sound. Instinct made him step backwards. My fingers kept hold of the knife as he stumbled, and as he reached the balcony railing, I screamed and pushed him. He tumbled backwards, still silent, his mouth opening and closing in shock. His arms flailed, and then he was gone. There was a distant, quiet thud – a strangely satisfying sound. Snowflakes blew into my eyes, and I blinked them out. Thudding music was coming from downstairs.

I looked down. I'd kept hold of the knife. It was smeared with slippery red blood.

I stepped forward and peered down into the ravine, looking for a body despite knowing that no one could have survived such a fall. It was too dark to see anything, though perhaps there was a smudge of darkness in the white snow.

Perhaps.

*

The doorbell rings as I'm putting my plate in the dishwasher.

I check the intercom.

Shit.

It's Mike Ross.

What's Cara's father doing here? I thank my lucky stars Lee's at work. I vacillate, recalling my last visit to the Ross house, remembering Mike's volatility. I grab a steak knife from the cutlery drawer and slip it into the front pocket of my hoodie. The hallway mirror shows me I'm still wearing my cap. I dump it on the hall table, fixing my hair.

At the door, I put one hand in my pocket and take hold of the knife handle. I open the door with my other hand.

'Hello, Nicola,' Mike says. He's unshaven, dishevelled, his eyes wild. The knife is slippery under my sweating fingers.

'Lee's not here, Mike.' My words are sympathetic. Apologetic.

'I know. I just left the station. We have to talk.'

I'm reluctant to ask him in given his state, though I can't see a polite way to avoid it. 'Please, come in.'

In the lounge room, Mike stands. He refuses my offer of a drink. Judging by the agitated way he paces the room perhaps avoiding caffeine is a good idea.

'How is the investigation going?' I ask, taking a seat on the lounge.

'I was hoping you could tell me that,' he says, turning to face me.

'What?'

'I've seen how these cases play out in the media. The father is always the main suspect. The father, or the boyfriend. But Cara didn't – *doesn't*,' he corrects himself firmly, 'have a boyfriend.' He pauses. 'I'm worried they're going to try to pin it on me.'

'Pin what?'

'Whatever happened to my daughter.' Mike has bags under his eyes that suggest he needs more sleep. He squeezes his eyes shut as if in pain, then continues. 'They're going to try to blame me. The good Lord knows I'm praying she'll walk through our front door, but I'm worried. Cara is young, an innocent. Anything could happen to her!' A sob escapes him. 'It's clear the police believe I have something to do with her disappearance. They asked me where I was when she went missing. She's my daughter! I would never hurt her!' He leans towards me, eager to convince me of his innocence. With an effort, I remain still, the knife handle reassuring under my fingertips. 'I was at church when she went missing! Hundreds of parishioners can attest to that.'

'I'm sure the police are just doing their due diligence,' I say, trying to placate him. 'It will sort itself out in the end.'

He starts pacing again. 'I can't go to jail,' he mutters.

'If you haven't done anything wrong then you'll be fine, Mike.'

'Don't give me that. The media are all over this, even the Sydney papers. They'll be desperate to close the case. I'm the obvious target!'

'I'm sure—'

'They talk about Orange Dawn as if it's a cult! We sing songs and pray, we don't sacrifice humans!' He sighs and drops onto the couch opposite, then leans forward. 'Can you do something for me?' he asks in a quieter, still urgent voice. 'Find Lee's notes – anything he's written about me. See if I'm a suspect. I have to know.'

'I can't do that. You must realise how much trouble Lee would get in if anyone found out.'

Mike's mood changes. 'Have you told Lee about the incident with Isabella Donovan?' he asks. 'Or that you came over to our house the other day?'

Heat rises in me. 'No.'

'And I very much doubt you want him to know now. Do this for me and I won't tell him. I promise.'

'You're threatening me?' I jump up, the knife still in my grasp.

'I wouldn't call it that. Just two friends helping one another out.' He gives me a big smile and stands as well. He's much taller than me. 'Lee doesn't have to find out you've peeked at his notes. It'd only be a quick read-through to give me some idea of what the police are thinking. Forewarned is forearmed.'

I pretend to mull over his proposition. Of course, I'll never do it. If Lee brings paperwork home he's very careful to keep it in his office. If it's not locked away then it's neatly stored in his briefcase and it would be clear straight away if anyone went through it. But Mike doesn't need to know that. I could tell him I'll try — even lie and tell him that I did search Lee's notes and found nothing accusatory about him.

That's the safest option. I can't risk Mike telling Lee what happened or about last week's visit.

It's better to go along with him.

'Okay,' I say, making sure to sound reluctant. I sit back on the couch. 'But I'm not happy about this.'

'And if you find any suspects, give me their names,' he says in a grim voice. Then his face falls. 'I need my daughter back and I'll get her myself if necessary.'

Mike's so forlorn at that moment I truly believe he's not involved in Cara's disappearance. But then the bruises on Donna's wrist return to my mind. Should I ask him about them? No, not even with a knife in my grip. There's no need to provoke him.

Instead, I dip my head slowly, as if I'm not happy about what he's asking of me. I won't do it, but it'll keep him out of my hair for a few days. Hopefully Cara will have been found by then.

'Thank you, Nicola,' he says, then he adds in a voice so quiet it can barely be heard, 'God will bring my girl back to her daddy. I have to believe that.'

Daddy.

Something prickles against the back of my neck. The way Mike says the word reminds me of something. It was a year after the thing with Isabella. I remember the timing because I was in Mode, Arundel's most expensive clothing store, trying on dresses for my second date with Lee.

He had started at the police station a month earlier. He'd asked me out after a chance encounter in the supermarket involving wayward shopping trolleys and much laughter. I rarely went on dates, partly because I was a single mother, and partly thanks to my destroyed confidence in men. But Lee had made me feel comfortable immediately. We had so much in common: the same taste in music – nineties grunge and Australian rock – and we were both runners back then, though Lee gave it up not long after we moved in together. It helped that he was a police officer too. It made me feel safe.

Our first date was a burger and a movie, but for the second Lee had organised to take me to the best (and only) French restaurant in Arundel. In desperate need of a new dress, I resolved to risk Mode, which had always scared me with its expensive price tags and slightly snooty staff. And, true to form, I had no luck that day. But in the change room, the outfits back on their hangers and slung over my arm, two voices carried to me.

'Thank you, Daddy! I love them all so much!' It was a young girl, obviously thrilled though a little breathless too.

'Try them on before you get too excited, Cara. You won't know if they're any good until you do.' It was Mike and Cara Ross. 'I'll wait out here. You can model them for me.'

Shit.

A curtain swished shut. I quietly unfurled the clothes from my arm and hung them over the hook on the wall, then peered through a gap in the curtain. Mike sat on a chair outside the change room.

A childish voice floated to me from the next cubicle along. 'Mummy doesn't let me wear crop tops.'

The curtains swished open.

'Oh, that's gorgeous, my darling. What do you think?'

'I love it!'

'Okay. We'll get it. Try the dress.'

Cara disappeared back into the change room.

After what felt like forever, the pair agreed on three outfits. 'So, like I told you before,' Mike told Cara, 'this is a special treat for being so brave this morning.'

'I wish I didn't have to do it, Daddy.'

The poor kid, what did she mean?

'I know, sweetie.'

Cara emerged from the change room, a ball of clothes in her arms.

Mike pulled Cara to him. 'Let's go buy these. A treat for being such a good girl at the hospital. But remember, don't tell Mummy. Hide them in the bottom of your closet. Put them in between a folded jumper or something. They're our secret.'

'Thanks, Daddy. I love you.'

'I love you too. Remember what I say—'

'That I'm Daddy's little girl.' She giggled.

'Nicola?' I'm jolted from the reverie by Mike, who's watching me from the opposite couch with a scowl on his face. 'Did you hear me?'

'Sorry. What?'

He has an arm extended, a business card in his hand. 'Here's my number.'

I let go of the knife, withdraw my sweaty hand from my pocket and take the card. On one side is a simple graphic of an orange sunrise. On the other it reads 'Pastor Mike Ross'. Below his name is a phone number and email address. There's no mention of the church.

'Call me.'

'It might be a couple of days,' I warn him. 'I'll have to be careful.'

He nods. 'That's fine. But please do it as soon as you can. I can't take this anymore.'

'I'll do my best. I can't promise anything, though.'

It's only after Mike leaves that my brain registers the tattoo on the inside of his wrist.

It's a knife, dripping with blood.

*

I didn't stand in the snow for long. It was too fucking cold.

That cold might have saved my life. Without it, I could have stood there in the dark, peering down into the abyss, for hours.

Instead the icy winter chill seeped into my bones and snapped me out of my stupor.

I'd killed a man.

I'd killed *Sam*.

Stabbed him and pushed him over a balcony to his death. Peering down, my eyes straining, I noticed a light coming from below the balcony.

Shit, the party downstairs.

My mind raced. Would anyone have seen him fall? I rubbed my forehead. It was pitch black outside and the party had already started. Surely no one would have been staring out the window at the exact moment he plunged into the ravine.

Oh God.

Sam had plummeted to his death. I had stabbed him.

Killed him.

I took a sharp breath and the cold air mixed with the bile in my throat. My breaths came fast and I felt light-headed. I had to call the police. An ambulance.

Somebody.

Nicola, you killed a man. In cold blood, a voice inside me said.

He raped me.

So? You know how these things go. Besides, it wasn't an accident. You chose to do this.

My gaze roamed the balcony without taking anything in. My body no longer felt like mine. The goosepimpled skin. The grey cotton undies with the tiny hole near the waistband. Beige bra. Feet mottled white and red, the snowflakes that melted the moment they touched my skin.

I relived the moment Sam pressed against my back, shoving his penis inside me, and doubled over, clutching at my stomach.

Breathe.

In, out, in, out.

The nausea passed as I hung there, my head between my knees in the snow.

In, out, in, out.

The mountains breathed along with me, their centuries-old ice seeping into my veins.

In, out.

I made a decision.

I wasn't going to call the police.

I straightened. I had to get out of here, and soon.

The falling snow was taking care of any sign that Sam had ever been out here. No blood, no footprints. A stroke of good luck.

There was no exit from the balcony, so unless I wanted to follow Sam into the ravine I had to go back inside and leave through the party.

Fine. My teeth ground together. Then that's what I'd do.

My eyes lit on Sam's phone where it still rested on the snow-covered table, snow settling over it.

An idea came to me.

I retrieved the phone with my unbloodied hand, shutting the balcony door awkwardly with fingers close to useless. In the bathroom, I sat the bloody knife on a wad of toilet paper and washed the blood from my hand, refusing to peep in the mirror above the sink. I took the phone back to the bedroom and climbed under the covers, careful to avoid the smeared blood on the sheets, trying to warm up my numb fingers and toes while I thought about what to do.

Think, Nicola, think.

You can't afford to forget anything.

I wiped Sam's phone clean of snow on the bedcover, then entered the code he had told me in the car earlier that day.

'Sam!' A voice came from the door. A fist thudded against it. 'You in there? You said you'd text me!'

I gasped, my heart rate spiking. Was the door locked? I held my breath.

The handle rattled but the door stayed closed.

Thank fuck.

The phone buzzed in my hand and I dropped it onto the bed as if it was venomous.

One new message.

You having another go? It was Angus. Heat flooded through me. *Jonesy told me you said him and me could have a turn next. Riley's not keen. As usual, the pussy.*

Fuck off, I typed with stiff fingers. *I'm busy. Find your own girl for a change.*

The banging on the door stopped and seconds later another message buzzed. *Prick.*

And then the phone and the voice were quiet, though the music thumped even louder from outside the door, making my head hurt.

I had to get out of there.

No one at the house knew my name. I replayed the day in my mind. The only person who might remember me was Wendy. Though for all she knew I might have left Sam as soon as we walked out the door. I hadn't paid for lunch or the ice-skate rental at Lake Louise, and none of the staff there knew me.

No one would find Sam tonight. Maybe not for days in this storm. He had a car sitting outside. He'd even left the keys in it. Was it possible to escape through the house without being seen?

I had to try.

I slid into my jeans and jumper, not bothering with my t-shirt. The wool of my jumper was soft against my skin, but the smell of beer made me feel ill.

Closing my eyes, I breathed deeply, trying to concentrate. I had only one chance to get this right.

Wiping any prints from the room was my first task. In the bathroom cupboard was a bucket filled with cleaning products. He'd said the cleaner was coming tomorrow, but I couldn't rely on her being thorough enough to remove all my fingerprints. I used paper towels and spray, wiping anything I might have touched, including the cleaning products themselves. Working up a sweat, I wondered if this was even necessary – my fingerprints weren't on file anywhere.

But then what if the police ever questioned me?

There was a roll of garbage bags in the bucket and I opened one, putting the paper towels inside, along with my t-shirt and the hand towel from the bathroom. I replaced it with a fresh hand towel from the cupboard.

I'd have to take everything with me.

The sheets, spotted with my blood, were a problem. It would be suspicious to take them, especially if any of Sam's friends came in later that night. Then I remembered that the cleaner would wash them tomorrow.

But that blood … would she contact the police? Or talk to one of the other guys living here? No, I reasoned, if she'd worked as their cleaner for a while, she'd probably seen worse than a little blood.

Where else had I left evidence? My mind flittered. Kitchen. Living room.

Shit.

The beer downstairs – there would be fingerprints on the bottle, and probably elsewhere in the house. But there was a party going on, so surely any fingerprints would be attributed to guests at the party? It sounded as if at least a dozen people were already downstairs, maybe more. And the cleaner would probably throw away the bottles in the morning, wouldn't she? I had to hope so.

I wiped down my knife and sat there, turning it over in my hands. It was a classic red Swiss army knife. My dad had bought it in Geneva, decades before my birth. I'd kept it as clean and as rust free as possible. He'd had his initials, AJM, carved into the side when he purchased it. They were the only things that distinguished it from thousands of other pocketknives just like it. My fingers traced the neat letters, before I put it in my back pocket. It would need to be disposed of eventually, but not here. It could be tied to me.

Besides, I might need to use it on my way out.

*

'Nicola?'

A hand on my shoulder shakes me awake. It's Lee. My swiftly beating heart begins to slow, though my mind takes a minute to catch up to my body. The television is on, some reality TV show. The room is too bright. I'm on the lounge. I must have fallen asleep waiting for Lee to come home.

There'd been a dream about knives dripping with blood and dead puppies in the middle of dusty roads, so I wonder if I'd made a sound, if I'd cried or screamed or whimpered. Lee's face tells me I haven't.

He is still dressed in his work clothes, though he's rather dishevelled.

'What's wrong?' My heart thuds again. 'Is it Abby? Did you find Cara?'

'No.'

The clock on the wall says it's almost 10.15 pm. Abby had said goodnight and gone to her room at 9.30 pm. I've only been asleep for fifteen or twenty minutes. I'd been watching the news, but there was nothing about Cara on it. I couldn't decide if that was good or bad. I sit up, wiping spittle from the corner of my mouth.

'I've had a call from Tom Foley, Nicola. He's accusing you of following him while he went to pick up a new puppy for his daughter.' Lee's tone is incredulous. 'Is that true?'

'Ah, that.'

'What the hell were you thinking?' Lee doesn't like arguing, so when he starts out this confrontational it's clear he's really mad. 'You're not a police officer.'

'I thought I might write a story.'

'Oh no. Not this again.' He stands up, shaking his head. 'You can't write about my open cases, Nic, surely you can see that? We've had this discussion. I thought I was clear.'

'You were. But this is just such a great story, Lee, and I'm in the best position to tell it. I need to do it for Cara. For Abby.'

'For Abby? You aren't doing this for Abby. This is for you. Look, if you want to apply for a job with a more hard-hitting newspaper then I'm all for you going out and getting one. But this … investigating my case on your own? It's not on.' I'm silent and he sighs. 'You get too involved. Last time—'

'I've already apologised for that.'

I'd spoken to several local women – off the record – who had said the police in town weren't doing enough to combat the abuse being dealt out by their husbands and boyfriends. Mum had encouraged me to write the story, she said it was the right thing to do. I'd convinced Petra to publish a snippet of it, with the promise of more to come, but when Lee's bosses in Sydney found out, the shit hit the fan.

I dropped the story, even though it had been important. Really important.

I'm still not sure it was the right thing to do.

I blink back tears – unsure if they are tears of anger or sadness. Either way, Lee softens.

'We need to find Cara. That's priority number one.' Lee kneels in front of me, takes hold of my hands. 'The police are best placed to find her. You, out there investigating, won't help.' His words are emphatic. 'Leave it alone, babe. Please. For me.'

I bite back the words that hover on the tip of my tongue and nod. 'Fine. I'll drop it.'

*

'Great to see you.'

Lucas greets me at the counter, then smiles at Mum. 'Mrs Miller! You're back! We must be doing something right.' He's a slim man with one of those moustaches all twenty-something hipsters currently seem to have. He's lovely, though he's far too old for Abby and he needs to know that. Besides, being nice in public is no indicator that he'd treat Abby well.

'You know me, Lucas. I'm all about the salads!' Mum says with a grimace and he laughs. When I called to see if she wanted to meet me at Nature's Café on my lunch break today, I completely forgot she and Abby had eaten here on Sunday. Something softens inside me; for Mum to agree to it without suggesting a change suggests she's worried about me.

'The usual?' he asks Mum.

'Yes, please.'

'For you, Nicola?'

There are so many salads on the board behind him. 'The miso chicken salad with cashews please,' I finally say.

'Peas in a pod!' He chuckles and Mum gives him a wry look.

'What?' I ask.

'Oh, that's what Abby and Joyce always get when they come here. Like mother, like daughter – or in your case, like mother, like daughter, like granddaughter.'

There's a long lunchtime queue behind us so I decide to warn Lucas off Abby later. We find a table outside on the footpath. I fetch water from inside, and as I return I notice Mum is yawning. She has dark circles under her eyes, and I berate myself. Mum is so self-sufficient that sometimes I forget she might need a daughter to lean on. I've neglected her lately because Cara had been spending almost as much time at Hillcrest as she did at our place and had grown quite close to Mum. It was cute how she followed her around the garden, listening to stories from Mum's time with Bert, my dad. Cara adored Dad's art and was fascinated to know we had a semi-famous artist in our family.

'Here you go, Mum,' I say, setting the glasses on the table. 'How've you been?'

'Fine, darling. Busy. People think the gardens don't need you in the winter, instead it's quite the opposite. There's lots to do.'

'Are you missing Cara's help? I can send Abby out? Or come on the weekend to lend a hand myself?'

'You?' She smiles. 'You haven't got your hands dirty at Hillcrest for ages. And you've got your own garden to take care of.'

My smile is wry. 'Ours pretty much takes care of itself.' It's full of low-maintenance plants like agaves and yuccas.

Mum waves at a group of women who've just arrived and we make small talk with them as they settle at a nearby table.

'I do miss Cara,' Mum says when we're alone again. 'I'm starting to get a little worried, I can't deny it. I had thought she might have turned up by now.'

'It's not good, is it?' We are silent for a moment. 'Mum? Do you ever worry about Abby?'

'No, of course not.' She gives me a sympathetic smile. 'There's no need to worry about her, my darling.'

I don't say anything.

'How's Lee?' she asks, taking a sip of water.

'Okay. Tired.' I don't tell her about our fight. I've told Lee I won't investigate, and I won't. Not physically. But asking a few questions and an online search or two can't hurt. I change the subject. 'Have you heard any rumours about Tom Foley?' Her brow furrows. 'Eva's husband?'

'No.'

'What about the Rosses?'

After Mike left yesterday I googled what his tattoo of a knife dripping blood might mean. According to an online tattoo dictionary, a bloody dagger commonly refers to death and sacrifice. So perhaps it signifies Jesus's sacrifice? Or that people need to sacrifice themselves for God?

'The Rosses? No.' She folds her hands together on the table. 'Do you know something about Cara?' She gives me a sharp look. 'You haven't been trying to do Lee's job for him, have you? You can be very determined when you get something stuck in your head.'

'Don't be silly.' I avoid her eyes.

'Here we go – two miso chickens.' Lucas arrives and puts the enormous bowls in front of us. Cabbage, sprouts, cucumber, toasted shallots topped with miso-marinated chicken. It smells delicious.

'These are certainly value for money,' I mutter, doubting we'll eat even half of what's in front of us.

It is excellent, and we fork it into our mouths without speaking for a minute. The women at the next table cackle with laughter.

'Mum,' I say, after chewing crunchy greens for an age, 'what was Dad like?'

My mother raises her eyebrows. 'Your father? What's brought this on?'

'Just wondering. Sometimes our family feels very … female.'

'Last time I checked Lee was a man.'

'Lee's great, obviously. But I can't remember Dad very well and sometimes I wonder about him.'

She half-smiles. 'Bert was, well, you've heard the stories. More myth than man.'

My father died when I was three. He was a great artist and an even bigger character. A couple of his landscapes are hung on my walls. They're bold and lush and sparse at the same time, worth quite a lot of money now. Occasionally someone bails me up at the pub to tell me a story about Bert Miller coming into town for a few nights, losing big in a poker game, climbing the telegraph tower for fun, or spending the night in the lockup for being drunk and disorderly. He was a big man, a big drinker, someone who lived life to the fullest. The kind of person who could charm the birds right out of the trees.

Abby takes after him. She's been the leader of every pack she's ever been in. As for her charm – she gets that quality from her own father too.

Which is something I try not to think about.

'Did you love him?'

'Of course, darling. He was my husband.'

My neck prickles. I have a strong sense someone is watching me. It occurs occasionally – a hangover from Canada. I know I'm just being paranoid so I force myself not to look around.

'Does Abby ask you about her father?' My voice is as nonchalant as I can make it, though I'm not fooling Mum.

'No. She's never missed having him in her life.' She pats my hand. Her knuckles are bony, speckled with sunspots. I'm hit with the notion that she won't live forever. My heart catches in my throat. 'You are enough, Nicola,' she says, leaning in to whisper it.

Someone grabs my shoulders and I gasp.

'Ha! Gotcha!' It's Petra. She's laughing and I force a smile. 'Lovely to see you, Mrs Miller.'

'Likewise, Petra.' Mum's tone is wry. 'Always a pleasure. When are we going to see you back on the golf course?'

'Soon, hopefully. Been busy with this little lady.' She grabs Sadie around the waist.

Sadie rolls her eyes. 'C'mon, let's order, I'm starving.'

'I'm going to bail her up about that domestic violence story when she comes out,' Mum announces as the couple go inside. I nod, distracted. The prickle is still there, deep in the back of my brain. It wasn't Petra, or the women who are leaving, their table not yet cleared. Further along is an unfamiliar couple in their thirties, and the final table is taken by Joe Pearce, who manages the bank downstairs from our office, and two younger men in suits. Joe gives me a wave when he catches my eye. None of them is the reason for my unease.

I glance at the street. Lunchtimes at Nature's Café are busy and cars are parallel-parked all the way along it. A black hatchback almost opposite us drives off, moving slowly. I open my mouth to ask Mum if that's the car Abby liked when someone calls out my name.

'What did you get?' Petra asks from the door. 'I can't choose.' I tell her and she returns inside.

When I look back, the car is gone.

*

The music downstairs continued with the addition of a chant. 'Chug! Chug!' Then something smashed and everyone cheered. The party was getting rowdier. That was good. That would help me.

I accessed Sam's phone again. *Change of plan*, I messaged Angus, since he'd texted last. *This one's worn out so I'm gonna drop her home and go on to Calgary. Might even head to NYC. Need a change of pace. New conquests? Ha ha.* I thought some more, then added, *See you in a week or so. Have a beer for me, boys!*

Hopefully the party had built to the point where they wouldn't hear or notice their phones and no one would think to check on Sam and his latest conquest, at least for a while.

I hit send, switched the phone off then wiped it over with a hand towel. Then, keeping hold of the towel, I flung the phone over the balcony. It disappeared into darkness. It would be found at around the same time as his body, hopefully. The balcony was completely white with snow now, no footprints visible, no rectangular phone indentation on the table. I wiped the door handle, then put the towel in the garbage bag and shoved the whole lot into my bag. The music was deafening as I walked briskly along the hallway, then down the stairs, desperate to leave without being seen. People sang drunkenly, their voices rising as they wailed along with the Black Eyed Peas. The house stank of pizza and beer and weed. I'd reached the entryway and was about to get my coat from the peg at the front door, when a ginger-haired man appeared from the kitchen. I set a hand to my back pocket, reassured by the presence of the knife.

The man was about Sam's age, so he was possibly Angus, Riley or Jonesy, or just a friend of a friend. A few blobs of white foam that might have been beer froth were hanging to his scraggly beard.

He whooped and grabbed my hand and I forced a smile and whooped back. He tried to dance with me to the Pussycat Dolls' 'Don't Cha', but he was in grave danger of falling and dragging us both down. I danced along for several more seconds, then yelled, 'Toilet!' and waved vaguely towards the door where he'd emerged from. He danced off in the other direction and I found my coat and pulled open the front door. My breath was loud in my ears as I jogged over the open ground, relief running through me as I reached Sam's pick-up and climbed in. I took the pocketknife from my jeans and put it in the centre console of the car, then yanked the visor down.

The key fell onto my lap, startling me, though I knew it was there. I stuck it into the ignition and turned it, thanking my lucky stars as the vehicle roared to life.

You can do this, I told myself as the lights came on, their beams highlighting the falling snowflakes and the driveway with several cars parked to either side.

You told them Calgary, so you'll have to go further. Edmonton, maybe.

A sob escaped me.

In a storm, in a car you've never driven, in the middle of the night.

Yep. Good plan.

It took thirty terrifying minutes to get to the hostel, with many wrong turns and a couple of episodes of me driving on the wrong side of the road. Once there I was in and out in ten minutes, my bill paid for in advance, my roommates off partying for New Year's Eve. The road to Calgary was pitch black, but the snow slowed, the promised storm never quite making it. The ploughs worked through the night, keeping the roads passable, if dangerously slippery. Even though it felt as if I drove at walking pace, I made it through to the outskirts of Calgary by 1 am, then went north to Edmonton, hitting the city around 5 am. Outside a strip of airport hotels I stopped, switching on the interior light as I wondered where to dump Sam's car. A group of inebriated revellers poured out of the nearest hotel. One of them ran over, yelling, 'Happy New Year!' and slapping my window with gloved hands. His unfocused gaze roamed over the interior of the car. The pocketknife was lying in full view in the centre console, so I opened the glove box and flung it inside. The man's friends called him and he stumbled away. I sped off as fast as I dared, aware he wouldn't have seen anything too suspicious, freaked out just the same.

Half an hour later, exhausted, I came to a rundown industrial area not far from the airport and a block from the main road. It would do. I parked the pick-up in a spot where it would hopefully remain unnoticed for a few days, maybe longer. I exchanged my cable-knit jumper for a hoodie and pulled the hood as far over my face as I could. After using the last of my energy to wipe over the interior, I stuck the key above the visor, took my bag and walked five hundred metres to the main road where I hailed a taxi. On the way I threw the garbage bag of bloodied towels into an industrial rubbish bin.

It was only as I sat nursing a vodka and Coke on the 10 am flight to Boston, my head drooping with tiredness, that I realised I'd left my father's pocketknife in the glove compartment of Sam's pick-up.

*

I'm early for my appointment with Eva Foley.

She runs her new business from home, which is a bonus for me since I've come to stickybeak. God only knows what I'll say to her. Hopefully it'll become clear when we meet. Lee doesn't know I'm here, though technically it is just a massage appointment. I don't let myself think about how angry he'll be if he finds out what I'm up to.

And then there's Tom Foley. What if he comes home for some unknown reason? Or if Eva tells him I've been to see her? My nerves are on edge, and yet I press the doorbell.

A dog barks in response to the chiming bell and, soon after, the door opens. Eva appears, carrying the puppy Tom collected on Monday. It's wriggling in her arms and trying to lick her face. Eva gives me the smile I remember from the golf club Christmas party.

'Hi. You must be Nicola,' she says. She is very blonde, and I'd forgotten her slight accent, which marks her as originally hailing from one of the Scandinavian countries. 'Please forgive me. It's chaos here. Olaf is a very new member of the family and so far he's chewed two pairs of the kids' shoes and weed on most of the carpet in the house.' She kisses the dog on its head. 'But how can I resist this little face?'

'Olaf?'

'Josie is obsessed with *Frozen*.' She rolls her eyes. 'Come in, come in. I'll put this guy in his pen and wash my hands so we can get started.'

She ushers me inside and I turn as she shuts the door. Before it fully closes, I glimpse a car sidling past, very slowly. It's black and sporty, with the windows tinted so heavily they must be illegal. Then the door is shut and Eva walks on. The house smells of curry, and there are kids' toys scattered around, with family portraits lining the hallway – the type where everyone's in jeans and white t-shirts, or the kids are sitting on Santa's lap.

'Please excuse the mess. I promised myself I'd be more professional with clients coming to the house, but things get away from me. Especially since Olaf came along.'

'Don't worry. I've got a daughter. I understand.'

'You do? How old is she?'

'She's seventeen now, and the house is still a mess.'

'Don't tell me that!' Eva laughs. We emerge into the kitchen and Eva gestures to a chair. 'Please sit, and I'll grab you a new client form to fill out.'

The kitchen is as pleasant and ordinary as the rest of the house. Eva bustles back in, dog-less and with a sheet of paper attached to a clipboard.

'Can you fill this out? Again, I'm very sorry for—' She waves a hand at the clutter.

'Don't worry. Clients will care about the job you do, not your house.'

'Thank you, that's very kind.'

My pen scratches across the form as I surreptitiously watch Eva move around the kitchen. She's the type of woman who never stops moving, the type capable of anything she puts her mind to.

My phone buzzes with a call and I fumble it from my pocket. It's Hudson. I let it ring out and set it on the table.

'So,' Eva says as she packs some crockery into the dishwasher, 'what do you want to focus on? You are very fit – perhaps you need a good loosening up? Do you have an event soon? A run? Triathlon?'

'Ah, no.' And suddenly I can't do it. I need to just be honest. 'I'm kind of here on false pretences, Eva.'

She stops what she's doing and turns to face me, her eyebrows raised. 'Oh?'

'Yes. I probably shouldn't have come. But ...' I hesitate, then continue. 'Did your husband tell you the police talked to him about the girl who went missing?'

'The police?' She straightens up, the dishwasher forgotten. 'You are with the police?'

'No, no. My partner is Sergeant Lee Cook. You know my mother too, Joyce Miller? And we actually met last year at the golf club's Christmas party. I had a dreadful headache and begged drugs from you?'

'Oh yes, of course.' She smiles, though it doesn't reach her eyes. 'The screaming that day, mine were probably the worst culprits.'

'Well, it's my daughter's friend who's gone missing. Both girls are at your husband's school.'

'Yes, Cara,' Eva says. 'Her poor family. I've heard about it, of course, though we don't watch the news. Our children are still so young and it's all a bit too much for them, you know?' She makes a face. 'Too graphic. We're trying to hold on to their innocence a little longer.'

My phone buzzes again, a text this time. Hudson again. *We need to talk. It's important. Call me.*

'Is everything all right?' Eva asks, glancing at the phone.

'Yes, fine. I'm … I'm trying to work out what happened to Cara. I want to help find her.'

Eva sits at the table beside me. 'What's it got to do with my husband?'

How much should I tell her?

Presumably, Tom hasn't mentioned meeting Cara at the gym to his wife. Or that the police asked him a few questions.

She has a right to know.

'It may be nothing, but I saw your husband with Cara two days before she disappeared.' Her eyes widen though she doesn't say anything. I fill her in.

When I finish, Eva is still for a long moment. Finally, she gives a sharp nod, as if she's decided something. 'Wait here.' She marches out and I hear rustling from the living room.

I need to tell her I'm a journalist, that I'm planning to write a story about all this, but I can't do it. Telling her will surely make Eva clam up. Instead, I promise myself I'll do it later and that I certainly won't publish something she's unhappy about.

But I'm not sure it's true.

A minute later Eva returns holding something in her hand.

'This!' An earring dangles from her fingers. It's gold, an elegant dagger. 'It's proof.' Her expression is part triumphant, part sorrowful. 'That girl. I wasn't certain it was her, you see, and then when I heard she was missing, well, I didn't want to go to the police without being sure. This, this could be the proof that it was her. She was here. Cara Ross.' In her accented voice the name sounds ominous.

Eva lowers the earring. She's pale now, resigned. She sits opposite me again. 'It's true then, isn't it? Tom was sleeping with her.' She squeezes her eyes shut. 'How could he? She's a child.'

'Slow down, Eva,' I say. 'What exactly did you see?'

She takes a deep breath and thinks before speaking. 'It was a couple of weeks ago now. I'd been driving the kids to after-school activities. It was a Friday. Can you believe we are booked solid on Fridays? I hate it. Josie does ballet while Elijah has maths tutoring, then we go to the scout hall and wait outside while Ollie has Scouts. But this day, when we arrived at Scouts everyone was already leaving and the other mothers told us that Johann, the scout leader, had called in sick. To be honest, I was thrilled.' She peers at me earnestly. 'I'm thrilled anytime the kids' after-school activities are cancelled. It's one less thing to do. So we headed home. Tom's car was here, as usual, and the lounge-room light was on. The kids ran inside while I rounded up the uniforms and water bottles, you know how it is.' She gives me a look. 'We were early, granted, though Tom would usually have started dinner by then. I'd left him a note requesting his famous spaghetti bolognese, and he cooks that mince for a couple of hours – that's why he claims it is so good. But the kitchen was in darkness. Tom bounded in from the lounge room with Josie on his back. He was all cheery – confused as to why we were early, of course – though underneath he was a little off. He told me he'd get dinner started and he asked Josie to help him. The boys had run off to play Fortnite.' She rolls her eyes. 'I told him I was busting for the toilet, but I went to the lounge room.' Eva puts her elbow on the table and bites a fingernail. 'It was empty. Still, I sensed something … I don't know what it was. I'd never had that kind of premonition before.' She lifts her shoulders. 'I opened the curtains and peered outside.' She takes a breath. 'It was that girl. Cara Ross. She was on the footpath by the kerb, staring off into the distance. She must have noticed the light when I moved the curtain because she turned around.'

'It was definitely her?'

'Yes. Blonde, pretty. I recognised her from the photo of my husband's Ancient History class on Facebook.' She rubs at her temple. 'This girl, she looked right at me. Then she spun around and walked away.'

'You thought something was going on between them?'

'I didn't want to.' Eva holds the dagger earring by the hook so that the point hangs straight down. She scrunches up her face, as if deciding what to say. Then she shakes her head. 'Look, Tom had a one-night stand after Ollie was born. She was an old flame, and he promised it would never occur again. It certainly wasn't a teenage girl from his school. I didn't think Tom could do something like that.' Eva appears embarrassed.

'I keep tabs on him. On Facebook. Instagram. Sometimes I even check his phone. I never used to cyberstalk my husband, you know, *before*. But now I can't help myself.'

'Were there incriminating messages on his phone?' I can't help asking as that would be evidence to take to Lee.

She shakes her head. 'No, there was nothing on his phone. Anyway, I let the curtain drop and turned around and that's when I saw this ...' She holds up the earring.

I examine it more closely. It's pretty, and it certainly resembles the jewellery Cara favoured. Perhaps her parents could confirm if it was hers.

'It was on the floor near the coffee table, glinting in the light.' Eva sighs. 'I told myself that he might have been tutoring her, or that she needed his help with something. Only, he never mentioned it to me later. Tom's been a model husband since that one time, so I had kind of relaxed about it. It's ... you never properly trust someone again after they do that. Not completely.'

I nod.

'I should have confronted him. But things have been good between us lately. I didn't want to believe ... So I hid the earring with my sewing needles and tried to forget about it.'

Why would Tom risk an affair with a student? If it came out it would ruin his life.

'Should I go to the police?' Eva asks me.

'Maybe,' I say, picking up my phone. 'First, though, we should be sure it's Cara. You've never met her before?'

'No, I've always been happy to stay out of Tom's work life.' She laughs bitterly. 'It seems that was a mistake.' Her shoulders slump.

'I'm so sorry, Eva.'

'It's not your fault,' she says, then takes a breath to gather herself. She drops the earring onto the table and it vibrates then lies still, the tip pointing at me.

'Look, it might be nothing. Cara's in Tom's Ancient History class. Perhaps he was helping her.'

She nods and I sense she's withdrawing, perhaps wondering if she's said too much to someone who's virtually a stranger. I search for Tom on Facebook and scroll down to the photo of him and his students outside the museum. There's a scrabbling sound and the next moment the new puppy comes bounding into the kitchen.

'Olaf! How on earth did you escape from your pen?' Eva leaps up and chases the dog, finally grabbing him. She sits back on her chair with the dog in her arms and presses her face into his fur.

'Here's that photo,' I say pointing to Cara. 'Is this the girl you saw?'

'Her?' Eva lifts her head from the dog and examines the photo with a frown. 'No. That's not her.'

It's my turn to be surprised. 'Really? You're sure?'

'Yes, of course. It's the other one. There.' Eva points to Abby. 'That's the girl I saw outside the house.'

'I WILL BRING SAM'S KILLER TO JUSTICE'

By James Wright

The death of a child is every parent's worst nightmare, so imagine the added anguish of discovering that your precious child was murdered.

Even the rich are not immune from this tragedy as property developer Andrew Cargill, and his wife, Lorraine, discovered almost eighteen years ago. I sat down for lunch this week at Double Bay Sailing Club with one of Australia's wealthiest men and his glamorous wife for their first interview in over ten years about their son's death. For the Cargills, Sam's murder feels like only yesterday.

The Cargills arrived in separate vehicles, Andrew having spent the morning in his office, atop the spectacular Sam Cargill House in The Rocks. Lorraine wore Chanel, fresh from a board meeting for the foundation the Cargills set up in Sam's name. They greeted each other warmly, and it's clear Sam's death has brought them even closer together. Our wide-ranging interview touched on how his murder changed their lives forever, their love for their charming boy and their ongoing hope that the killer would be found. Read a snippet here; the full interview can be found in this Saturday's Weekend *magazine, along with images of the pair wearing the best of Australian-made sustainable fashion in the glass-fronted penthouse of Sam Cargill House.*

'Samuel was every father's dream,' Andrew Cargill tells me. 'Smart, funny, adventurous. We knew he'd be a success in whatever field he decided to pursue, and I was thrilled when he told me he wanted to take over the family business.'

'Lorraine, what do you miss about Sam?'

'His laughter. His sweet face. His kindness.' Lorraine pauses for a moment. 'I'm sorry, James, this is very difficult for me.'

I ask Andrew to tell us what happened to Sam in Canada.

'I think most of your readers have heard the story by now. Sam was murdered during a party at the home he was renting. He was stabbed and pushed over the balcony into a ravine. It was a cowardly act. His body wasn't found until almost three months later when the snow melted.'

'His housemates didn't notice he was missing at the time?'

'The murderer planned it well. He used my son's phone to text his friends to tell them he was going away, then cleaned his prints from the room. The cleaner came the next day, so all forensic evidence was lost. He took Sam's car. And as it took some time to report Sam missing, it was too late to recover surveillance footage from Banff. The car wasn't found in Edmonton until several weeks later.'

'There were no suspects?'

'No.'

'Is it true you hired private investigators to find your son's killer?'

'The Canadian police botched the original investigation, blaming the weather and a lack of forensics for results. They simply didn't do their jobs, which meant I needed to step up.'

'And have your investigators found anything?'

'I can't comment too much on that as it might compromise what's been uncovered so far. I can say that I'm still very hopeful we'll find Sam's killer and bring him to justice. I do have a key piece of evidence in my possession.' Cargill eyeballs me and I've never been the focus of such an intense gaze before. That drive is what helped him take his father's modest development company and create an empire. 'I won't let this rest,' he tells me. 'I believe we'll have an important announcement to make soon. It would have been Sam's fortieth birthday on September fifteenth.'

'It sounds, as if you are still very much invested in finding your son's killer.'

'I am. There is someone out there who is guilty of murdering my son. They believe they got away with it. They think they can just live a normal life. However, they should know that I am going to find them and bring them to justice.'

PART II

BEFORE

ABBY

'Oi! Chuck it here, moron!'

Zach jumps from the picnic table onto the back lawn with a grunt, waving his arms about. Moments later a football whizzes past my head, flicking my ponytail on the way past before landing in his arms.

'Hey!' Grace yells from where she sits beside me on our regular bench. 'Watch it, losers!'

I want to roll my eyes or sigh, but I don't. It's lunchtime on the first day back at school after the summer holidays so it's hardly surprising the boys are trying to get our attention.

'Abby's got balls of steel, fellas! She didn't even flinch.' Zach dummies at me and I turn away from him as he laughs and runs back to his mates.

I take a bite from a carrot stick and turn around to see who almost took my head off, shading my eyes against the sun with my other hand as I chew. It's a stinker today and I'm glad that we seniors wear white shirts so I don't have to worry about sweat stains under my arms. Jamie Drummond grins at me self-consciously. His acne has cleared up over the summer break; he must have seen the doctor and started Roaccutane. He's had his hair cut into a short mullet too. It doesn't suit him. Who looks *better* with a mullet?

'Sorry, Abby,' he says. I ignore him and swallow the carrot, which is hot and unappetising after being in my school bag all morning.

'Somebody's got a little crush,' Lili mutters. She's jealous. She's had a thing for Jamie since year seven, even with his acne. She shouldn't. Jamie is a moron. She could do better; I'm always telling her that. Lili has terrible taste in guys.

'Don't pay them any attention, Bethan. They're idiots.' Grace speaks in a deliberately loud voice, glaring at the table of boys. Bethan started at Arundel today, but her parents are friends with Grace's parents, so she receives a free pass to our group. She's still got that townie look about her – her make-up is wrong, and she wears the wrong school shoes – though I can tell by her sharp eyes and eagerness to please that she'll be one of us soon enough. She'll phase out the fringe and grow her hair longer, adopting a casual high pony and dumping her homemade friendship bands for a simple silver bracelet. That'll make five in our group. Me, Lili, Grace, Hayley and now Bethan. 'I can't believe they're in year twelve,' Grace adds with a grimace. 'They seem so much younger than us.'

Grace says she's waiting for university before she starts dating. She reckons the guys will be better in the city. Lili catches my eye and smiles. We have an in-joke that Grace will only date private school boys from Sydney. Even Arundel Christian College boys aren't good enough for her.

'Snob,' Lili mouths to me when Grace isn't watching. I grin.

The school has been spruced up for the start of the year. The freshly mown lawn smells amazing, and everything is green, despite the stinking heat. Jeff – Hudson's partner – has been busy. I see him around the school sometimes and he's always up for a chat, even though he's a pretty reserved guy. The sandstone and red-brick buildings with their pleasing spires and arches and stained-glass windows are behind us and to our left. On our right is the gym and pool, and in front is the oval, with the grandstand on the far side marking the school's boundary. Above me, the sky is the same bright blue as the Post-it notes I use for Ancient History. Last year we celebrated the school's one hundred and thirtieth anniversary, many of those years as a boys' school, though for the past thirty it's been co-ed. Along with the equally attractive Arundel University, Arundel Christian College is considered an essential part of the town's old-world charm.

Arundel is surface-level pretty; underneath it's as messed-up, gossip-laden and secret-filled as anywhere else.

Jamie runs over and wrestles Zach into a headlock. I tune them out.

One more year, I tell myself. *One year and you're out of here.*

'I swear I'm not dating any of those boys anymore. It's my new year's resolution,' Hayley says. This time the rest of us stifle giggles. She's been at Arundel since halfway through year ten and she's slept with two of the boys at that table and has done 'other stuff' (her words) with at least two others. Her resolution will last until the first party at Isaac's property – his parents are notoriously lax, and all sorts of shit goes on out there. Mum doesn't let me go to Isaac's parties, or at least, she doesn't let me go to the ones she hears about. Missing parties where most kids drink until they pass out is fine by me. I just don't tell my friends that.

The boys mock wrestle and swear at one another. Zach and Jamie. Cooper, Isaac and Josh. They are 'our' boys, the popular boys. Josh slow claps as Cooper leaps around in imitation of a ballerina and I almost smile. They might be morons, but they aren't all bad. I made out with Cooper in year nine, and Isaac early last year. Mostly to keep the rumours in check, the ones that say you're either frigid or gay if you don't. Not that I'd mind being thought of as either of those things, usually; it's more that I'd prefer to play it safe. Being the most popular girl in school is working for me, and while it does, I won't rock the boat.

One more year.

My eye is caught by movement beyond the morons. Taj Fielding emerges from the canteen, followed by Grace's twin brother, Jin. Taj holds a meat pie by its clear plastic wrapper as if it's too hot to handle. He's a step up from Zach and the other boys, at least in the looks department. I've always been attracted to the sun-bleached, sandy-haired type. Cute dimples. Taj has clear skin, and shoulders that lead me to presume he's a swimmer, as I am. I mean, yes, he has a mullet, but at least he wears his well.

Taj is one of the new kids, like Bethan. We usually get an influx in year eleven then a few more in year twelve as parents finally reject the local public high school. They think switching over here will magically give their little darlings better marks, as if the school is at fault, not the kid. I suppose sometimes that's true. Anyway, I'd noticed Taj straight away. I found out his name during period three English roll call, pleased to see him in the Advanced class. I appreciate a boy with a decent number of working braincells. Towards the end of the lesson I'd caught him staring at me and my stomach gave a little flutter.

Now, I watch Taj and Jin approach the other boys from the corner of my eye. Taj rips open the packet and starts eating his pie, glancing over at me. I force myself not to touch my hair or sit up straighter. There's something about him, even with his mouth full of sloppy gravy and pastry. The girls move on to discuss which best fake tan to buy, examining one another's arms as if it's the most important decision they'll make this year. Finally, I can't help myself. I tip my head back and move it from side to side slowly, as if it's stiff, then I lean back, exposing my throat and dropping my shoulders, stretching languidly, before sitting back up. I risk a look. He's watching me, along with Isaac, Jamie and Zach. I'm pleased – on the inside. On the outside I'm as cold as ice, baby. I hold his gaze. His eyes are dark brown, with long lashes.

Taj might make a worthy distraction from my studies this year.

Only a little one.

But then he peers past me. All the boys do, their conversation petering out. I sit up and turn around. There's a girl approaching our table. She looks exactly like one of our group. We're all blonde and either slim or sporty – except for Grace, who is Korean and slim and sporty. I squint into the sun and blink stupidly.

And then I realise who it is.

My pulse races, heat flooding through me in a wave. No, not a wave. A fucking tsunami.

No. I will her away. *It can't be.*

'Who's that?' Grace murmurs, and I wonder if I'm imagining the fear in her voice. Is there some part of her that can tell everything's about to go to shit?

'Fuck me,' one of the morons says. Zach, I think. 'She's hot.'

Bile rises in my throat, carrot flavoured. I know this girl. She's in my thoughts almost every day.

Because, long ago, in a time I want to forget and in a place I haven't returned to since, she and I almost killed a girl.

I hoped and prayed to God I'd never see Cara Ross again.

And now she's here.

*

How did I miss seeing her in assembly?

She's in our uniform, which means she's starting at this school. Today.

Shit.

A figure appears behind her. Miss Crofts, my Maths teacher and our year adviser. She hurries out of A Block in her sensible flats.

'Girls!' she pants as she reaches Cara. I have no idea how or why it was agreed that Miss Crofts would be a suitable year adviser. She's eighty-five years old – fine, probably fifty-five, though her *soul* is a solid eighty-five – never had kids, never married, and her idea of fun is attending caravan shows with her sister and telling us all about it. I swear she's been talking about buying a caravan ever since I started here, though I doubt she'll ever get one. She and her sister will keep going to caravan shows, lying beside one another to test the beds for comfort, opening and closing cupboard doors until one of them carks it. 'I'd like to introduce you all to Cara Ross, our scholarship recipient. She'll be boarding during term time and doesn't know anyone at Arundel. She's planning to do Extension Two Maths, Grace, so at last there's some competition for you and Jin.'

Grace hates being an Asian cliché; however, she genuinely is very good at Maths, as is her brother.

'I thought you girls could show her the ropes.' We must seem unhappy at the idea, as Miss Crofts adopts a serious expression. I risk a glance at Cara. She's examining me frankly, but there's no sign of recognition in her expression. My spirits lift, perhaps she won't remember me. 'I'll leave you to introduce yourselves. Girls, I expect you will show Cara all the courtesy you would appreciate should you be thrust into a new school at such an important time of your lives.' Miss Crofts gives us a meaningful look, then turns on her heel.

The others wait for me, so I reluctantly introduce myself and the others to Cara.

Zach wolf-whistles.

'Ignore those dickheads,' Grace adds, flashing the boys a glare.

'So, where are you from?' Lili asks. She looks the new girl up and down like she's competition.

Which she is.

It's apparent to us all immediately – even Bethan – that Cara isn't a townie who'll have to learn our style. She has her own style. Her blonde hair has been pulled into a low, side pony, which shouldn't work and yet it does, and she wears gold earrings in the shape of writhing snakes. Edgy and effortless. She's exactly how I remember her, maybe even prettier, with a large mouth and wide-set eyes. She's short, very slim with a narrow waist. Suddenly I feel like a giant, with my height and broad swimming shoulders. She even has perfect olive skin, quite different from our bottle-orange tans. I sense Lili sees all this too and is worried she'll go from hot girl number two to hot girl number three. It's superficial, but there you go.

'Calder Head,' Cara answers.

'Oh, not too far away then,' Grace says. 'Why'd you want to come here? You're right on the beach out there.'

'Yeah, we live a block from the beach, which is so amazing.' Cara grins. The gap between her two top teeth is endearing. I remember thinking the same thing the day I met her. 'I came because I want a good HSC mark. I want to go to university somewhere really cool and study medicine.' She dumps her school bag on the ground.

'Wow. Medicine,' Hayley says. She's bummed to hear this. Our group is smart, though Hayley gets the lowest grades and I'm sure she was hoping the new girl wouldn't be smarter than her.

'In Sydney?' Grace asks. Grace is dying to go to Sydney Uni.

'I'd prefer to go overseas. London. Maybe even Oxford or Cambridge.'

'Abby wants to go overseas too, don't you, Abby?' Grace prompts.

'Yeah.'

'She wants to go to America and study psychology. She will too. She's very smart,' Lili adds, claiming my intelligence as though she's partly responsible for it.

'We'll see,' I say. I don't want to tell Cara anything about me, though there's only benign interest in her expression. Maybe she hasn't linked me with the girl she befriended outside her house when we were kids.

'It sucks that you're boarding. You'll be stuck eating the school food day and night. At least we only have it for lunch. Avoid the pink dessert thing that looks like mousse.' Grace pulls a face. 'There's only a few of you boarders this year, isn't there?'

'Yeah. Eighteen. We each get our own room.' Cara shrugs. 'And if I board I can get away from my parents during term.'

'Well, that is appealing,' Grace says. She moves down the bench seat and gestures for Cara to sit. 'What's wrong with yours?'

'My dad's a pastor.' Cara sits on the end of the bench, swinging her legs over it and crossing her arms on the table. 'He's the head of the Orange Dawn Church.'

'Really? So you have to pray and go to church and shit? We do that here so at least you'll be used to it.'

She nods. 'Yeah, but my dad's church is all about singing knock-off rock songs and swaying.'

'Like Hillsong?' Grace makes a face. 'Weird.'

'And he's strict. He acts cool, but he doesn't let me do anything.' She gives a mysterious smile. 'So I have to sneak around behind his back.'

'Love it.' Grace has been telling Lili and me that we're boring ever since we refused to try the cigarettes she stole from her uncle back in year eight. 'My parents are too busy to take much notice of what I do. But Abby's mum is overprotective.' She nudges me.

'She's all right.' I shrug.

Zach and Jamie saunter over. 'Are you going to introduce us to your new friend?'

'This is Cara, idiots. Cara, these two idiots are Zach and Jamie.'

The boys mock bow and ask a few more questions. She soon has the boys eating out of her hand, hardly surprising given the low and superficial bar they've got for girls. Then, while she keeps half an eye on the improvised footy game they've started in an effort to impress her, she opens her bag and withdraws a small make-up bag. The girls ooh and ahh over the contents, and Cara lets them try her lip gloss and the small bottle of perfume that none of us has ever heard of. She wins them over effortlessly too. As they giggle I wonder if I've been too hasty in my concern. Perhaps she's different now.

Then, when she leans over to put the make-up back into her school bag, I catch her eye. Her expression doesn't change, though there's a glimmer in there that tells me Cara Ross knows exactly who I am. She hasn't forgotten. And she wants something from me.

Something I don't want to give her.

'We're allowed to have friends come to our dorms after school, so if any of you get sick of your parents you're welcome to take refuge there. I look after my friends.' She smiles, then adds, with a glance at me, 'What's the saying? Keep your friends close—'

'And your enemies closer,' I finish.

Something in me rises to the challenge and I smile broadly at Cara, ignoring the dread that sinks like a stone into the pit of my stomach.

*

Cara Ross is part of our group now.

I don't quite know how it happened. Well, I do.

It's because she's *Cara Fucking Ross*.

You see, Cara is very similar to me in some ways. We're the kind of people who want to be in control. I study, not because I enjoy it, but because it gives me a semblance of control come exam time. I bake, because following a recipe precisely gives me perfect results.

I carefully control my food intake for the same reason. When I injured my shoulder back in year nine and I couldn't swim for three months, I put on five kilos. Lili told me she adored my 'fuller face', and Grace said that if I had to give away any outfits because they didn't fit me anymore, then she really loved my red floral dress. *Just sayin'*, she'd added.

I lost the weight in two weeks.

I control *me*. I can't control *everything* in the world around me, though I do my utmost to try.

I'm good at controlling things. And people. My friends, my teachers, even Mum and Grandma. I know how to get an exam date moved to suit my schedule, with my teacher believing they wanted it changed themselves. I can persuade my friends to buy me anything from an eyeliner pencil to breakfast, with no complaints. It's a talent, though I don't abuse it. At least, I don't think I abuse it. Sure, Lucas gives me the occasional free salad at Nature's Café, but I'm careful not to go there every week.

Cara Ross, though; somehow she has my number. When she's around, things don't go so smoothly for me. It's in the small things. No one sees it but me. I hate to admit it, but she's smarter than I am.

Better.

More in control.

It's *concerning*.

Things have changed in our group since she joined us. Zach and our other boys throw balls past Cara's ponytail now; they wrestle where she can see them. All except Taj, so at least something's going my way. There's only been one party in the month since school started, and we kissed. It wasn't exactly magical – he'd tasted of Bundy rum – but we can work on that.

He's sweet. He sits next to me in English, and when Miss Smith turns to face the smartboard, we roll our eyes at how she attempts to use big words in every sentence. He's also an artist – though thankfully not one of those pretentious types. For his HSC major work he's threatening to sketch me. I haven't agreed to do it yet.

I like him. *Really* like him.

Of course, I'll be gone at the end of the year, so it's not serious, but it's nice.

While walking through the gates that afternoon to wait for Mum to pick me up, I'm daydreaming of Taj's shoulders so I don't hear Cara approach.

'Abby.' She touches my arm and I flinch. 'Or should I say Abigail?'

My stomach clenches. 'I don't go by that name anymore.'

'Fair enough.' She gives me an appraising look. 'Abby, then. Perhaps I could come over one afternoon next week to talk about this Persia topic we've started in Ancient History? Mr Foley's notes are confusing. Could you help me make sense of them?' She gives me her sunniest smile. I frown. Cara is as capable at Ancient History as she is at everything else she does. I'm certain she's doing better at it than me.

'Maybe we could go through it at lunchtime one day instead?' I demur. 'After school doesn't always work for me. Sometimes Mum interviews people from home and I have to be quiet.' Mum's car pulls up. 'I'd better go, she's here.'

'Okay, no problem.' Cara seems to deflate, and against my better judgement, I feel bad. And then she tucks her hair behind her ear with that low finger twirl I remember from when I was eleven as we lay on towels on Calder Head Beach. 'Have a great weekend.'

I hurry towards the car. Mum has pulled into a drop-off zone and gets out with a heavily loaded bag. Something leafy sticks out of the top.

'Hi, hon. I have to give this to the ladies in the office. Grandma's orders.'

'Sure. I'll wait here.' I open the passenger door and throw my bag in the footwell.

'Hi, Mrs Miller.'

I straighten up and turn around.

Cara stands there, her binder in one arm, her backpack on. 'Do you remember me?'

All the colour has left Mum's face. She looks Cara up and down, taking in her school uniform and her confident smile.

'Cara,' she says, her voice breathy. 'I didn't know … how are you?'

'I'm doing really well.' She smiles. 'Abby probably told you I've started at Arundel this year. I got that new P and C year twelve scholarship.'

Mum's mouth opens and closes like a fish. 'That was you?'

'Yes. I love it at Arundel so much, and it's been so nice seeing Abby again. We've become very close.'

'Oh,' Mum says.

I keep my expression blank.

Cara takes a step closer to us. She lowers her voice. 'I want you to know I haven't mentioned anything about what occurred … about Isabella. I want to put it all behind me – behind us.'

'That's … I'm glad.'

'Okay, great. Well, lovely to see you. You're exactly the same, Mrs Miller. Still so fit! My mum doesn't exercise much anymore. Do you swim? Abby does. Do you know I couldn't swim at all until I was thirteen? And I'm now a surf lifesaver at Calder Head, though that's mostly for my resume. Volunteering is so important for fattening up a resume.' She flicks a glance at me, then turns back to Mum. 'Perhaps we could talk more next week? Abby asked me to come over to your house to work through some Ancient History stuff. I hope that's all right?'

Mum's eyes flash to mine. I'm not sure what to say so I remain silent.

'Sure,' Mum finally answers. 'That would be nice.'

'Thanks, Mrs Miller.'

'Oh, it's Miss Miller actually. I mean, call me Nicola.'

'Thanks, Nicola.' Cara beams. 'I can take those to the office for you if you want? It's on my way to the boarding house.' She walks around the car and takes the bag from Mum.

'Um, thank you. Sure. Tell them they're from Joyce Miller. For the admin staff.'

'Will do. Have a lovely weekend.' She walks away, her ponytail swishing cheerfully.

And that's how it's done.

*

Mum has loads of questions after Cara strolls away with that bag of vegetables.

Why didn't I tell her Cara was at Arundel? What is she like? Have I seen her parents? Is she in my classes? Et cetera. Et cetera.

Et fucking cetera.

This is why I didn't tell her in the first place. Well, one of the reasons.

'Mum, everything is fine,' I say, staring out the window as we cut through the back streets to get home. 'I'll deal with her.'

She's silent, and I realise my tone might have been a little darker than intended.

'I mean, she's all right,' I continue, smiling at her. 'She hasn't mentioned the Isabella thing to anyone and she's part of our group now. She's –' I hesitate '– my friend.'

'O–kay,' Mum says in that voice she reserves for those times she doesn't believe me. Still, we both let it go.

That evening Cara texts an apology for inviting herself around, blaming it on loneliness. I mean, I get that. There are only two other year twelve boarders, the McAllen twins, girls who live on a property out west. They're joined at the hip, spend more time on horses than with people, and aren't riveting company.

I'd prefer it if she doesn't come around, though at least I'll be across what she's up to if she does.

Cara suggests a Thursday, which isn't ideal as Mum sometimes works from home on Thursdays. However, with all Cara's volunteering, hockey and netball, and other extracurricular activities, that's the only available afternoon she has.

We set it up.

*

A week later and Mum's waiting at the front of the school when Cara and I arrive at the end of the day.

I'm in the front, Cara's in the back behind Mum.

'Thanks so much for this, Mrs Miller – sorry, Nicola. It's so nice to escape school for a couple of hours. Don't get me wrong, I'm happy to be at Arundel, but ...'

'It's not exactly homey, I suppose,' Mum says as she pulls away from the kerb. She manages to sound normal, though I know she hasn't yet decided what to make of Cara. We're all silent for a minute, then she continues, 'Do you miss Calder Head? The beach?'

'Yeah, absolutely. I love the ocean. It's only that I'm super keen to go overseas to study next year and I have to get good marks to have any hope of getting in somewhere good. Arundel is my best shot.'

'What degree do you want to do?'

'Medicine.' She sighs. 'I know, I know. I'm aiming high. Oxford or Cambridge, ideally.'

'Oxford or Cambridge! That's impressive.'

'We'll see. I haven't got in yet.'

'The UK is a long way to go for university.' Mum is fishing now.

'Yeah. I'm kind of ready to get away, though. To escape.' She laughs but doesn't say what she wants to escape from.

'Abby wants to study overseas too. I'm still hoping she'll change her mind and choose somewhere a little closer.'

'You did exactly the same at my age, Mum. The only difference is that you came back early.'

'Where did you go?' Cara asks.

'Canada and the US. I was on a gap year, but I ended up pregnant with this one. I love you, Abby, but some advice, girls – don't get pregnant at seventeen.'

'I'm not planning on it,' I mutter.

'Me either.' Cara grins.

We share a look and I wonder at the possibility of becoming real friends with Cara after all. Then she leans back into the seat and tucks her hair behind her ear. My smile fades.

*

I first met Cara when Isabella and I walked to the supermarket for icy poles. There were tonnes in her fridge at home, but we were sunburnt from a morning on the beach and an afternoon in her pool and it was that time of the day where we were out of things to do and a little sick of one another. Her mum gave us a ten-dollar note and shooed us out of the house.

We wore no shoes, and the pavement was hot enough to force us, single file, onto the strip of grass alongside it, dodging bindies and glass from broken bottles. I led the way, pleased to be out of Isabella's enormous house and away from her holidaying parents, who spent most of the day drinking margaritas on their sun loungers. The house – with its hundred-and-eighty-degree view of the water, a plunge pool and five bedrooms – was their *holiday* house. Isabella's parents owned a couple of hotels on the Gold Coast, which is where they lived. We'd met at a swimming camp and stayed with one another overnight here and there, mostly because our parents encouraged it rather than due to any real connection between us. Isabella was friendly enough, with an obsessive interest in pop music that I leaned into when I was with her.

'Hey, Isabella.' The voice came from the house on the corner, the one with the veranda that ran all the way around it. A little girl sat on the porch stairs, watching us. She was very skinny and had black bags under her eyes. She wore a stiff white nightgown that highlighted how pale she was. Her blonde hair was lank and loose.

'Hi, Cara.' Isabella's voice had a note in it I hadn't heard before.

'Who's your friend?' the girl asked.

'This is Abigail. She's from Arundel.'

'Hi, Abigail,' Cara said.

'Hello.'

'Want to see what I've got?' The girl had her hands cupped together in her lap. She grinned, exposing a gap between her two front teeth. Something about her smile was exciting. Different.

'Sure.'

I led a reluctant Isabella across the grass to stand in front of Cara. Up close it was clear she wasn't as young as I'd thought, probably closer to our age. She smelled of soap, despite it being 4 pm in the summer holidays. She opened her cupped hands to make a chink for me to peer into.

A tiny gecko sat motionless on her palm, its tongue flicking in and out. Creatures that moved too quickly scared me, but I wouldn't admit that. 'A lizard! Cool.'

'You want to hold it?'

My mouth went dry, but something made me say, 'Okay.'

She motioned for me to move closer. I held my hands together and she dropped the lizard into them. It was just a whisper against my skin, still for a long moment, then it moved, tickling my palm and making me jolt. It skittered off, falling from my fingers to the stairs before disappearing under the house. Isabella squealed but Cara met my eyes.

'I'm sorry I lost your lizard,' I said.

She shrugged and twisted a lock of hair between her fingers, tucking it behind her ear. 'It's all right. There's heaps of them around here. I'll find another one later.' She had a sheen of sweat on her face. 'How cool would it be to be a zookeeper?' she continued. 'Looking after lions and tigers all day!'

'Yeah, that'd be excellent.'

'You'd have to pick up poo,' Isabella chimed in.

'I wouldn't care.'

'Me either,' I said, though privately I agreed with Isabella that it was pretty gross.

'I'm going to be a flight attendant when I grow up. I'm going to travel everywhere and never come back to this dump.' Cara gestured around us. I didn't say anything. I loved Calder Head – I even quite enjoyed living in Arundel back then. 'Or I'll be a fashion designer. Or a lawyer. I'll definitely live in New York. No, London!' Her eyes shone.

Suddenly, I wanted part of that life too. 'London would be amazing!'

'Wouldn't it?'

'I'm going to marry Shawn Mendes,' Isabella said, 'and have two children, a boy and a girl.'

Cara frowned at Isabella. 'Shawn Mendes? Why would you want kids? Kids are boring. I want to experience everything! Have adventures. Like riding on camels and flying in hot-air balloons.' She glanced at the cloudless blue sky with a longing I hadn't ever felt.

Something sparked inside of me.

Adventures and balloons.

'Do you want to come to the beach with us one day?' I asked. 'I'm here till Saturday.'

'Maybe.' She looked at Isabella. 'If I can. And only if you won't be mad, Isabella. I don't want to get in the way.'

'She doesn't mind, do you, Issy?' I answered for her. Isabella opened her mouth then closed it.

'Cara!' A woman's voice came from inside, then she materialised at the door. The woman appeared cuddly and kind, as if she'd smell of washing powder and cupcakes. She smiled at us, but I could see worry in the lines around her eyes. 'Hello, girls. Cara, you shouldn't be out here, honey. You need to be in bed.'

'I'm all right, Mum.' She kept her back to her mother.

'Cara.' It was a warning, though said in a nice way. 'You need to stay inside until you get a little bit better, darling.' The woman's brows came together as she addressed Isabella and me. 'My daughter isn't feeling well, girls. I'm afraid she'll have to say goodbye now.'

'I'm fine!' Cara said, trying to stand. She must have done it too quickly as she swayed on her feet.

'Oh!' her mother called out and Isabella and I gasped.

There was a sound from inside and a man appeared. He was very tall and wore shorts and a t-shirt. The skin of his arms and legs was covered in tattoos. I shrank back. 'What's wrong?' he asked.

'She's dizzy again, Mike.'

The man scooped her up. Her mother hovered near him, looking as if she wanted him to put her down. He regarded Cara with a tenderness that made my throat tight.

'Time to come inside then, little one.' He sounded nice. It made him seem less scary. 'I'll call the doctor.'

'No, Daddy!' Cara struggled a little, but she was too weak to pull free. 'I want to stay out here!'

The woman gave us an apologetic smile. She held her fine silver necklace in her fingers, twisting it. On it was a small silver cross. 'Sorry, girls, but she really isn't well.'

As they reached the door, Cara spoke, her words breathy. 'Nice to meet you, Abigail, I'll see you soon.'

The screen door squeaked shut and they were gone.

'What's wrong with her?' I asked Isabella. I'd never seen anyone who was really sick before.

'Dunno. She's always been like that,' Isabella said as we walked away. 'Mum said I should stay away from her in case I catch it.'

As we walked back, licking our icy poles – lemonade for Isabella, raspberry for me – I wondered how it was that, despite Cara's poor health, she was somehow more vital – more alive – than we were. Isabella seemed even less interesting now. She didn't want to live in London or be a fashion designer. She talked about Shawn Mendes, 5SOS and boys from her school I'd never met.

I dragged my feet as we passed the house again, hoping Cara would appear. The curtain twitched, then nothing.

I didn't see her again until two days later.

'Abby?'

I snap back to the present and realise we've arrived home. Mum is watching me, her car door open.

'Sorry,' I say. 'Just daydreaming.'

I risk a glance at the back seat. Cara watches me, a gleam in her eyes.

*

'She's nice,' Mum says, watching Cara walk down the street.

Cara had insisted she'd catch the bus back to school, then Mum had insisted she would drive her before Cara insisted again. It was a whole thing. Cara won. I hadn't been alone with Cara for long, as she spent most of the time chatting with Mum, then Grandma, who was suspiciously not fazed to see her here. So much for our Ancient History study.

She had charmed both of them within minutes. Smart, articulate, pretty.

What wasn't there to like?

Now Grandma nods her agreement to Mum's observation. 'Yes,' she says. 'Cara seems very nice. I'm glad she came over.'

We're all silent for a moment. I tidy up the coffee mugs we'd used for afternoon tea, then start prepping my bowls and whisk.

'You're baking? Now?'

'Yeah. It's only five. There's a recipe for peanut butter macadamia biscuits I've been wanting to try.'

I need this. Mum looks at me and for a split second I think she's going to talk about the incident, but she won't.

The three of us don't talk about Isabella.

Ever.

Don't get me wrong, I'm glad of it. I don't feel the urge to talk about that day in Calder Head. And my mum and my grandmother and I, though we might not agree on everything, we understand one another.

We know when to be silent.

Grandma stands up. The last rays of the setting sun fall across her face and she squints. 'I have to say something.' She waits while I set the whisk down on the bench and give her my full attention. 'What happened to Isabella was an accident and it was a long time ago,' she says, startling me and disproving my assertion. 'This afternoon shows us that we have been worried for nothing. Cara seems prepared to keep the whole thing under wraps, and I, for one, believe she will. Let's take this as a win and move on.'

Mum shoots me a glance. 'Abby? What do you think?'

What choice do I have?

'Sure. I believe her.'

Do I?

I pick up the whisk again, then put it down when I see my hand is trembling.

'Me too.' Mum smiles and there's relief on her face.

'Wonderful,' Grandma says. I'm pretty sure she's noticed my shaking hand but doesn't comment. 'It's done, once and for all. I'll see you Sunday for brunch, Abby?'

She waits until I murmur agreement. That seems to satisfy her because she picks up her handbag and begins to leave. Mum follows, coming to a halt when Grandma swivels around.

'Oh, one more thing. Let's not tell Lee any of this, okay? It's all in the past now.' The sun has dropped below the horizon and Grandma's face is in shadow as she speaks. 'There's no need to open up old wounds.'

Mum steps around her and switches on the light. It's too bright. We blink at one another, then incline our heads.

It's all in the past.

*

'You really like Taj then?'

My eyes meet Cara's in the mirror. It appears to be a genuine question.

'Yeah.' I shrug. 'But I'm going overseas next year so it can't last.'

'It could be fun while it does, though.' She grins.

'True.'

Mum's now actively encouraging me to hang out with Cara. She overheard us talking about the school dance and next thing I knew Cara was getting ready at our place, Mum offering to drive us.

'It's a shame Lucas won't be there,' she says.

'Lucas?'

Cara gives me a look. 'He's cute, don't you think?'

I shrug. 'He's old.'

'Not that old.' Cara grins and pulls out a small bag of jewellery. 'Fine. Tonight, I'll be a good girl.' She holds up a pair of gold cross earrings and I smile. Her jewellery does seem clearly divided into good and evil. Snakes, daggers and the evil eye versus crosses, hearts and suns.

'Sure you will. You have so much great jewellery.'

She grins and holds one to her earlobe, admiring it. 'You like it? I'm in love with yellow gold at the moment.' She names a brand I've only seen on TikTok. It's expensive. Too expensive for teenagers.

'How do you afford it?'

She slips the earring through her ear and glances at me in the mirror. 'I have a job.'

'Oh? I didn't think boarders were allowed out to work.'

'It's not a regular job, but it pays well.'

'What do you do?'

'I'd rather not say.' Her tone is coy, and it's clear she wants me to ask more about it, so I don't.

'Well, it must pay better than the hospital café. Speaking of disgusting food –' I grin, changing the subject '– how's the boarding house going? Not sick of the grey lamb chops and lumpy mashed potato yet?'

She wrinkles her nose. 'Kind of. But I don't mind boarding.' She gives me a sideways glance, a tube of lip gloss in her hand.

'My parents aren't like your mum. Dad's always telling me what to do.'

Cara's told me this before, though I don't believe it. Her parents might be full-on, but it sounds like they dote on her.

'Don't you miss them?' There's a lot I'm looking forward to about going away next year, but I'll miss my mother and grandmother.

She smears gloss onto her lips, then rubs them together. 'No. Persuading them to let me come to Arundel is the best thing I've ever done.'

'They didn't want you to apply for the scholarship?'

'The school's not strict enough, apparently. And I don't think Dad likes me being away from home.' She rolls her eyes. 'But I got Mum onside and she worked on Dad.' She grins, then puts the lip gloss in her bag. 'I'm done. You ready to go and blow Taj's mind?'

'Absolutely.'

*

Hudson and Mum, wineglasses in their hands, are sitting on the lawn in the last of the sunlight.

'You girls good to go?' Mum calls as I step out the back door, Cara right behind me.

'Yep,' I say. 'Hey, Hudson.'

Hudson waves at me. 'You're as gorg as usual, darling,' he calls out. 'Oh, by the way, I've got a seafood challenge for you. I'm cooking mussels with a curry consommé for starters, then crispy fried schnapper with hot and sour sauce for main. What's dessert?'

'Well, those are delicate flavours, but strong too, so dessert needs to hold its own. I'd do a yuzu orange cake with pineapple sorbet and caramelised pineapple.'

'I love it,' he says, waving his wineglass in the air.

Cara's looking at me strangely.

'It's this thing we do,' I tell her. 'Hudson's obsessed with cooking. He does savoury, I do sweet. Mostly we just tell each other what we'd cook, though sometimes we do actually get together and cook it.'

'She's bloody good!' Hudson calls out. 'You're Cara?'

'That's me.'

'Lovely to meet you, gorgeous.' His words are pleasant, but he gives Cara a thorough once-over – he's almost as protective of me as Mum.

'Hudson's staying?' I ask Mum as she comes over. He's lying down on the grass, his empty wineglass now beside him.

'Yes, we're having pizza. You two look lovely! You know your grandmother is collecting you, Abby?'

'Yep.'

'And you'll walk back to the dormitory, Cara?'

'Yes, other boarders will be at the dance. And a matron.'

'Okay. I'll use the toilet and then I'm ready to go.'

We're in the kitchen, laughingly applying lip gloss for the final time using spoons as mirrors when the garage door slams and Lee walks in.

He places his briefcase on the benchtop, beholds us with bemusement, before he turns to Cara and smiles. 'I'm Lee. You must be …'

'This is Cara.'

'Nice to meet you. Where are you girls going?'

'The school dance. Didn't Mum tell you? Apparently you're getting pizzas with Hudson. He's out the back.' I gesture vaguely behind me.

Lee opens the fridge and retrieves a beer, twisting the cap off. 'Jeff too?'

'No. He's working.'

Lee scrunches his face up.

'Hudson's not that bad, you know.'

Lee never says too much but it's obvious he's not Hudson's biggest fan. The feeling seems to be mutual.

'Yes, I know.' He sounds defensive. 'I'd hoped for a quiet night, that's all. I'd better go say hello.'

Cara watches curiously as he goes out to greet Hudson. 'They don't get on?'

'They do. They're just not buddies.'

'Maybe your stepdad is jealous of Hudson? He's hot!'

'No, he's gay. Very gay. Also very taken.'

'That's too bad.' She gives me a smile I don't like, then changes tack. 'Maybe I could stay over tonight? We could bitch about the outfits everyone wears at the dance.'

'Oh, sorry, I'm staying at my grandmother's house.'

'No worries,' Cara says. A flash of annoyance crosses her face so quickly I almost miss it. She puts her lip gloss in her clutch. 'Joyce is very cool, by the way.'

'You think?' Grandma is fun, but she's not cool. I fetch my heels and sit at the table to buckle them up.

'Absolutely. She's a crack-up. And she has the best stories. I love hearing old people's stories! All my grandparents are dead.' Cara pulls her own heels on while standing, her balance impressive.

'I'm sorry. Did you know them well?'

'Not Dad's parents. I knew Mum's mother, but she died a few years ago now. What was your grandfather like?'

I stand up, trying not to totter. 'I never met him. He was an artist. A fun bloke, though, not your tortured artist type. He was a farmer too, a larrikin.'

'Like Taj,' Cara says, looking at me slyly. 'He's an artist.'

I hadn't thought of that before. Mum reappears. 'Okay, we'd better go, girls.'

'Lee's home,' I tell her.

'He is? I'll check what pizza he wants, though it'll probably be Hawaiian.' She makes a face and goes outside.

'When did your mother remarry?' Cara asks.

'They aren't married. But they've been together since Lee moved to Arundel when I was twelve.'

She leans towards me, then whispers in a loaded voice, 'Does he know? About *what we did*?'

'Cara.' The word is a warning.

She holds her hands up in surrender. 'He's a good stepdad, though?'

'Yeah, he is. And he adores Mum.' Lee says something outside and Mum laughs. 'He's great.'

'That's good.' Cara looks at me sharply. 'Why would you want to go away and leave all this behind then?'

'I need … I think …' I can't find the words. 'Actually, I first decided I wanted to travel when I met you. You made it sound so exciting. Exotic.'

'Truly? I was eleven, Abby. If I had a functioning family I'd stay right here. You're lucky. A mother who loves you. A father who doesn't …' She spins away, setting her empty glass on the sink.

I open my mouth to ask what she means but she speaks

again, her voice almost a whisper. 'I have to get out of here. Away from my parents. Before—'

Right then, the screen slides open and Mum reappears, talking about pizzas and pineapple and how embarrassing it is to order a Hawaiian pizza, and the moment is gone.

*

A weight lifts from my shoulders every time I crunch onto the gravel driveway leading up to Hillcrest.

Life is simpler here.

No Cara. No Taj.

Just me and Grandma. I weed her garden, make lemonade, or cut flowers to take home for Mum. Sometimes we just sit and chat.

However, today my pleasure is marred when I see a white hatchback parked outside the house. Part of me wants to turn around and leave, but curiosity gets the better of me. I let myself in.

'Grandma?'

There's laughter from the kitchen and I brace myself before opening the door. Grandma and Cara look up from where they sit at the bench, their heads together over a pot of tea.

'Abby!' Cara smiles. She wears old clothes and a small pair of gold heart earrings.

'Darling! What a lovely surprise,' Grandma says, rising and giving me a hug. 'Cara's been helping me with some planting. We brewed some raspberry leaf tea to help with her period pain. Made from the raspberry plants in the garden. I used to find it worked a treat. Tastes all right too, doesn't it, Cara?'

'Yeah, it's pretty good.'

'I brought an apple teacake, it's still warm,' I say, keeping my eyes averted from Cara.

What's she doing here?

'Lovely. I'll cut some slices. Cara? You'll have a piece?'

Cara hesitates. 'Ah, no. I'll go. I'll come next weekend if you need me?'

'That would be wonderful.'

Grandma walks her out while I cut a slice of teacake. She's back in less than a minute, and bustles over to fetch new mugs.

'Well, thanks to your lovely friend, we don't need to do anything more in the garden today. How about we take a cuppa outside? Have a wander?'

'Sounds good. Does she visit you often, Grandma?'

'Oh, not too often. She's at Calder Head this weekend, so she probably wanted to get out for a bit.' She sees the single slice of cake. 'None for you?'

'No. I had a late breakfast.'

She doesn't say anything.

We sit on the back porch until Grandma finishes her slice. 'Delicious, darling, as usual. Shall we walk in the garden while we finish our tea?'

As we stroll, the sun and the tea thaw me until finally I regain my equilibrium. I point at plants and Grandma tells me about them; something we've done since I was little. 'Marj's delphiniums,' Grandma says when I gesture at a bush with leaves shaped like maple leaves. It looks a little like a weed. She smiles, as she always does when she mentions Marjorie. Hillcrest's caretakers were long gone before I was born. Dougie keeled over in the field, a bag of feed in his hands, according to the legend. And Marjorie moved to Sydney to live with her sister after Grandma sold the rest of the land.

'They'll flower in summer. The seeds are deadly.'

'Why grow them if they're deadly, Grandma?' I ask. 'Surely there are other flowers that aren't toxic you can plant instead?'

'Of course there are!' Grandma speaks sharply. 'Does that mean we should never grow the more dangerous plants?' She strolls over to a green shrub almost as high as her waist. Several electric blue flowers dot it. 'For example, this is aconite, one of the deadliest plants in the whole garden. It's also called wolfsbane or monkshood. Don't touch it without gloves. It's almost finished flowering. Gorgeous, isn't it?'

'Yes,' I say. 'Very pretty.'

She motions to a large tree by the back fence. 'That's oleander. The leaves and flowers can cause vomiting, seizures or a coma if ingested.'

Her eyes lock on mine and I'm not sure what she'll say next. She surprises me when she changes the subject. 'I'll pay for you to go away to study psychology, Abby, if it's genuinely what you want. As long as you aren't running away from anything.' She takes my hand in hers, her grip firm and sure. 'Run *towards* your future. Towards your true self.'

I look at the unassuming aconite flowers and swallow.

'Embrace who you are, Abby. That's what we all need to do.'

*

'Cara! Get over here!' Lili yells close to my ear and I wince.

It's almost the end of lunch and Cara's been at a student representative council meeting. I have no idea how she got elected to the SRC so soon after starting at Arundel, but that's Cara for you.

As a prefect, I can't be on the SRC. Thankfully universities regard prefects as more prestigious than student reps, and I do feel a petty pleasure one-upping her this way.

It's Monday and Lili's been excitable all lunchtime, giggling and peering across the quad expectantly. Now it's clear why. The rest of us have no idea what she's on about, and it's been a little bit annoying. Like when someone gets a great mark in a test and they keep asking you what you got, just so you'll ask them what they got and they can act all coy about how well they've done.

Nauseating.

Cara, who was talking to a group of attentive younger students, makes a beeline towards us. Heads swivel as she passes, and boys preen in front of her like peacocks. I'm embarrassed for them. But I understand. Cara's pull is strong.

'Can we do it now?' Lili is almost bursting out of her skin. She gives me a sly smile. 'We've got something to show you, Abby. It's so cool.'

Cara comes over and Lili jumps up from the bench to stand beside her. Together they're gorgeous blonde twins. Lili even wears her hair on the side in a low pony now, like Cara. I resolve then and there that tomorrow I'll wear my hair out. And then I'm annoyed I care what they're doing with their hair. These games are beneath me.

They glance at one another then lift up their school shirts to expose their flat stomachs and ribs.

There. Right up on their bony rib cages, just below where their bras start, they both have a tattoo.

That's why Lili is so excited.

They got matching tattoos.

Not a heart or a butterfly or some Chinese character meaning 'best friends'. The tattoo they chose is a knife: a thick, sharp knife, with a small drop of red blood dripping from the blade. It's not big, only a couple of centimetres in length. The sight of it there, inked onto their bodies, marking them for the rest of their lives, makes me uneasy. It connects them.

Grace, Bethan and Hayley gasp, offering oohs and ahhs. 'I don't think any other girls at school have tattoos yet!' Bethan says. 'You're the first!'

'Don't let the teachers see you,' Hayley adds. 'You'll get suspended or something.'

'It's so bad arse!' Grace sounds a little jealous. 'Very cool.'

'Are you insane?' The words burst from my mouth. 'Have your parents seen this?' I'm staring at Lili, ignoring Cara.

My oldest friend gives me an injured look. 'Not yet.'

'You realise they will? The first time you wear a swimsuit this summer.'

She shrugs, but a flash of concern flits across her face, followed by irritation that I'm not fangirling like the others. She and Cara share a look.

'So? I'm eighteen.' Her birthday was a month earlier. 'There's nothing they can do about it now.'

'They can renege on their offer to pay for half of that car you want so badly, the one you're still saving for. And they can make you remove the tattoo.'

She's sullen now, staring at the ground. She didn't expect this. She thought I'd be on Team Cara.

'My dad will absolutely kill me when he sees it,' Cara says, sounding unbothered. She lets her shirt fall and grins at us. 'I don't give a shit.'

Her attitude and vocabulary are markedly different when there are no adults around.

'Doesn't your dad have, like, a thousand tattoos?'

'He does.' She grins again. 'But he doesn't think it's "ladylike" for girls to get them. Especially his daughter. He'll freak out.'

Lili drops her shirt too, regaining some of her confidence. She pokes Cara in the shoulder. 'You should show them what else you've been doing.'

'Oh.' Cara shakes her head and sits down beside Grace. 'I don't think so.'

'Go on.'

She shoots me a challenging glance. 'Nah. Abby wouldn't approve.'

Approve.

I don't react. Does she think I'm the same girl I was at eleven? That she can manipulate me as easily now?

Back then, I was an innocent. For two days after my first meeting with Cara, I pestered Isabella to walk to the shops, or to the beach, anywhere that took us past her house, where I'd linger in the hope of seeing her. We didn't, not so much as a twitching curtain. Then, on the afternoon of the second day, as the two of us lay on the beach trying to look older and nonchalant for a group of teenage boys who threw a football to one another and totally ignored us, a shadow fell over me.

Cara. She blocked the sun, so she was little more than a dark silhouette.

'You made it!' I said.

'Yep.'

'Hi, Cara,' Isabella said.

Cara ignored her.

She wore a yellow two-piece swimsuit with frills on the side of the bottoms. It was a bikini for a younger child. She was very skinny, with a flat chest the same as me. Isabella already had little mandarin boobs and a string bikini, both of which she was very proud of. I wore a black bikini – the first 'adult' one my mum had ever let me buy, though it offered far more coverage than Isabella's. Cara's skin had evidently not seen the sun in a very long time, while Isabella and I were browned from weeks of summer.

'Do you need sunscreen?' I asked her a little worriedly, as Mum was constantly going on about skin cancer.

'Nah, I'll be fine.' She had no towel, so I shuffled down to let her sit on the end of mine.

'Want to swim?' I asked. The water – pool or ocean – was my happy place.

'No.' The way she eyeballed the waves, which were almost non-existent that day, told me that maybe Cara couldn't swim. That shocked me. *Everyone* learned how to swim. My friends and I had all had swimming lessons as soon as we could walk, and our parents were insistent we could swim well enough to be safe.

'I can't stay long,' she said. 'Mum has gone grocery shopping. I'm supposed to wait inside.'

Why? I wanted to ask. I didn't, though. It wasn't polite.

'Won't you get in trouble?' I queried her instead.

Cara lifted her shoulders in a languid manner that told me she genuinely didn't care. It didn't matter that she wore the wrong clothes or wasn't tanned like us. She was different. Freer. More interesting. Then she coughed and her slight frame shook. Her arms were twigs. Even if Cara knew how to

155

swim, she would be far too weak to swim in the ocean, even on a calm day like this.

The sound of 'Greensleeves' floated over on the wind. The soft-serve ice-cream truck had arrived. In summer it parked at Calder Head beach twice a day.

'Should we get soft serves?' Isabella asked. She kept an eye on the footy-throwing boys who were approaching the van. 'The cute guys are going over there.'

'Maybe you should get ice creams and we'll stay here,' Cara responded.

'On my own?' Isabella replied, her tone unsure. 'Don't you want to come?'

'The boys will focus on you if you're on your own. And you look so much older than us in your bikini. We don't have a chance with them.'

Isabella puffed up a bit but still seemed nervous. 'Really? I can't carry three cones.'

'Just get two. I don't want one,' Cara said. 'Go, Issy! They'll think you're at least fifteen! Tell us everything when you come back.'

Isabella stood up. 'Should I put my dress on?'

'No way! You want to tempt them?' Cara giggled.

Isabella smiled and walked towards the car park, turning back to us once, then continuing on when she saw we were watching.

Once Isabella reached the grass, Cara pushed herself up then bent over Isabella's towel, removing the other girl's dress, beach bag and sunglasses and dumping them on the sand. She lay down in her spot, shading her eyes with her hand as she looked at me with a smirk. 'I can't believe she's going over there! Those boys are so not interested in her.'

'Right?' I agreed, though I was confused. Cara had sounded sincere. Why did she lie to Isabella?

'Have you been friends with Issy long?' She rested her head on the towel and spoke with her eyes closed.

I shrugged. 'A few months.' Then for some reason I added, 'She's okay.'

'Oh yeah. Issy is … nice.' She made the word an insult. 'I've known her for ages. She's just, I don't know, boring, don't you think? All she's interested in is boys.'

I didn't say anything. I was desperate for Cara to like me and I didn't want to be lumped in with lame Isabella.

'I love your swimmers,' she said. 'They're cool.'

'Thanks.'

'Mine are so old. Mum won't buy me new ones. She doesn't like me coming to the beach.'

'Why?'

'I'm sick.'

'What's wrong with you?'

'No one knows.' Her eyes were still closed and her chest rose and fell with each breath. Every rib was visible and her collarbone stuck out far enough for someone to grab hold of. 'Mum keeps taking me to the doctors. They've done all these tests and can't find what it is.'

'I'm sorry.'

She shrugged again. 'Yeah, it sucks.' She pushed up onto one elbow. 'Hey, why don't we bury her sunglasses in the sand?'

'Why?'

'For fun.'

'But she loves those sunglasses.' Isabella had only bought them last week, and she kept going on about how they cost her mother thirty-five dollars and wasn't that a lot of money for something so small. 'What if she can't find them?'

Cara scanned the sand and picked up a scraggly piece of dried seaweed. 'We'll put this on top so we don't forget where they are.' She sat up and faced the ice-cream truck with her legs crossed. 'She's still in line, we have time. You dig, I'll keep watch.'

I scooped the hot sand from between our towels. Cara handed me Issy's sunglasses and I dropped them into the hole and filled it in, then she placed the seaweed on top.

We watched Isabella mill around awkwardly near the ice-cream truck, the older boys not even noticing. Cara dragged Issy's bag over to her and peered inside. She pulled out an orange pouch, pencil-shaped, only larger.

'That's her EpiPen,' I warned. 'Don't open it.'

She ignored me, removing the large syringe and examining the instructions. 'This is what she uses if she eats peanuts, right?'

'Yeah. Her mum showed me how to use it. It's a bit scary.'

'What, you have to stab her?' She made a stabbing motion with the EpiPen. 'Cool.'

'Yes. But it's not likely she'll need it. She just needs to stay away from peanuts, or anything that might have peanuts in it.'

Isabella was walking back towards us with the cones. I wished Cara would put the EpiPen away. She studied Isabella and then me, as if she knew exactly what I was thinking. Then she slowly put the EpiPen back in its case and then into the bag and sat back on my towel, returning Isabella's dress and bag where she'd found them.

Isabella had a sheepish look on her face as she handed me a rapidly melting ice cream. 'They didn't talk to me.' She licked ice cream from the side of her hand.

'You did so well!' Cara told her. 'The one in the blue and yellow boardies was totally checking you out.'

'Yeah?' Isabella plonked onto her towel, doubtful but pleased.

I ran my tongue around the ice cream, sweating and staring at the water. We were all silent for a minute, then Isabella asked, 'Hey, have you seen my sunnies?'

'No.' I couldn't look at her.

'What do they look like?' Cara asked. She sounded so innocent that I stared at her in awe.

'They were right here. You remember my new ones, Abigail? They're black.'

'I haven't seen them,' I said. The ice cream churned in my stomach.

'Maybe you left them over at the van,' Cara said, before I could crack. 'You had them on when you walked over there.'

'Did I?' Isabella seemed confused.

'Yep. Didn't she, Abigail?'

'Er, I think so.'

Isabella regarded me through narrowed eyes, then stood up and huffed off. Cara grinned.

'I'm glad we got rid of her again. She's so boring. Boys, boys, boys. Uh, look at them.' They were kicking the footy again. 'Why would you bother?'

'She isn't only interested in those boys. She also loves Shawn Mendes,' I said, rolling my eyes.

Cara laughed. 'You're not the same as Issy. You're like me.' She picked up the seaweed she'd used to mark the sunglasses burial site and threw it as far as she could. 'You're going to do great things. You're going to get out of here.' She held my eyes, then touched my arm with her warm hand. Something ran through me. A feeling like nothing I'd ever felt before. It was thrilling.

'I'd better go,' she said, after a glance towards Isabella, who was peering under the ice-cream truck and all along the footpath, her movements agitated. Cara examined the sand covering the sunglasses then raised her eyebrows to me but said nothing.

'Come back tomorrow. Earlier though. Around twelve. Mum helps Dad serve a free lunch to uni students at church tomorrow and I'll have a couple of hours free. I'll meet you here.'

'I'll have to bring Isabella,' I said apologetically. 'I'm staying at her house.'

'No worries, I have a plan.' She grinned, then rose and walked back towards her home, veering away from Isabella.

When Isabella came back, I didn't tell her where her sunglasses were.

Not even when she started crying.

*

'Go on, show her!' I snap back to Lili's voice in the present. She's holding Cara's arm possessively. 'Or I will!' It's a teasing threat.

'Okay, okay. Fine.' Cara takes out her phone and, after fiddling, passes it to me. 'It might not be your cup of tea, Abby, but it's making me a fortune. So, don't judge.'

'I don't judge,' I say, trying not to sound defensive. Cara raises her eyebrows.

At first I'm not sure what it is. It's a video, obviously, though I can't quite make out what's going on. Skin and clothes. There's the sound of breathing. I'm queasy for a minute until I realise it's not sex. The skin becomes a woman's foot as she moves away from the screen. I can't see her head, but I guess it's Cara. It's a woman's foot. The toenails are neatly manicured and painted a deep purple and the toes are flexing and stretching. There's a fine yellow gold chain around the ankle. One foot rubs against the other. I give her a disgusted glare.

'What is this?' I ask. 'Is this you? What on earth are you doing?'

'It's my new account on—'

'I know what site it is. It's WatchMe. It's revolting,' I say. 'This is the site celebrities are joining to post sex stuff on for money.' I've never checked it out myself but I know it's subscription-based and people can post anything – *anything* – for others to watch. Mostly pay-per-view live porn.

My gut churns.

'It's not only celebrities, though. Anyone can do it. And now I do it.'

'Freud said that people have foot fetishes because feet resemble dicks,' Lili says, giggling. She widens her eyes at my glare. 'What? It's true.' She shrugs. 'They do look a bit like dicks.'

'You do this for money?' My tone is incredulous. Looking back at the screen, I scroll down. There's a photo of a stockinged foot, two hands starting to peel the stocking off, with a play button in the middle of it. Below that is a headless girl wearing a black lace bra, and on and on – dozens more videos ready to play, all suggestive, most centred around feet.

'Not just "money".' Cara uses air quotes around the word. 'Fuckloads of money. You wouldn't believe how much people will pay to watch a girl do stuff with her feet.' She mouths the word 'fuckloads' again, slowly, her eyes wide. 'And not only feet stuff. I do other things too.' She puts a hand up to forestall my question. 'Not sex. Nothing like that. You never even see my face. And I use a fake name – caramel_69.' She grins. 'I earned well over a thousand dollars last week. My parents won't be able to keep me here if I have my own funds.'

'I'm thinking of setting up my own site,' Lili interrupts.

I stare at her. 'You aren't serious?'

'It's my body. I can sell it for cash if I want. I don't even have to show my face. It's better than working at Macca's or as a checkout chick!'

I frown. 'So you don't do actual sex?'

Cara laughs. 'I'd want way more cash for that!'

'Who knows about this?' I wave an arm at the playground. 'The boys? Our teachers? They'll find out eventually. This sort of thing can't stay hidden forever.'

'If it comes out, I'll deal with it.'

'I can't imagine your parents would be happy.'

She rolls her eyes. 'As if I care what they think.'

I click on another video. Cara's feet flex and writhe. Behind them a desk and shelves are visible. 'Oh my God, this is filmed at school! Do you have any idea of the shitstorm that will rain down on you if this gets out? You'll lose your scholarship!'

'Calm down, Abby. It's under control.'

I shake my head and thrust Cara's phone back at her. 'You're insane.' I stand up. 'I'm going to French.'

'The bell hasn't even gone yet!' Grace objects.

I stride off. Behind me Lili mutters something and the others laugh.

My cheeks burn. I'm not a prude, but this is wrong. And it's not only that. Cara thinks she's taking precautions, but what if someone finds out who caramel_69 really is? What if the school finds out, or her parents? Or someone who wants something more from caramel_69, something they can't get online?

God, Abby it's not as if you care about Cara, anyway. Unease slithers down inside me, coming to rest in my stomach like a large slice of dark chocolate tart with heavy cream.

Too rich.

Too much.

I'm not sure why it bothers me, but I have a bad feeling about this.

*

'Thanks for the lift, Lee.'

'Anytime, Abby.'

Lee's work car smells of pine air freshener. Grace was supposed to drive me to school but bailed at six this morning while I was still at squad, and Mum had an eight o'clock interview across town to promote a new trampoline park.

It turns out my friends are taking the day off school to go to Sydney for the weekend to attend a couple of university open days. Cara, Lili, Grace, Bethan and Hayley. They'd organised this trip several days before, though no one had thought to tell me. Or invite me, for that matter. When I suggested I might tag along, Grace said she was sorry, the car was full, the Airbnb booked. She said they didn't expect I would want to come, since I was set on going overseas next year.

I didn't say it would have been nice to be asked.

'I thought Cara was going overseas next year too?' I couldn't keep a bitchy note from my voice.

'Yeah, but she offered to buy snacks and she's paying for petrol. Sorry, Abby.' Grace had the decency to sound embarrassed. She was calling from the highway. In the background the other girls giggled. 'Sorry, Abby!' they called over speakerphone.

'No worries.'

The ache of being left out surprised me. I thought I was ready to leave Arundel and my friends behind. Until Cara claimed them as her own.

Maybe I don't like someone taking what's mine.

'What happened with Grace this morning?' Lee's driven me halfway to school while I've been morosely staring out the window.

'Oh, nothing really.' The smell of chlorine in my hair is giving me a headache. He raises an eyebrow so I exhale dramatically, then fill him in.

'God, that's a bit much! Leaving you out. Not even mentioning they were going.' Tears prick the back of my throat. I love that Lee is on my side. Maybe I'm not being oversensitive about this after all. 'Well, fuck 'em!' he says cheerfully, as he changes lanes. 'How about we get pizzas tonight? The gourmet ones from Bella Napoli.'

'Sounds great. Thanks, Lee.'

'I'll call your mum and tell her later. She's on a crusade to save money at the moment but I have ways of convincing her.' He wiggles his eyebrows.

'Gross! I don't want to know about that!' But I can't help smiling.

He has a strange lightness about him for a policeman. A happiness. It's as if all the shit stuff he's seen in his life has made him appreciate Mum more. Grandma says he's good for her.

'We could do something fun together this weekend too, if you want? Bushwalking? Or shopping?' That's a joke. Lee hates shopping and he knows I'm not a bushwalker.

'Oh, that sounds *lovely*,' I say in a sarcastic tone. 'Unfortunately, I'll have to study. Trials start in a week or so.'

'Ah well, I tried.' He grins. 'You don't go to school during the trials?'

'No, we only have to go in for the exams.'

'You'll be able to cook a few dinners for us then.'

'Ha! I told you I'll be studying. Plus, I'm picking up more hours at the café. I'll need spending money when I move to Massachusetts.' I observe him from the corner of my eye.

'That's Harvard?'

'Yes. But I won't get in there. I'm still aiming for Brown or Dartmouth, though.'

There's a short silence. 'Your mother hopes you'll change your mind and stay in Australia.'

'I won't. Grandma has said she'll pay—'

'It's not the money. Well, we couldn't afford it without Joyce's help. But that's not why your mum doesn't want you to go.'

'I know.'

'She'll miss you.'

'She'll have you to take care of her.'

'And I will.' He pauses again. 'I won't tell you to stay in Australia, Abby, I'm aware you have your heart set on this. Just … make sure it's what you really want. I mean, I've seen you bake, and Joyce has offered to set you up in Arundel with your own bakery. One of those fancy French ones.'

'A patisserie?' I give the word a lovely French accent.

'Yes.' He glances at me. 'You're good enough.'

We're quiet again. After a couple of minutes, I give him a sideways glance. 'What do you know about those websites where people post sex stuff? Videos and photos? The ones gross old men subscribe to?'

His brows come together. 'What do you want to know?'

'Are they legal?'

'To post on?'

I nod.

'Yes, if you're over eighteen, though the verification process is pretty easy to get around.' He tries for levity. 'You haven't got something to tell me, have you, Abby?'

'Ha.' My tone is droll. 'I was just wondering if it's dangerous to post on them.'

'In what way?'

'A pervert could find out where you lived or threaten to expose you.'

'Any sex work has dangers, even online stuff.' Lee hesitates. 'This is not about Grace, is it? Or Lili?'

I force a laugh. 'God, no. I just heard about those sites recently.' Lee doesn't judge, which is why I can ask him, but I can't dob Cara in. He raises an eyebrow at me. I lift my hand as if swearing in court. 'Truly, Detective, I was only wondering.'

We're almost at school. 'Remember, you can come to me,' he says.

'Thanks.'

He finds a park in the drop-off area. 'And about uni, I get that you have dreams and hopes and plans for the future, Abby. I'll talk to Nicola. We'll figure it out.'

I smile. 'Thanks. You're my second-favourite stepdad.'

'Well, you're my third-favourite stepdaughter, but if you make me some more of those macarons – chocolate ones, this time – and don't let Joyce take them to golf, you might move up the rankings.'

'See you, number two.'

'See you, number three.'

*

'Are you coming to Isaac's party?' Taj murmurs.

His lips are soft against my ear, his stubble sandpaper against my temple. The words hum in my head, like the purr of a cat. My back is against his chest as we sit on the warm concrete behind the brick fence separating the quad from the back oval. Younger students stay clear of this area, it's for year twelves only. And even the year twelves steer clear when they sense someone in our group wants the area to themselves, so we're alone.

'I wish I could. Mum won't let me.' I haven't told Mum about Isaac's party, though Taj doesn't have to know that.

'I really want you to come.' He breathes into my ear again and heat blooms deep inside me. 'Can't you give her some excuse? Say you're staying at Lili's or something?'

I take a deep breath. His hands creep under my shirt, one on each side. He slides them up towards my ribs.

God, I'm tempted.

I put my hands on his, halting their progress, disappointing myself almost as much as him.

'I'm sorry, Taj. Really I am.'

We've been together – properly together – for more than two months now and we still haven't slept together. He wants to, he's made that clear. We've done *stuff*, there's just something preventing me from taking that final step. A part of me wants to go for it. I'm seventeen – almost eighteen – not a child anymore. And I trust him. Plus, he's gorgeous. Lean and strong, yet soft too.

But there's this voice in the back of my head.

It's my mother's voice, of course. When I was thirteen, Mum sat me down and gave me the talk about boys. About how sex was a wonderful thing but that I shouldn't rush into it. About respecting myself, about not doing anything I wasn't comfortable with.

What I wasn't comfortable with was that conversation.

It was excruciating.

'Be careful, Abby,' she'd finished. 'Not all boys are nice. Some of them seem lovely at first – perfect, even.' She had hesitated for a long moment before continuing. 'Those are the ones who'll destroy you.' Something in her eyes told me she knew what she was talking about.

So, in a way, it's Mum's fault I'm still a virgin.

'Sure.' Taj says the word lightly, then sits up, his hands slipping out from under my shirt. I fight the urge to grab them and put them back on my skin.

He's silent and I can tell he's a little annoyed. Which annoys me. Can't he tell I'm conflicted?

'It's not that I don't want to …'

'Sure,' Taj says again, irritable now. 'Look, I'd better go. I need to visit the library before the end of lunch. I have to choose a new English text.' He disengages from my body and rises. The sun disappears behind a cloud and I shiver as the warmth of his body leaves mine.

'See you in class.'

'Okay.' He smiles, though I can tell he's holding something back.

He walks away and I almost call out, almost tell him, *Wait, Taj, I'm sorry, I'll come.*

Then he's gone.

*

That afternoon I stay behind to talk to Miss Crofts. My Maths results aren't up to scratch so we work through some examples to help me get ready for the trials. It's almost four when I leave, my head filled with sin, cos and tan as I set off for the bus stop.

Cara's laugh stops me near the corner of the library. It's a throaty laugh, sexy; she must be talking to a boy. My guess is they're sitting on the bench around the corner. I consider my options. Since school hours are over, the only way out is through the administration office.

Shit.

I'm not up to interrupting Cara as she flirts with whichever boy is currently her favourite.

'Aww, it suits you!' she says, then giggles again. 'Who knew pink was your colour? I've always admired a guy confident enough to let me put nail polish on him. It shows you aren't afraid of your feminine side.'

Oh God. The sad thing is that this kind of flattery would be lapped up by every boy at Arundel. They're all infatuated by her.

'Sit still or I'll get it all over you.' Cara laughs again. I cringe, though there's something else that feels an awful lot like jealousy.

No, you're annoyed that Taj ditched you at lunchtime, Abby.

I make a snap decision to go to Isaac's party. I'll text Taj from the bus and tell him Mum changed her mind. He'll be thrilled. The thought fills me with warmth.

Now my head's clearer, I feel almost sorry for the poor guy Cara has bailed up.

Just as I decide to interrupt them — they don't sound as if they are leaving anytime soon, and my bus is due shortly — the boy speaks.

'Pink is good on me, hey? Maybe I'll use it in my next painting. They'll call it my *pink period.*'

A sharp, white-hot pain pierces my heart.

It's Taj.

My boyfriend is flirting with Cara.

'Expect to see me with pink socks on next week,' he says. 'Pink Converse, pink—' He pauses, then says in a voice loaded with meaning, 'undies!'

Cara giggles. I squeeze my eyes shut.

That laugh. It hasn't changed. Even at eleven years old, when she was sick and pre-pubescent, Cara had a laugh you wanted to grab hold of with both hands. Infectious, slightly wicked. Impossible to resist.

The day after we buried Isabella's sunglasses in the sand, I was determined to be on the beach at twelve. Isabella and I had formed a habit of going to the beach early and heading back to her house for lunch. So at eleven thirty I went for a long swim, then insisted on lying in the sun to dry off before we left. Isabella suspected I had something to do with her missing sunglasses, so she was already a little standoffish, and my stalling didn't endear me to her.

'I'm hungry,' she complained for the third time in ten minutes. 'Let's go home.'

The clock on the surf tower behind us told me it was almost five past twelve.

Come on, Cara.

'Oh, but it's such a nice day!' I stretched my arms over my head. 'Five more minutes?'

Issy muttered something about passing out from hunger, but she was a people-pleaser at heart, so she relented, dropping back to her towel with an exaggerated sigh.

Then Cara arrived wearing cut-offs and a t-shirt. Isabella peered from her to me suspiciously, apparently guessing that we'd arranged this meeting.

Issy greeted Cara, then turned to me. 'We've got to go, Abigail.'

'Oh, don't go yet!' Cara said. 'I just got here.'

'Sorry, but I'm hungry and we don't have any money.'

Cara widened her eyes as if she'd just thought of something. 'Why don't you come to my house? I have loads of snacks.'

'You do?' Isabella asked. 'Like what?'

'Um, salt and vinegar chips, muesli bars, fruit. There's chocolate!'

'Mum doesn't like me eating at other people's houses. Because of my allergies.'

'We'll be careful, won't we, Abigail?'

Something stirred in the pit of my stomach. The glint in Cara's eyes. The smile that suggested we were in this together. In what together, I wasn't sure, but I liked it. It scared me too, though. That was the look she'd given me when she'd thrown the seaweed away.

'Yeah,' I said.

Isabella glanced from Cara to me. Her stomach decided it for her, growling loudly. She laughed. 'Okay. Let's go.'

Ten minutes later we were sitting around Cara's table while she pulled things out of the cupboards. 'See there's heaps of stuff. Biscuits, chips ...'

'Your house is nice,' I said, remembering my manners. Honestly, the house wasn't very impressive, though it was neat and tidy and smelled strongly of cleaning products. The kitchen cupboards banged noisily when Cara closed them. I tried not to look at the only décor in the room: a simple timber crucifix with a silver Jesus nailed to it by his hands and feet. But something about it kept drawing my gaze. Jesus was emaciated and appeared resigned to his fate, with his head bowed and eyes lowered. My family weren't churchgoers and the cross made me uneasy.

Who would do that to a person? Nail them to a cross?

And why have something so unsettling looming over you while you ate your cornflakes every morning?

'Can I use your toilet?' Isabella asked.

'Yeah. It's down the hall.'

As soon as Issy had left, Cara came closer, talking to me in an undertone. 'We need to give her one of these.' She pulled a box of muesli bars from behind her back. 'They've got nuts in them!'

My stomach fizzed. 'We can't do that! She'll have a reaction. She could die!'

'Nah.' She waved her hand, dismissing my reaction. 'I'm at the hospital all the time and I've seen people with nut allergies. She'll probably just get sleepy. And she has her EpiPen. We can use that if we have to.' She set the box on the table.

I regarded it as I would a bomb. 'I'm not sure about this.'

'If she sleeps we can leave her here for a while. We could take one of the surf club's kayaks out on the water and check out the seals around the headland. There's not enough room in the kayak for three.' As she spoke she searched under the bench and found a large plate, then started opening packets of food and adding them to it. A pile of chips, a mound of choc-chip biscuits. She went to the fridge and grabbed a container of grapes, adding some to the plate.

'I don't know.' As much as I wanted to do something alone with Cara, this plan seemed risky. 'Maybe Issy could come with us, anyway? We could take turns?'

'I don't want her to come. She's lame.' She sighed. 'Don't worry. If you're scared, we don't have to do it. I'll go see the seals later when you go back to Issy's house.'

Cara coughed, the sound wet and nasty. I didn't like the idea of her going off in a kayak on her own. She wasn't strong enough for that.

She picked up the box and waved it at me. I shook my head. She grinned and pulled out a muesli bar, which was individually wrapped. With a glance towards the door, she ripped the wrapper off and set it on the plate, then did the same with two more.

'Cara, this is a bad idea.'

'It'll be fine.' She shoved the wrappers into the bin.

Without warning, Issy appeared at the door and I gasped. She laughed. 'You scare easily,' she said. She must have seen something in my face, though. 'Are you all right?' she asked.

Before I could answer, Cara carried the snack-laden plate over to the table.

'Come and eat.'

'I'm starving,' Issy said as she took a seat. 'What can I eat on here?'

'Everything,' Cara answered, with a glance at me.

My heart leapt into my mouth.

We can't.

Issy reached for the plate—

'Taj!' I'm thrust back to the present when Cara says my boyfriend's name in a breathless tone. I lean against the brick of the library wall, my jaw clenched tightly enough to make my temples throb.

I know what Cara is like, so I shouldn't be surprised that she'd go after my boyfriend.

But Taj.

I trusted him.

It turns out Mum's right. You can't trust boys.

Cara laughs. 'Come back to my room!' she says, and I jerk upright.

Shit. They're going to come this way. My moment of panic almost immediately turns to rage.

Fuck this.

Fuck them.

I take a deep breath and step around the corner. Cara and Taj both freeze, their mouths hanging open so stupidly I want to laugh. Taj's bitten nails are painted flamingo-pink and he holds them out from his sides as if they're wet.

'Oh sorry!' Cara says. Then she sees it's me. 'Abby ...' The look on her face is not what I expected. She's not gloating or embarrassed or even happy. She seems sad.

'I'm ... We were—' It's Taj who's talking.

My stare is withering.

'Excuse me.' I push past them. A few steps on I spin back around. 'Cara, I'm sorry but I can't meet after school tomorrow anymore. Something's come up. In fact, it's probably best if we don't see each other for a while.'

My eyes focus on Taj and I hope he can see the hatred in them. 'As for you, Taj Fielding, you can go fuck yourself.'

I walk away, my head held high.

*

Plating up a ham, cheese and tomato toastie, topping it with a sprig of curly parsley, I wonder if I should have had sex with Taj after all.

Perhaps I shouldn't have listened to my mother.

The lunch rush is almost gone. My shift finishes at 3 pm though the café stays open late as there are so many night workers at the hospital. It's a weekday and I'd usually be at school, but our trial exams have started, giving me more free time. We've had English and Maths already, and tomorrow is French, but I told Christos I could work a few hours today. I should be studying but need the distraction.

All I can think of is Taj and how I stuffed everything up. I hate that I believe it's my fault, but I do.

Not very feminist of you, Abby.

I carry the plate over to Dr Patrick. He's a regular, a tired-looking oncologist who always has the same thing – a toastie and a diet Coke – and then does a sudoku from the book his wife gave him for Christmas. He gives me a distracted thank you and writes a number in a box.

I take a couple more coffee orders, passing them to Christos, who's manning the espresso machine. Coffees are at least two-thirds of all our orders. There's nothing hipster or cool about the hospital café. Easy-to-wipe-down surfaces, metal chairs and plain laminated tables, a newspaper stand in one corner and a TV up high on a wall tuned to Sky News, which is sometimes blaring, at others showing only subtitles, depending on Christos's mood. We do have an excellent espresso machine, but other than that our offerings are standard sandwiches, muffins and chocolate bars.

'Hi, Dr Grange, what can I get for you?' Dr Grange is at the counter.

'Quiche and salad and a latte.' He doesn't smile, which is normal for him, but it seems out of character for a paediatrician.

He waves his phone at the machine then spies Dr Patrick. He strides over and takes a seat at his table. Dr Patrick closes his sudoku book with resignation. He values his half-hour of quiet at lunchtime, I can tell, and Dr Grange should know better than to interrupt him, they've been colleagues for years. Dr Grange starts telling him something and even though I can't hear the details, his gestures are animated; no doubt he's explaining in detail how someone wronged him. He's a charmless man.

Christos chats to a nurse over the scream of the milk frothing, so I go into the kitchen to heat up Dr Grange's quiche. It's in the microwave when Christos calls out to tell me there's a customer, so I walk back out, then freeze. On the other side of the counter is Cara with her mother.

'Abby, hi.' Cara plays it cool.

I haven't seen her since I caught her flirting with Taj. She's in a light blue crop top and black jeans. Her earrings are the same gold crosses I'd admired the night of the school dance.

I bet your mum hasn't seen your new tattoo, I think.

Both Cara and Taj have tried to call me heaps of times, texted too. I've ignored them. Thankfully there were only two more days of school before the trials and I'd told Mum I had my period so she let me stay home.

I couldn't face either of them.

'Hello, Abigail,' Mrs Ross says. She's still got that soft, squishy look about her, with lines between her eyes suggesting she's a worrier. She wears a beige cardigan over a beige turtleneck, and blue slacks. I see her at the hospital sometimes, but we are happy enough to avoid one another. She rarely comes to the café.

'Hi, Mrs Ross.' I can't bring myself to address Cara. 'What can I get you?'

'A couple of lattes, please.' She sees me glance at her daughter and adds, 'Cara's been helping me with some auxiliary work this week between exams. It's good for her university applications to do a variety of volunteer work, although obviously it's more important to impress God than get into university.'

'Volunteer work. Of course! I mean, Cara's basically a saint,' I say. Mrs Ross blinks in confusion, then smiles uncertainly. 'The things she does out of the kindness of her heart.'

Cara's eyes widen briefly before she's back to her cool self.

'Well, I hope her father and I have taught her the value of helping others.'

'Oh, I don't think there's much she won't do for others. Many times.' I keep my voice deadpan, then, after an awkward silence, I laugh as if I've made a joke. Mrs Ross tilts her head at me, then pays with her phone and I tell her I'll bring their lattes over. She greets Dr Patrick and Dr Grange as she and

Cara take seats at a table in the corner. Five minutes later, I carry their mugs over to them.

'I've got a pashmina in my handbag, honey, it's no trouble,' Mrs Ross is saying to Cara. 'You must be cold, they never have the heating up enough in here.'

'I'm fine, Mum.' Cara's voice is firm, bordering on rude.

'Thank you,' Mrs Ross says when she sees me. She appears embarrassed by her daughter's tone.

I leave them and start tidying up before my shift ends.

'Abby?' Christos calls to me. 'Be a darl and grab some milk from the back fridge, please?'

When I come back out with the milk, Cara has returned to the counter.

'God, I hate hospitals,' she says, holding out a chocolate bar to buy. 'I need chocolate to survive being here.'

I deliver the milk to Christos before acknowledging her. My hand is stretching out for the bar when I see it's a Snickers. I eye her but she doesn't say anything else.

Snickers have peanuts in them.

I grip the counter as heat floods through me and I remember the moment Isabella reached for that plate. The way her hand had hovered over the muesli bars, how I'd held my breath.

'Are you sure I can eat this?' she'd asked, frowning at the platter. 'I can't have most muesli bars because they have nuts.'

'These ones don't have nuts. Only chocolate,' Cara had said in an unconcerned voice.

Isabella glanced at me. I didn't say anything. Then her hand dropped. She ignored the muesli bars, instead taking a chip and shoving it in her mouth before grabbing another.

I let out my breath.

'These chips are my favourite,' she said, her mouth full. 'Mum doesn't buy them because she prefers the chicken ones, but chicken chips suck.'

'Yeah,' Cara agreed, her curious eyes flitting between Issy and me, as if wondering what I'd do. 'Drinks?' she asked. 'We have orange juice. You aren't allergic to that, are you, Issy?'

Isabella shook her head and Cara pulled a carton from the fridge. She opened a corner cupboard and selected three glasses. 'We might have straws,' she said, opening the next cupboard along. There were no straws, just several shoeboxes sitting beside one another with no lids on them. All of them were filled with medication. There must have been twenty pill bottles, blister packs sitting loose among them. I'd never seen so many pills. Cara saw me staring. She frowned. 'I take heaps of different things every day. They don't help.' She slammed the door shut.

Issy sipped her juice so I grabbed a muesli bar and took a bite, then grimaced. 'Urgh, sorry, Cara, but these are terrible. They taste like baby vomit.'

Isabella laughed. 'How do you know what baby vomit tastes like, Abigail?'

I dropped it in the bin. 'I think they're off.'

Cara smiled at me, perfectly aware of what I was doing.

'Have one of these instead,' I said. 'They look delicious.' I passed Isabella a choc-chip biscuit and she took a bite.

'It is good,' she said, biscuit crumbs falling from her mouth.

'Mum made them today, a double batch,' Cara said. 'She takes them to church but left a few behind. They're my dad's favourite.'

I chose a biscuit for myself, nibbling it. It was soft, perhaps a little undercooked, with chunks of chocolate in it, and something harder. I chewed more slowly, glancing at Cara, who smiled at me in what could only be called a triumphant manner. We both turned to Isabella.

Issy frowned, then looked from Cara to me. Her face was red. She spat the biscuit into her hand. 'Does this have nuts in it?' Her voice was raspy, her eyes wide with fear.

'Um, I'm not sure,' Cara said. 'I don't eat them.'

I knew the taste. 'These have macadamia nuts in them.' My words sounded odd in my ears. 'Are you allergic to—'

Isabella couldn't talk. She spun away from the table, searching for her backpack. 'I—uh,' she gasped and grabbed at her throat. Her eyes focused on mine and she reached for me as she stumbled backwards. She fell against the wall and then to the ground, waving one hand frantically towards her tote bag, which she'd left by the door.

I watched her, frozen, the biscuit in my hand. Her eyes bulged and the fear in them was like nothing I'd ever seen before. Her face was clammy and getting redder by the second. Other than her wheezing and the scrabbling of her hands against the floor, then the wall, it was deathly silent.

I turned to Cara and found her staring at me, a smile on her face. She didn't move.

A door slammed, and Cara's expression flashed with annoyance. She ran to Isabella's tote bag and searched through it, finding the EpiPen.

'Mum! Come quick!' Cara called as she tugged the lid from it and ran to Isabella, jabbing it into her thigh and holding it there. Mrs Ross ran in and regarded us with confusion.

'What's going on? What are you girls doing here?'

'It's Isabella,' Cara said. 'She ate nuts. I've done the EpiPen.'

Mrs Ross took in the girl on the floor, her hands now at her throat. Issy's eyes bulged, and she moved her mouth, though nothing came out.

'Oh, dear Lord. I'll call the ambulance.' She grabbed the EpiPen from Cara's outstretched hand and ran back to the hallway, returning with her phone to her ear.

I hadn't moved. Mrs Ross spoke to the dispatcher, her words drowned out by the whooshing in my head.

'What did she eat?' she asked us, moving her phone away from her mouth.

'The biscuits you made,' Cara answered.

Mrs Ross nodded. 'Macadamias,' she said into the phone. 'Okay. Yes, sure.' She hung up, worry etched into her face. 'They'll be here as soon as possible. Isabella, honey? Are you all right?'

Isabella could sit up now, her breathing coming more easily. She nodded, still not speaking. I turned away from her, my eyes alighting on the crucifix and Jesus on the wall. His resigned expression was now judgemental, disapproving.

'Abby? Are you okay?' I'm back in the café, Cara staring at me with something approaching concern.

I clear my throat. 'What are you up to, Cara?' Behind her, Mrs Ross is on the phone.

'You don't answer my texts.'

'Can you blame me?'

'No, not really.' She clears her throat. 'Seriously, though, it was nothing. Taj isn't interested in me. He likes you.'

'Mm.' I motion at the machine and she scans her card.

'I'm sorry.' Surprisingly, she appears to mean it. Not that I care.

'It's too late for that.'

She fiddles with the wrapper of the Snickers, her eyes lowered. 'You didn't tell your mum about me and Taj, did you? Or your grandma?'

'No. Why?' I ask, my tone sharp.

'I mean …' She exhales. 'It matters to me what they think.'

I cross my arms over my chest and stare at her.

'I made a mistake, okay?' She lifts her head. 'I shouldn't have talked to Taj that way. It's just that he's nice, and what you two have …' She hesitates, then goes on. 'I guess I envy that. But, honestly, Abby, I wouldn't do that to you.'

'That's not what it sounded like.'

'I wouldn't. We're friends.'

I remember her laugh. The teasing note in Taj's voice.

Heat rises in me.

No.

It's too late. For both of them.

'Truthfully, I don't think we've ever been friends, Cara. Not back in Calder Head. Not now.' My voice is hard. 'I'm done with you. Stay away from me. Stay away from my whole family.'

Her face crumples. 'You can't, Abby. We're …' She takes in the hardness of my expression, and something changes in her. It's as if she makes a decision in that moment. Her face becomes blank. 'Okay, if that's the way you want to play it.' She's calm now. In control again. She touches her ribs at the place she and Lili got tattooed. 'I just hope you aren't too attached to your current *friends*.' She gives the word particular emphasis. 'If I can make them get tattoos and cut you out of their plans, it won't take much more effort to have them dump you for good.'

'What do I care? School's almost done anyway. I'll be out of here soon.'

She leans over. 'You just keep telling yourself that, Abigail.' My name is glass shards in her mouth. 'I know you better than you know yourself. You need them.'

I roll my eyes and turn my back on her then march around the counter and start clearing tables. I sense her stalk back to her table, though I refuse to look that way again.

A few minutes later, Mrs Ross's phone call ends and they leave. Once they've gone, I walk over to collect their mugs, my legs suddenly weak.

I fall onto a seat behind the two doctors and take deep breaths. I might have won this round, though something tells me it isn't over.

*

The French exam came with no nasty surprises and within a couple of hours of completing it I'm working another shift at the cafe. There's another staff member on with Christos and me today. Mandy. She's almost Mum's age and is what Grandma would call 'rough as guts'. I like her. She doesn't take any shit from the customers and keeps an eye out for me if any of them hit on me. They do that more than you'd think.

There's one more exam, Ancient History, on Monday. It's one of my favourite subjects and I'm good at it, so I don't feel too much pressure. After that, it's not long till the HSC, and then school will be done. A few months working in the café to save some cash and then I'll be on the plane to ... *somewhere.* The thought doesn't fill me with the joy it should.

'Abby, can you turn up the TV for me, please? The news is on in a minute,' Christos calls out.

He says the customers enjoy watching the evening news, but he's the one who loves it. There are only a dozen or so customers in the café, mostly eating alone or in pairs. It's pretty quiet for the early evening.

I locate the remote from under the counter and turn up the volume.

The newsreader starts off with war, touches on corruption, before moving on to pestilence, so I tune out. I have enough doom and gloom of my own to deal with.

It's then that Cara strides in, her gaze raking the room. I curse under my breath. She sees me and weaves her way between the tables and chairs towards me with a sense of purpose. She's furious and I know why.

The rest of our group deleted her number and unfriended her the previous night after I told them what went on between her and Taj. There's a lot of things those girls will forgive, but stealing someone else's guy isn't one of them. They'd spent the evening at my place, comforting me and making emphatic promises that none of them would ever, ever befriend Cara Ross again. It seems she's received the message.

Cara stops at the counter. 'You dobbed on me, Abby? Everyone hates me now.'

I search for Mandy. She's wiping tables but she sees me. I hold up my hand, my fingers splayed to gesture five minutes. She nods, which is pretty nice considering I'm about to finish and she has several hours still to work. 'Thank you,' I mouth, leading Cara over to the drinks fridge, which is far enough away for our conversation not to be heard by most of the tables.

'That's not my problem.'

'You feel that strongly about Taj Fielding?' she asks, incredulous.

'I feel strongly that what you did was wrong. Unforgivable.'

She looks at me. 'That's how you want to play this?'

'Yes.'

'So you've never made a mistake? What about Issy?' She tilts her head and my mouth goes dry. I know this Cara. I remember how ruthless she can be. 'Perhaps I'll tell someone. The school? Your friends? The lovely Taj?'

'I'm not the same gullible girl I was back then.' I won't let her see my fear. 'Don't push me. Besides, nothing happened. There's nothing to tell.'

'You handed her the biscuit.'

'I *didn't know*.' I lift my chin. 'If you tell anyone about it, I'll tell them the truth, and you come out of that whole thing worse than I do. Mum and Grandma will back me up.'

'I'm sure they will,' she says, dryly.

'So there you go.'

She gives me a tight-lipped smile, though her eyes are pleading. 'I thought we were friends. I've helped Joyce at Hillcrest and watched episodes of *Sex and the City* with your mum. I'm virtually part of your family after all the afternoons I've spent at your house.'

'Family?' I am scathing. 'You've known my family for all of five minutes. I can't help it if your own family are weirdos. Your dad, all creepy and obsessed with you, and your mum, the perfect Christian doormat.' Her face darkens. 'My mum mightn't be perfect,' I continue, 'but she won't give you the time of day after I tell her what you've done, and that makes her perfect, in my opinion. Oh, and Joyce asked me to keep you away from her house. She said you never shut up.' That last part isn't true. I want to hurt her.

And I have. Her shoulders slump, if only for a millisecond. Then she blinks. She straightens up, pulling herself together in true Cara style. I don't care, I've had enough. 'Just go, Cara.'

'I'm not done.' She takes her phone from her tote. 'Actually, that's not even the reason I came to see you.'

'Oh, in that case, can I get you a sandwich?' I ask facetiously. 'A muffin? We have lovely raspberry and white chocolate ones.'

'No.' She scrolls on her phone. 'I came to show you this.'

She hands it to me. For a second I'm tempted to fling it at the wall or drop it into the bin, but something in her eyes makes me decide to take a look.

A quick glance shows me a similar scene to what she posts on her disgusting foot fetish webpage. A shot of her dorm room, with the bed in the background. In the foreground are two people, kissing. One is Cara. The other is probably Taj.

'I don't want to watch any more of your sex tapes, thank you very much.' I thrust the phone back at her.

'You'll want to see this one. And it's not a video, it's a photo. I'm not that cruel,' she says.

'I get that you're with Taj, okay. I don't need to see it.'

She laughs, bitterly. 'I'm not interested in your precious Taj. There are so many men – real men – who want me.'

'Great. Enjoy all your men, then.'

'Look at the photo before you say anything else.'

I re-examine the image. The people are side on. She must have a camera sitting on the shelf above her computer. The man's back is a little more to the camera than hers is, so I can't see his entire face, only his jaw and cheek and his hair, or lack of it.

It's not Taj.

The man has a short beard and a shaved head. Cara's hand is on the back of his neck.

My stomach churns and I think I might throw up.

Cara is kissing Lee.

She smiles when she sees the blood leave my face. 'Check the date on the screen. This was Saturday. It seems he isn't as keen on your mum as you thought, is he?'

This betrayal kicks me hard in my gut. I trusted Lee. Mum trusts him.

How could he do this?

I inspect Cara's face. She's calm, with a glint in her eyes.

'What the fuck have you done?'

'Shouldn't you be asking your precious stepdad that question?'

'Did he see you on that website? It's not a feet thing, is it?' I can't keep the disgust from my face. 'How could you do this to Mum?' Her face falls. 'You just told me she was like family to you.'

'That's what I thought.' Cara's words are bitter. 'But I've learned that families don't always treat you the way they should. That's why I always have a back-up plan.'

'Everything all right here, Abby?' It's Mandy, looking guarded and concerned, a dishcloth in her hands. I lower the phone and manage a smile.

'We're all good, thanks.'

She turns from Cara to me slowly then disappears into the kitchen.

'Have you and Lee ... you know?' I hiss.

'What do you think?'

'Cara ...' I take a step towards her.

'Fine.' She waggles her eyebrows. 'Turns out he's got a thing for younger women.'

I ball my fists, only just resisting the overwhelming urge to punch Cara Ross in the face. To shove her into the fridge. To knock her down and stomp on her stomach. I want to see blood streaming from her head. To make her scream for mercy.

To hurt her.

Cara's chin is raised in defiance. It's as if she knows what I'm thinking and wants me to do it.

The image of Isabella on the floor of the Ross house, her hands to her face as she tried to catch a breath, flashes through my mind.

The fear in her eyes.

Death.

It was so close that day.

'You better be careful, Abby. I tried to be your friend, but you're ruining it. I could destroy your family. I could send this photo to the media and ruin Lee's career.' She's speaking in a singsong voice as she ticks her points off on her fingers. 'Or tell your mum what he did. Or tell your friends about how you had another friend once, who you nearly killed. So many options.' She sighs theatrically. 'I could even send anonymous letters to the universities you're going to apply to, telling them what you did to poor Isabella. What were your top choices again? Dartmouth? Brown?'

I open my mouth but no words form.

'Oh, and I have to say that Lee was *lovely*.' She lingers on the word. Without thinking I'm up on my toes ready to launch myself at her, until her expression changes. I swivel around.

And see the worst thing I could imagine.

Mum. She's at the café entrance, watching us.

She's looking at me as if I'm a snake about to strike. As if she's afraid of me.

Fuck.

Control yourself, Abby.

I exhale, letting it all go in one long breath.

You can do this.

It takes all my willpower to give Cara her phone back. As she takes it, I notice my hand is trembling. I can't meet her eyes. Instead, I walk over to my mother.

'Is everything okay, hon?' she asks. She's wearing her gym clothes and her hair is damp from sweat.

'Yep. All good.' I'm surprised how normal my voice is. 'Cara's leaving. Give me a couple of minutes and I'll be ready to go.'

Her eyes flick to something behind me.

'Hi Nicola.' Cara's voice is light, as if nothing has happened.

'Cara.' Mum speaks coolly. 'What are you doing here?'

'Oh, I've been helping my mother with the hospital auxiliary. I can study a little while I sit at the desk, so it's not wasted time.'

'Lovely.' Mum's voice is tight.

Christos comes out from behind the counter. 'Nicola! How are you?' He kisses her cheeks and she smiles. He offers to make her a coffee.

'Oh, you don't have to do that, Christos!'

He insists, and I excuse myself to go into the kitchen and get my things. Mandy's back there, eating a muffin. She gives me a guilty look. 'I'm off the fags and I need to eat something.' She drops the wrapper in the bin. 'I get so fat when I quit smoking.'

My smile is distracted and she frowns.

'You all right, love?'

I sigh. 'Yeah.'

'Wanna tell me about it?'

'No. I'm fine. It's just boy stuff.'

'Ah,' she says.

I hear Cara's laugh so I grab my things and say goodbye to Mandy. I can't leave Cara alone with my mother. Fuck knows what she'll say.

I hurry out, past Christos and the screaming coffee machine and walk around the counter, ready to herd Mum away from Cara, but Mum's staring at the television in the corner with an expression of abject terror.

Cara is watching her, too, and we both turn to see what's caused Mum's fear.

On the screen is a man in his sixties. He's handsome, with a chin dimple and an expensive suit. He's standing outside a renovated warehouse beside a young female reporter in a red coat. The caption at the bottom of the screen reads SYDNEY DEVELOPER ANDREW CARGILL and under that it says OFFERS GENEROUS REWARD MONEY.

'Yes, thank you, Jean, it's been eighteen years now since Sam was murdered,' says the man, in a pleasant voice, though he speaks sombrely. 'However, to me it feels like only yesterday. I'd hoped to have handed the reins of the Cargill Group over to my son by now. He should be standing here beside me in front of this building I dedicated to him not long after he died, talking about his own children. Sam's death was a tragedy from which I will never recover.'

The journalist addresses the camera. 'For the viewers who don't remember, let me remind you that Sam Cargill was stabbed and then pushed from the balcony of his rented accommodation in the Rocky Mountains eighteen years ago. His killer has never been found.'

My eyes flicker to Mum. All colour has leached from her face.

'That's right,' the man continues. 'Sam should have turned forty on September fifteenth – that's a little over one month from today. With that in mind I have something to announce.' The man turns to face the camera. There's something very likeable about him, something that makes you want to help him. 'I have vowed not to rest until Sam's killer has been brought to justice. I am offering a reward of one million dollars to anyone who comes forward with information that leads to an arrest.'

'One million dollars?' Jean shakes her head in disbelief. 'You heard it here first, viewers. One *million* dollars.'

Mum stumbles and grabs the counter. Cara reaches for her elbow, and I want to push her away. Just then Christos calls, 'Nicola,' and Mum spins around as if under attack.

'Your coffee.' He lifts it, then sees her face. 'You okay?'

'Oh yes.' Mum clears her throat and gives a little shake of her head. 'Thanks, Christos. A little light-headed, that's all. I should have eaten more than a salad for lunch!'

My head spins.

Sam Cargill. Dead in Canada eighteen years ago.

Eighteen years ago.

I keep my expression neutral, though inside I'm a mess. It can't be a coincidence. Mum was in Canada eighteen years ago. Mum abandoned her travel plans and came home in a hurry. Pregnant.

My mum couldn't have …

No, it's *Mum*.

I glance at Cara and see she's watching me with a curious expression.

Fuck. We've got to get out of here.

I drop my gaze. 'Mum, you ready? Let's go.'

The man is still on screen. Mum keeps her eyes averted. 'Yes, let's go. Lee's doing steaks on the barbeque tonight.'

At the mention of Lee's name, I glance at Cara. She smiles. 'I might watch the rest of this interview,' she says, leaning back against the counter.

I take Mum's arm and we scurry out. Her skin feels icy cold under my hand. We don't speak on the way to the car park. What can I say? What can I ask her?

Did you kill a man?

Did you kill my father?

We reach the lobby. Across the other side, Mrs Ross emerges from a door with a sign on it that says, 'Staff Only'. She's dressed in her usual drab attire and she stops to greet an orderly, offering him a hug after he tells her something. She pulls away and tilts her head at him sympathetically, pats his arm and then enters the nearby female toilets.

Breathe, Abby.

In, out.

In, out.

Suddenly, I feel much more like myself.

As we continue through the lobby, I jiggle my backpack before opening the front pocket and rooting inside it. I halt and turn to my mother. 'Sorry Mum. I left my water bottle in the café. I'll run back and get it and meet you at the car.'

Mum gives me a distracted glance. 'Sure. I'm in the usual area.'

I turn back, walking with a purpose. As I stride along, I can't help thinking of the irony of my earlier words to Cara. I'd called her mother a weirdo.

When it seems mine's a murderer.

*

It throws me, I can't deny it.

My mother, a murderer.

And my father ... well, who knows what he was?

That night, after sitting through the most awkward meal of my life with Mum and Lee, I google Andrew Cargill and Sam Cargill.

Andrew Cargill, a multi-millionaire property developer. Sam Cargill, his beloved son.

I do the math, as Americans would say, and it adds up.

Sam Cargill was my father. And Cargill senior is my grandfather.

My mind boggles.

It takes a couple of days to process it all. By Friday I have read through what feels like everything the internet can tell me about Sam Cargill. He was very similar to the man on television, only much younger. Sam smiled more freely than his father – perhaps because he'd been spared the same grief. It was the sort of smile that told me he was popular. Maybe a little wild. Untouchable. In contrast, his father appears more tightly wound. Something about him makes me shiver.

I won't be contacting Andrew Cargill anytime soon. It's doubtful he'll want to meet his granddaughter, given the circumstances.

Part of me wants to spend more time researching my father, yet I need to put that desire away for now. There are bigger things to worry about. Such as the fact that my mum might have killed a man. Not just any man, either – the man who gave me life. If anyone finds out what she did, she could go to jail. I can't risk it.

Another is that Cara saw Mum's reaction to that news item. If I've figured out what Mum did, then surely she has too. And she'd be pretty bloody happy to get her hands on a million dollars. That would set her up nicely in Cambridge. Far away from her parents, and Arundel, like she's always wanted.

Then there's my other problem.

What to do about Lee and Cara.

My head hurts thinking about it, not to mention my heart.

By Friday afternoon, I can't deal with the issues facing Spartans or Athenians anymore. I shut my computer, planning to bake something super complicated, perhaps even the croquembouche I've had in the back of my mind for a while now. I check my phone to see what my friends are up to. An app shows me their locations. Lili is all the way across town, and I realise she's at Jamie Drummond's house. So, she's finally bitten the bullet and gone for it with him. I shake my head – *stupid, Lili* – yet something about it makes me happy as well.

Then another location lights up, somewhere unexpected.

I think about what that means and what to do, though not for long.

I grab my things. On the landing, I hear the shower. Mum's been to the boxing gym this afternoon, even though she ran this morning, even though it's not her usual day. Exercise has always calmed her and she's been a woman possessed ever since she saw Andrew Cargill on television.

And she doesn't even know about Lee and Cara.

Darkness swirls in my head when I picture my stepdad and Cara together. I've been avoiding Lee ever since I saw that photo. When I have to see him I act as normal as I'm able, though I want to kill the bastard.

In their bedroom, the sound of the shower grows louder. 'Mum!' I call, approaching her ensuite. 'Hello?' I stick my head around the doorjamb, averting my eyes from her nakedness.

She gives a shriek. 'Oh, Abby!' she says. 'You scared me.'

'Can I take the car?' She turns off the tap. I grab her towel and pass it through the gap when she opens the screen door.

'Where are you going?'

'To the library. To study. I'll be a couple of hours.'

'Of course, hon. But are you sure you don't want to have a break from study? It's Friday night. Lee's going to pick up Chinese takeaway. We'll get the prawn dish you love?'

'I can have a study break after exams.' It sounds brusquer than intended. A flash of anger stabs me at the thought of Lee acting all normal. 'I'll re-heat it when I get back.'

'Okay. See you later.'

I'm not gone for as long as I expected. Lee and Mum are watching a romcom on Netflix and the house smells of Mongolian lamb. Lee greets me. He's on the lounge, my mother's head on his shoulder.

I'm tempted to say something I shouldn't.

Instead, I go to the kitchen and pull out a bowl and a wooden spoon, deciding to make scones. Simple, delicious and comforting.

God knows I need some comfort. Lee – a man I consider my stepfather, and a *policeman*, for fuck's sake, a man I've come to love and trust – has betrayed my mother in the worst possible way. Not just Mum, he's betrayed *me*.

But what can I do about it?

I can't tell Mum what he and Cara did, it would destroy her. My teeth grind together, making my head throb.

As I see it, I have two problems.

Lee.

And Andrew Cargill.

I rub the flour and butter together, the texture sending a shiver down my spine.

Cara.

She's the common denominator in both scenarios.

Lee will have to wait. But Cara … Cara can be dealt with.

The tray of scones is sliding into the hot oven when I make the decision.

Something has to be done. So, I do what I usually do when I need help.

I call my grandmother.

Thursday, 8 August

Dear Mr Cargill,

I know who killed your son.

Sorry to lead with something so blunt. However, I'm sure that's what you want to know.

All you need to know.

I am more than happy to pass on the details of this person to you. I have their name and their address, which should make getting your revenge very easy. And, after seeing you on television, it's clear it's revenge you're after, not justice. I would want the same if I were in your shoes.

As a gesture of good faith, I need you to transfer $100,000 to the bank account I have nominated below. Once that money has cleared I will tell you everything.

In return, I understand that you will need some information to prove I'm not wasting your time.

The person who murdered your son was a woman. I know for a fact she was in Canada at the time of his death, and she returned to Australia pregnant.

I was with this woman two days ago when she watched you offer the million-dollar reward on television. I saw her face. I can guarantee, given her reaction, that she killed your son.

If I can have your word that the rest of the reward 10 AUGUSTney will be mine, I will email you again with her name and address.

Regards,
Your newest friend

Friday, 9 August

To my newest friend,
Money will be transferred ASAP. Once you have it, email me the person's name and address. Send it, and the million is all yours.
AC

PART III

10 AUGUST

JOYCE

'Grandma? I need your help. Or advice. Something. I don't know.'

Abby had been close to tears when she rang me last night. I'd paused *Killing Eve*, my pulse quickening.

'Oh, my lovely girl! What's wrong? Tell me. Grandma can fix anything.' I hesitated, then asked, 'Is this about Taj?' Abby had told me they'd broken up but had been reluctant to tell me why.

'No. I mean, yes. A bit.' She blew her nose before continuing. 'It's Cara.'

My adrenaline spiked at her name.

'What about her, my darling?'

'Taj and Cara, they …'

She paused and the silence told me all I needed to know. 'Oh, darling, I'm so sorry.'

'Yeah, it sucks. But that's not my main concern. There's more. It's Lee. Cara showed me a photo of them. They were together.'

'Lee and Cara?'

There was a moment's silence. I pictured my almost-son-in-law. The way he smiled at Nicola when she was watching TV or reading a novel on the lounge. How he put his paperwork aside when she had a funny story to tell him, giving her his full attention. His obvious happiness when he arrived home from work to find her laughing in the kitchen with Abby.

Lee was with Cara? No, it couldn't be.

I didn't want to believe it.

Abby told me the sordid details. There was a photo of Lee kissing Cara, a girl all of us Miller women had befriended. For a moment my vision clouded. I'd been here before, was familiar with this anger, the rage of a mother who has discovered that a man has hurt her child. But Abby's words still shocked me. Wounded me, too.

Lee had been the best thing to happen to Nicola since, well, since Canada. I didn't think she'd ever be able to be vulnerable with a man again after what transpired over there. But he is good for her. He *was* good for her.

Was.

I sighed. Perhaps I could ask Abby to bake him some macarons. Hazelnut ones. He's the only one who likes them. I could add a little something extra to the batch while Abby was out of the room …

Not yet. Too risky.

Lee could wait.

Cara, on the other hand.

I redirected my rage at the girl.

How *dare* she? Yet my fury was tinged with pain. I'd grown attached to her. At first I'd been wary – very wary, given her history with Abby. And yet she'd wormed her way under my defences. Smiled at my stories, helped me work in the garden.

And now she had betrayed me. Not only me, Nicola and Abby too.

I had trusted both Cara and Lee.

And I didn't enjoy being proved wrong.

'What do I do, Grandma?'

Abby's voice was small and I felt a pang. It was as if she was a child again, coming to me after being accused of making that annoying Timothy Owens eat a sandwich out of the bin, or of causing rifts between other girls in her class.

'Leave it to me, darling. Don't mention any of this to anyone,' I said. 'Not to your mum, or to Lee.'

'What will you do?'

'Don't you worry about it, my darling. I'll sort everything out. I'll talk to Lee and to Cara and we'll go from there.'

'Grandma, Mum adores him. This will kill her.'

'She's stronger than you think, Abby,' I said, softly. 'Much stronger. She'll get through it. First, though, we need to find out the truth.'

*

I still remember the day I learned Nicola was pregnant with Abby.

She'd been back a week from her ill-fated gap year. After abruptly leaving Canada for the east coast of the USA, she'd stayed in hostels in Boston and New York. During her rare phone calls she sounded homesick and distant, nothing like the excited girl she'd been when she left Arundel. It became clear something was really wrong two days earlier when she'd called (reverse charges) to say she was coming home after only three and a half months away. I worried about what it would be, even though I was pleased to have her home.

At the airport it was immediately clear she'd lost weight. She was pale. But, I reasoned, she'd come from winter, and probably had to sacrifice food for her travel budget. She slept for most of the five-hour car trip home. Jet lag, I told myself. But then she spent the next few days sleeping.

I was worried. I wanted to ask her a million questions. I wanted to shake her. I wanted to hug her nonstop. Instead, I kept busy, pruning the deadwood from the trees, top-dressing the lawn. I even repotted most of my houseplants.

And then one morning she finally told me.

We were eating breakfast. It was already stinking hot. Nicola was sweaty and had bags under her eyes that suggested that, despite all the hours in her room, she wasn't getting much sleep. In hindsight, it was blindingly obvious she was pregnant. She'd barely eaten a thing all week, so that day I'd made her favourite – scrambled eggs and smoked salmon on rye. She went ashen on seeing the glistening coral fish and mound of soft eggs, pushing it away and grimacing. I was the same when I was pregnant.

But I was still oblivious, suggesting she make an appointment with Dr Searle for a check-up.

At that, she blurted it out.

'I'm pregnant, Mum.'

I tried not to appear shocked and failed miserably. She started crying, which made me feel terrible. Nicola had always been a good girl. Smart, keen to study, with never too much interest in boys. All she wanted was to travel. She'd saved up the money she earned at the supermarket, and I'd promised her some too – just for the flights, mind you – giving it to her the day she received her very respectable HSC marks. She had it all planned out. Canada, to work in the ski fields, then the USA to see New York and Washington. Then on to London where she'd get a job in a bar and go to Paris for weekends on the Eurostar. She'd tell me all her plans. We'd watch old episodes of *Absolutely Fabulous* or new ones of *Sex and the City*, places that seemed so exotic from our lounge room in Arundel. She'd say, 'I'm going to live there, Mum!'

She was nothing like me. Nicola dreamed big. Believed she could do anything. That the world was her oyster.

And now she was pregnant. How would that affect her plans? She had wanted to be a journalist. That was the second part of her travel-the-world plan. She was going to go to university in Sydney, then become a foreign correspondent.

I know what Bert would have said, if he was alive. He'd have told me not to be such a *stickler*. He'd have said, *These things happen, don't worry about it, Joycie,* as he drank too much scotch and painted those grey-trunked eucalypts with the bold brushstrokes and thick paint that made his art so powerful, so beloved. He'd have said, *Don't worry, we'll deal with it, another baby in the house will be wonderful.* When the baby came, Bert would have disappeared for days at a time, leaving me to organise everything, cook everything, clean everything.

Just the way he always did.

And the townsfolk of Arundel would have accepted Nicola's illegitimate child, because, after all, this was *Bert Miller's* family. In the town's eyes he could do no wrong.

But, you see, I'd discovered – too late – that Bert was *often* wrong.

Life did not always work out the way you thought it would.

Obviously, I reassured Nicola everything would be fine. I carefully asked her if she wanted to keep the baby and she said yes straight away, with that determined look on her face I knew so well.

'Who's the father?' I had asked. It was the wrong question because she clammed right up again.

A one-night stand, that's what I thought at the time. Some toothy, drunk American frat boy like in the movies, or a floppy-haired Canadian ski instructor. Someone who took advantage of my beautiful, innocent daughter.

At the time, I thought it was probably good I didn't know who it was.

If I knew, I'd be tempted to kill the bastard.

*

'Granola, darling?'

At six months pregnant, Nicola had a neat, rounded belly and I'd come around to the idea that there would soon be a baby in the house. We had money. Nicola and her baby would be fine.

I would make sure of that.

'Thanks, Mum.' Nicola sat down at the bench with a groan.

'The cot and pram should be here next week.' I placed a bowl in front of her. 'And here are the paint samples.' I slid the small pieces of cardboard across the bench. 'Yellow might be nice?'

I had this idea we'd redecorate Hillcrest's nursery, turn it into something more cheerful than the old beige and white room.

'Yellow is good,' Nicola said, pouring some milk into her bowl. I passed her a banana to slice on top.

I had come clean to the ladies at the golf club and the CWA about Nicola's pregnancy. For a while I'd thought about telling people the father was a US soldier in Afghanistan or that he'd died in a terrible car crash; however, in the end I refrained from lying. Instead, I maintained a dignified silence.

Gossip was no doubt flying thick and fast around town, though one of the good things about living out at Hillcrest was that we didn't have to hear much of it. There were stolen glances my way at CWA meetings and across the greens but I was confident enough in my position in Arundel society to feel that we would get through it without too much blowback.

'Should I roast a chicken for dinner or cook a small piece of steak?' I asked. Nicola made a non-committal noise so I decided on steak. She could do with more folate.

As we ate breakfast, we watched the small flat-screen television I'd had installed up high in one corner of the room. It was tuned to one of those morning shows. We'd watched the news and weather for the third time when I finished my granola and took the bowl over to the sink. I was about to hunt down the remote control and switch the television off when they started a new interview. I opened my mouth to ask if Nicola was still interested in watching the show when I heard her gasp.

She was staring at the television, her face so pale I thought she might throw up.

On screen, the female host was seated alongside a handsome man of about fifty. He had good hair and reminded me a little of Michael Douglas.

'Andrew, your new building conversion is really going to be something, isn't it?'

'I hope so, Sarah.' He smiled, and his teeth were perfect. 'I believe Sam Cargill House will become a Sydney icon.'

It panned to a shot of a building. 'The Cargill Group plans to develop the old tea factory warehouse right on the harbour in The Rocks. The building will include a business hub over several floors, and a cutting-edge art gallery. It's certainly striking with outer walls made entirely of glass, to maximise the spectacular city views.' The camera returned to the man, who was smiling.

The host put on her serious face. 'And you've named the building after your late son?'

'I have.' A shadow passed across the man's face. 'My brilliant and wonderful son, Samuel Cargill, who was murdered in Banff, a town in the Canadian Rocky Mountains, earlier this year. This building will be his legacy.'

The host turned to the camera. 'In April, Samuel Cargill was found at the bottom of a crevice below the mountain chalet he and his friends had rented. He had been stabbed, the murder weapon a small pocketknife. Canadian police are still searching for the killer. Twenty-one-year-old Sam had been a keen snowboarder and had planned a winter of adventure before he returned to work with his father.'

I glanced at Nicola.

In Banff.

On the television, Andrew Cargill was composed, but his loss was etched into the lines between his eyes.

'I'm working with the police to ensure we find out who killed my son. And when we do, I'll be putting all my weight behind the prosecution case to ensure Sam's killer is brought to justice.'

Nicola appeared to be in shock. I could only see her profile as she blinked at the screen, one hand rubbing back and forth across her stomach, her jaw tight. I stepped towards her, but before I could do more she looked over at me, a smile in place. 'Should we switch this off, Mum?' she asked. 'It's such a nice day, perhaps we should plant those delphinium seeds?'

She now seemed perfectly composed. I was ready to ask her if she knew him, that man who was in Banff at the same time she was. That man who was *dead*.

Murdered.

I swallowed.

I didn't know what had happened, I only knew what was important now. My daughter. My grandchild.

Nothing else.

I returned her smile. 'I'll fetch the trays and meet you in the laundry. They'll be blooming by the time your baby is here. These seeds are from the plants Marjorie gave me. Have I told you that?'

'Yes. Only every year when we plant them.' Her eyes are soft. 'I remember Marjorie quite well, you know. I used to run down to the cottage when you wouldn't let me eat junk food after school. She was a soft touch, despite that crusty exterior. Dougie was even worse, but he was usually out fencing.'

'I'm surprised you remember.' It touched me that Nicola hadn't forgotten Marjorie. I thought of the caretaker often. I put my hand on Nicola's stomach. 'New life. Isn't it wonderful, darling?'

'It is,' she agreed. 'It's everything.'

*

I wake with a clear head. Cara is an early riser, so I call her bright and early, even though it's Saturday.

She answers straight away. 'Joyce. I didn't think I'd hear from you. You haven't been answering your phone. Neither has Nicola.' She sounds repentant, though wary too.

'I'm sorry, Cara darling. Abby was upset and asked me to keep my distance.' A beat passes. 'But we should talk. There are two sides to every story, after all.'

'Abby didn't tell you what we were fighting about?' she asks, a note of worry in her voice.

'Not exactly, darling, no.'

'I can explain everything, Joyce, I swear,' Cara continues, hopeful now. 'It's all a big misunderstanding. I'd never hurt Abby. Or Nicola.'

'Why don't you come over later? Perhaps you could help me with some planting. We could have afternoon tea when we're done.'

'That would be lovely. I'll borrow Mum's car. She and Dad will be out all day. Dad's got an event at church tonight that they need to prepare for.'

'Wonderful. See you at about three?'

'Will Abby be there?'

'Let's keep this between ourselves for now.'

'Okay.'

'We'll work it out and I'll talk to her for you, darling. I'm sure you'll be best of friends again in no time.'

*

I couldn't quite believe it. I had a grandchild – a granddaughter.

Abigail.

The love I had for that baby, it was nothing I'd ever felt before.

Of course, I fell in love with Nicola the moment she was born too. This time, though, it was different. There was none of the fear that possessed me back then, none of the worry for her future. For *my* future.

After Nicola's birth, I'd held on to her like a lifeline. Tightly. Too tightly. Part of me had hoped she'd help bring Bert back to me. At the same time, giving birth to Nicola felt as if I'd created something just for myself. This magical little baby that was all mine. I didn't want to share her with him. I didn't even want Bert to hold her when he arrived at the hospital the next morning, and that was only partly because he reeked of bourbon and another woman's perfume.

Nicola was a weight. A blessed weight, but a weight nonetheless.

Not so Abigail. She arrived lightly into this world, despite her troubled conception, or perhaps because of it.

There was no father to interfere. No man to try to tell Nicola what to do.

Instead, I could help her – help them both.

'She's beautiful, Nicola. Just perfect,' I said after the midwives left us alone. I'd been with Nicola for the birth. As a nurse I'd attended many labours and she seemed happy to have me there as her supporter and advocate. The birth was straightforward – a six-hour labour and vaginal delivery with no complications. It was a sign, surely. Far more auspicious than my eighteen-hour labour, forceps delivery and third-degree tears.

Everything would be perfect for Abigail. She would have the best of everything. Nothing would hurt her.

Nothing.

'How'd I get so lucky?' Nicola said, awe in her voice as she held her sleepy daughter in her arms. Abigail's eyes were squished, and her head flattened, yet she was flawless, we both saw that.

'We'll be all right, won't we, Mum?'

'Absolutely.' Nicola was exhausted and radiant at the same time. 'Abigail has you and both of you will always have me.' I smiled. 'I have enough money to support you both. You can stay at home and take care of her for as long as you want.'

'Oh, I'll find a job. I can't be totally dependent on you.'

'If that's what you want, darling.'

'I might need to lean on you for help with Abigail, though.'

'Of course.'

I smiled as my baby touched her own daughter's hair, which was dark, though coated white and damp with vernix.

'It's just like yours was,' I said. 'So dark and thick. It will probably fall out after a few months, though.'

'It's thick, like—' she started, then stopped herself from saying his name. A haunted look passed across her face; she shook it away. 'Her eyes are the same as Dad's.'

I didn't want to agree, but she was right. I'd noticed it too.

'I wish Dad was here.'

I nodded my agreement, though was eternally grateful Bert was no longer here. 'He would have adored her.' That was true.

Bert adored so many things.

We sat for a long moment, listening to Abigail breathing as if it was the most delightful sound in the world.

'Nicola, I need to ask you something,' I said in a low voice. 'I'll ask you now and then we'll never talk about it again.'

'All right.' Her hand was stroking her daughter's tiny, balled-up fist.

'That man we saw on television,' I started. 'Cargill. He's the father of the man who—'

'Yes.'

I took a deep breath. 'And the pocketknife? It was the one Bert left you?'

She nodded, confirming my worst fears. I closed my eyes for a moment.

The pocketknife had Bert's initials engraved on it. AJM.

I shook a terrible feeling off. 'Obviously the police don't know you were there.'

'No,' she said, looking me in the eyes, passion back in her voice. 'And they won't link it to me. I wasn't in town long; no one knew I was with ... Sam.' The name was drawn from deep within her and she paled as she said it. 'We are safe. Abigail is safe.'

I inclined my head. Nicola wasn't stupid. I trusted her.

'And I'll keep you both that way,' I told her. 'If you ever hear anything about this Cargill again, you tell me. At the first sign of trouble, you hear? I'm your mother and Abigail's grandmother and I'll never let anything hurt you.'

Nicola teared up. Abigail gave a whimper.

'She's hungry. Let's try breastfeeding again.' I moved closer to my daughter and put a hand on her arm. She nodded.

We understood one another.

*

After calling Cara, I fertilise the lemon, orange and cumquat trees I keep in pots to protect them from frost – a job I've been meaning to do for some time – then drive into town.

The paddocks flash by, so familiar I usually notice anything out of the ordinary – the grazing sheep in a different paddock, a flock of cockatoos settling in a gum tree, a slasher rumbling across a field. Not today. Today I'm lost in thought.

As I reach the 'Arundel: Pop 27,912' sign, a wombat waddles onto the road and I'm forced to brake and swerve, the car skidding as my heart jumps into my mouth. I barely keep control of the vehicle, wrenching it across the double lines, counting my lucky stars there's no oncoming traffic. Once I'm safely back on my side of the road, a glance in the rear-view mirror shows the wombat scurrying off into the sparse undergrowth. Thick black skidmarks scar the tarmac like ligature marks.

I'd been nursing less than a year when I saw my first attempted strangulation.

Mrs Allen, choked by her husband with her own stockings from the washing basket as she sorted out their smalls. The dark bruises around her throat that she was too scared to blame on the prick who'd attacked her had horrified and sickened me.

Genevieve Allen had been in hospital three more times before finishing up on a gurney in the morgue. By then I wasn't nursing any longer. Nicola and I were living at Hillcrest on our own, renovating the old place with the help of several burly tradesmen. I'd taken a huge bunch of lilies from my garden – which was very much a work in progress back then – to the funeral. They'd stood out beautifully among the sea of carnations. I've never been a fan of carnations. Genevieve deserved more than those sad, drooping flowers. At her wake I'd turned aside when her husband – who had inexplicably avoided any official punishment for his abuse – tried to take my hand. He'd come to the golf club several times after that, had a steak in the bistro. He died one of those nights. Nicola and I were there, a rare night out for us. A sirloin, medium rare, he ordered, with a side of vegetables and mashed potato. Three schooners and a couple of bourbons afterwards, he hit a tree with his car. Drunk, apparently.

I shake my head. I haven't thought of poor Genevieve Allen in years. Ten minutes later I arrive at Nicola's. She opens the door wearing sweatpants, her hair wet from the shower. She smells of jasmine, her favourite essential oil. When she wears that she's happy. Today that makes me sad.

'Mum, what are you doing here?'

'Can't I call in to see my favourite daughter?'

'Sure. You usually ring first, that's all. Come in.' She stands back as I enter. 'Can I get you a cup of tea?'

'That would be lovely.' She calls upstairs from the entryway, 'Abby! Grandma's here.' We walk through to the kitchen. 'Where's Lee?'

'Running a few errands,' Nicola says, switching on the kettle. 'He's been promising to clean the driveway for months so he's gone to the hardware store for a high-pressure hose. And a fluorescent lightbulb to replace the one that's been out in the garage.'

'My, my, what's brought this on then? You usually need to nag him for much longer before he gets his handyman on.' Of course, I know the answer.

Guilt.

'Tell me about it! He's been lovely all week. Tonight we're going out to Sadie's brewery for a beer and some hot wings.'

'How nice!' The kettle clicks off. 'A date night. I haven't missed your anniversary or something, have I?'

'No. Lee just said we don't do this nearly enough.'

Abby appears at the kitchen door. 'Actually, he said every day with Mum is perfect and he never intends to forget it.'

She pretends to gag. 'Yes, I was listening this morning.' She addresses me. 'They were kissing near the front door before he left.'

Nicola laughs. 'More fool you for eavesdropping!'

'You were loud.' Abby rolls her eyes. 'There was way too much kissing.'

'That's enough out of you, young lady. Oh, I need to choose a dress to wear for dinner. Can I model them for you two? I'll be right back.' She leaves and Abby throws me another look.

'We can't tell her,' she says in a low voice. 'It'll kill her.'

'No,' I sigh. 'Not today, anyway.'

'What if Cara says something?'

'I'll talk to her. She's coming to Hillcrest this afternoon. Is there anything else I should know? About Cara?'

'No.' She stares me straight in the eyes, doesn't flinch.

'What do you think?' Nicola practically skips back into the kitchen in a floral dress with tones of pink and orange. It's lovely against her dark hair.

'It's gorgeous. Won't you be cold, though?'

'I've got a jacket. A denim one. And the forecast's pretty good. Do you like it, Abby?'

'Yeah, it's good. Lee will love it.'

'I've got one more. I'll be back in a sec.' She races off again, giddy as a schoolgirl.

It's been a long time since I felt that emotion.

Love.

I hope I don't have to destroy it for my darling daughter.

*

It was a whirlwind. A lovely, perfect, romantic courtship.

When I described it to people, those were the words I used. They'd sigh in response, tell me how lucky I was to have found my perfect match, especially at such a young age. I would smile and keep a faraway look in my eyes. Let them believe what they wanted. No one needed to know my business and it made them happy to think my life with Bert was all sunshine and roses.

The truth was far more pragmatic, more like storms and oleanders.

We met at work – my work, the hospital. I was twenty-two. Bert was forty-three.

As usual, the hospital was understaffed so I was rostered on for most of the weekend. It didn't help with Maria at a wedding on the Gold Coast and Jenny on maternity leave. The late shift finished at eleven and here I was, back again, six hours later.

Nursing was a safe job, or so Mum had advised me. 'People will always need nurses, Joycie. Don't depend on a man. Make sure you can support yourself.' Sometimes when she said it, I had to bite my tongue, given her situation, but she had a point. I desperately wanted money. I knew what it was like to have none, and I would have given anything – everything – to have enough of it to buy clothes that didn't come from an op-shop or to purchase a dress simply because it was pretty on me.

'We've a couple of new arrivals,' Beth, my boss and friend, told me that day. 'Genevieve Allen, again. Two stitches on her jaw.' I grimaced. Mr Allen must be back on the Bundy and Cokes.

'What did the police say?'

'The same as usual,' Beth said, rolling her eyes. My outrage must have shown, as she raised a hand. 'Joyce,' she said, a warning in her voice. 'Our job is to take care of Genevieve, not do the police's job. Understand?' She raised an eyebrow and I reluctantly agreed. There was far too much of this in Arundel. Seeing the pain these deadbeat husbands and fathers inflicted on their wives and children was one of the few times I was glad to be the child of a single mother.

'Our other patient is a little more interesting.' Now she had a twinkle in her eye, unusual for a Sunday morning. 'And he's kind of famous.'

'Really?' I perked up. I hadn't met anyone famous before, not unless you counted the local radio disc jockey, an overweight man with wandering hands who came in once with food poisoning and, despite continually vomiting, still managed to pinch my bum.

'He's an artist. Bert Miller.'

I gave her a blank look.

'Albert Miller? He lives out past Wallis Flat on a huge property that's been in his family for generations. He comes to town every month or so to be' – she made air quotes – '"inspired". Which seems to be code for drinking at the pub.'

'I've never heard of him. Is he old?'

'Kind of. He's forty-three.'

A forty-three-year-old artist I had never heard of was not my definition of famous. I sanitised my hands as she continued.

She told me he had crashed his motorcycle into a tree outside town at two in the morning, his main injury being a broken arm. He was lucky. Other than the break he had superficial cuts and bruises.

'He's a charmer,' she said, biting her lip and giving me a double eyebrow pump.

'Beth! What would Rich say if he saw you now!' I laughed.

'It's only a bit of fun, Joyce. Rich doesn't need to know.'

'What did the police say? Had he been drinking?'

'They didn't test him.' She saw my expression and shrugged. 'He sent them on their way with promises he'd bring them a carton of beer when he was discharged. You've seen how it is, Joyce. It's a small town. And famous people don't live by the same rules as the rest of us.' I clucked my disapproval as she went on in a gushing tone, 'He does the most beautiful landscapes. Sydney people can't get enough of them. He has paintings in fancy galleries in London and New York. They sell for *thousands*.'

'Why does he still live out here then?'

'He loves the land, I guess. Or Hillcrest, more specifically. However, there are things in town that you can't get out on an isolated property, not when you live by yourself, if you get my drift. I've heard he's in the market for wife number four.' She winked.

'He's been married *three* times?'

'Yes, he's an incurable romantic, apparently. Loves getting married.'

I snorted. 'Seems silly if you ask me.'

'Oh, and where he lives – Hillcrest – is the most amazing house! I drive past it with Rich when we visit his family out west. You can see it up on the hill on Grange Road. It's gorgeous, one of those two-storey, big old rambling places with about seven bedrooms. It's run by caretakers, so Bert has time to paint. They're an old couple, friends of his parents from before they died.'

I tried to imagine living in a seven-bedroom house and couldn't. Mum and I had shared a two-bedroom flat on the edge of town until she died the year before. Now I shared a three-bedder with two other nurses.

A seven-bedroom house, a handsome husband and a few little tykes running around my feet. Add a nice big garden with fruit trees, and that was my idea of heaven.

Dr Madden strolled in, holding a chocolate croissant in his hand that dropped crumbs all over our lovely clean floor. I started my rounds, my thoughts creeping back to that imaginary house and whether I'd paint the interior completely white or add wallpaper or feature walls in muted colours.

I'd decided on the muted colours by the time I reached Ward B. Laughter carried down the hallway, so I followed the sound to a single room, finding Bert Miller sitting up in bed. Standing beside him in a white coat was Dr Bell. Both men were belly laughing. Dr Bell was a new doctor who most of the single nurses batted their eyelashes at, but I found him pompous. He tried to stop laughing when he saw me enter, wiping at his eyes. Bert waved me in.

'Girl!' he called, his voice deep and animated. 'Help us settle an argument. I visited an old flame last night. What a night it was! However, Trevor here doesn't believe I couldn't possibly have managed to—'

'That's quite enough, Bert.'

'Not once, but three times!'

'Bert!' Dr Bell had reddened. 'No need to make our young nurses uncomfortable.'

'I'm fine, Dr Bell.' It annoyed me how the doctors thought they needed to protect us nurses. I could take care of myself.

And I'd thank any man to remember that.

I turned my attention to the patient. 'How are you feeling this morning, Mr Miller?'

He was initially disappointing, physically. He didn't look like a famous person. He was thickset, his facial features strong. Wide mouth, large nose. His face had a warmth to it, an attractiveness that made you want to please him, though he wasn't classically handsome. That morning he had several cuts on his forehead and cheeks, and a graze on his chin. His hair was unbrushed. Bert Miller was more farmer than artist, with his weathered hands and tanned face.

And then he focused his gaze on me. There was something in that gaze. Something irresistible, almost primal. Powerful.

Bert Miller was different from the boys I usually dated; he was something else entirely.

'Call me Bert, Joyce,' he said, and it was as if we were alone in the world. His smile was infectious, though it was his eyes that sucked me in. Bright blue, lively and dazzling one minute, deep and intense the next.

He intrigued me.

I checked his cannula. Dr Bell gave me some instructions about medication, Bert watching all the while, then the doctor departed, wagging a finger at Bert that he thought I didn't see.

I made some more notes on the chart and hung it over the rail at the end of the bed. When I finished, I saw Bert appraising me. 'How old are you?'

'Twenty-two.'

'God. You make me feel old,' he said, shifting in the bed with a groan. 'Am I going to live, Joyce?' he asked in a mock-concerned voice.

'You won't die on my watch, Bert.' I smiled. 'I don't think you'll be on a motorcycle again for a while, though.'

'We'll see. This won't keep me down for long.' He waved his cast at me, then winced. 'Not too long, anyway.'

I moved around closer, reaching for his arm and gently placing it by his side. My fingers pressed against his wrist. The skin was warm, his pulse strong. I sensed him staring at me. I turned to him and smiled. 'All good.'

'Yes, it is.' He held my gaze. 'Do I make you nervous, Joyce?'

'I—Ah, a little,' I said. He didn't. But even at that tender age I knew what men wanted to hear. And I had a reputation to think about. Women were expected to be modest. Small towns were notoriously small minded, especially when it came to people like me.

He grinned.

'I have to finish checking the wards,' I said.

'Of course.' When my back was to him, he spoke again. 'Joyce?'

'Yes?'

'Come back and see me when you have your break, will you?' He tilted his head to one side, his eyes flashing. 'I want to know everything about you.'

And I did. I spent every spare minute with him after that.

At first, I was concerned about what people would think – I was half his age. But people in Arundel respected Bert. He was one of those larger-than-life figures, and Beth was right, he was famous. Not only Arundel-famous; Sydney-famous. Apparently he was untouchable, and this meant I was too.

After spending two nights in hospital, he moved into the best hotel in town. He wanted me to stay with him. I didn't, obviously. I wasn't that sort of girl. He could have gone back to Hillcrest, though he told me that even forty-five minutes was too far away from me.

I knew I was a very pretty girl. Short, but with curves I was good at accentuating. Dark curls and full lips. And I admit it was nice to have a man – a powerful and rich man – admire me. For two weeks we ate at the fanciest restaurants in Arundel – steak and cocktails at the Cattleman's Club, duck à l'orange at the Little Snail – plus several dinners of crispy skin chicken and special fried rice at my favourite Chinese restaurant, Red Palace. I went to the member's lounge at the golf club for the first time in my life. I examined the – surprisingly ordinary – room with a mixture of scorn and satisfaction. That moment summed up my relationship with Arundel. The town was like a neglectful mother. I wanted her approval yet despised her at the same time.

Bert collected materials from the art shop and painted me, sitting by the window of his hotel room, a riot of autumn leaves on the liquidambar maples behind me. That painting is still on my lounge-room wall. Sometimes, even now, I stand and stare at the expression he captured on my face, and I am dumbfounded. I look content; happy.

It seems incomprehensible to me, given what happened later, that I was ever content with Bert.

You'd think I'd sell that painting, or hide it, or tear it to shreds and burn it in the forty-four-gallon drum hidden around the back of Hillcrest that I use to burn the diseased branches of plants.

But sometimes it's good to be reminded of your past.

'Come back to the farm, Joyce,' Bert had said as we sat in the pub. He poured me another one of those sweet white wines, which is all I drank back then. 'Live with me.'

'What?' I'd laughed. 'I've got a job. Your farm is forty-five minutes out of town and I don't even have a driver's licence.' That was true.

'You don't need to work. I have enough money to support you. Come on! You'll adore Hillcrest.' His hands moved down my arm, light as a feather, slowly and with great assurance. I broke out in goosepimples. He was an attractive man.

'I can't, Bert.' My mother's experiences had been too harsh a lesson. I wouldn't be an easy prize.

'You're killing me,' he murmured, straightening up and glancing around the pub. 'I need you,' he said in my ear, the words urgent, his breath hot.

'I can't.' I'd told him I was a virgin and intended to stay that way until my wedding. 'You'll have to marry me,' I said the words lightly, having caught sight of my housemate Maggie at the bar.

'What a sterling idea,' Bert murmured.

'What?' I replied, distractedly, waving at Maggie, who grinned and gave me a thumbs up. I blushed. My friends all thought it was a great lark that I'd snared the one and only Bert Miller.

'Marry me. Move to Hillcrest.'

'Are you serious?' I spun to face him.

'Deadly.' Bert grinned. 'Marry me.'

Soon after I became Mrs Bert Miller, mistress of Hillcrest. I might not have believed in love, but I was happy.

All my dreams were coming true.

Or so I thought.

*

I'm not sure love – the romantic kind – is worth it. In my experience, it only leads to betrayal.

Nicola has been betrayed by a man. Again.

Sam Cargill, she took care of herself.

I'll take care of Lee.

I'd hoped to see him at Nicola's that morning. No matter. I decide to sort Cara out first.

As I back out of Nicola's driveway, I conclude that this might in fact be a better plan. Cara likes me. I need her to tell me what the devil she's been up to, why she's messing with us.

Then I'll deal with Lee.

It's almost lunchtime and Cara is coming to Hillcrest at three. Plenty of time. My first stop is at one of the big discount pharmacies in a local mall. I buy two syringes, a bottle of eye drops, some latex gloves, a pre-packaged chicken and avocado sandwich and two rolls of bandages. I don't expect to need most of that, though it's good to be prepared. I pay with cash at a self-serve checkout, for once pleased that being a woman of a certain age makes me invisible to the high-school-aged staff stacking shelves around me.

Next, I visit three garden centres I don't usually frequent. They all have some of the plants I want, so I buy a couple from each, along with other random purchases – some potted herbs, a new trowel and bags of potting mix. At the last place I'm forced to duck behind a row of bamboo plants when I almost stumble right into Bev and Judy, a chatty couple from the CWA. They're gossips, and they'll remember me for sure. Fortunately, they choose two poinsettias and depart soon after, so I remain unseen. Again I pay cash, keeping my conversations with staff to a minimum.

At home, I park in the garage, leaving the plants I need at the front of the house and dumping my pharmacy haul on the bench inside. In the shed I skirt around the mower and line trimmer, the many other bags of potting mix and the towers of plastic pots as I locate my gardening gloves. They go into an old plastic bucket in the far corner of the shed, covered with a tarp for good measure.

Back at the turning circle at the front of Hillcrest, I examine the garden beds. Currently these are home to flowering cyclamen, lavender, violets, impatiens and pansies, mostly in purples and white. They are gorgeous against the sage, wrought iron and red-brown brick of the homestead. Rather reluctantly, I choose the violets as they are easiest to replace. I climb into the raised garden bed and trample them, digging with my hands in places to really make a mess. When I'm done, I wash the soil from my hands and eat my sandwich.

And wait.

*

'Doug?' I called out, knocking on the caretaker's cottage front door. 'Marjorie? Is anyone home?'

I cupped my hands on the glass of the window. Inside, Marjorie's laundry was arranged in neat piles on her kitchen table ready to be ironed. The ironing board had been set up nearby, but there was no sign of anyone. I bit my lip. What if they were out all day? Was it shearing season? Or maybe they were fencing? Marjorie was often out helping her husband with chores in one of the distant paddocks.

Why don't you know more about the farm? I berated myself.

Although Mum had impressed on me the importance of relying on no one but myself, since moving to Hillcrest I'd grown far too dependent on others. On Bert, and on Doug and Marjorie too. They virtually ran Hillcrest. Everything that went along with running a thousand-hectare sheep farm, they did for him.

For us, now.

'Joyce?' Marjorie came around the far side of the house, a bucket swinging from one hand. 'Can I help you?'

'Oh, Marjorie, thank goodness! I mean, good morning.' I stumbled over my words. 'Would you or Doug be able to take me into town later this afternoon? Sorry to put you on the spot again. I have a doctor's appointment for Nicola, and Bert is away.'

Marjorie gave me a dour look. She took her time climbing the steps onto the porch. She shook her head. 'Where's he gone this time?'

'Sydney. He's seeing an exhibition.'

Marjorie grunted. It was obvious she didn't believe me.

Not that I blamed her.

Bert had been doing this almost as long as we'd been married. Four years. I'd fallen pregnant with Nicola almost immediately and was only five months along the first time he disappeared.

He wasn't at an exhibition, Marjorie had that right. He had gone to see *her*. As usual.

Trish.

Patricia Hopkins.

Trish was a barmaid at a pub in Byron. I was with Bert when he met her. Pregnant, with swollen feet and horrible heartburn – I certainly wasn't 'glowing' as my pregnancy

books led me to believe I should be. And there was Trish
Hopkins, trim and perfect and sexy. With her long hippy hair
and free spirit. Three drinks in and he was flirting with her
right in front of me. And Trish fell for him, hardly hiding it.
That night Bert and I had our first big row. Bert told me I
was being silly and I threw a plate, though afterwards we had
incredible make-up sex on the couch.

He disappeared the next day and stayed away three days.
I thought he was dead, or that he had left us for good. When
he came back, telling me he'd been up the coast, touring on
his motorbike – part of his creative 'process' – my relief was
so great I didn't make a fuss. That's when their affair started.

Then it became more frequent. It wasn't until the baby
shower and farewell my work colleagues threw for me that I
found out more. I'd said my goodbyes and taken the flowers,
vodka and nappies out to the car when I realised I'd forgotten
the spare clothes in my locker. At the staffroom, I heard my
name and halted.

'Do you think Joyce knows?' asked Renee, who was across
all hospital gossip.

'Maybe.' It was Beth. 'She's a smart girl.'

'I couldn't deal with it.' Renee spoke with the conviction
of someone who'd never had to.

'It's *Bert Miller*. He's not someone you can keep tabs on, is
he?'

'Yeah, she'd have known what a player he was when they
got together,' one of the newer nurses piped in. 'Men like him
can't help themselves.'

Humiliation and anger punched me in the chest.

'Trish says he's with her at least a few days a month,' Renee
said. I remembered she used to live in Byron Bay. It seemed

she was friends with Trish. 'Sometimes more.'

'Doesn't she care he's married?' Beth asked and I could have kissed her for it.

'Trish is all about free love and following your heart. She enjoys seeing Bert on her terms. He's … "intense" is the word she used. This way, she gets the great sex and then sends him back to his wife.' The others laughed and my face burned.

I didn't pick up my spare clothes, instead I turned and fled.

I should have confronted Bert that day, but I was almost eight months pregnant. How could I raise a baby on a nurse's salary? Who would take care of my child during night shifts?

I needed him.

'What time is the appointment?' Marjorie asked, drawing me back from the memories.

'Two forty-five.'

She gave a curt nod. 'I can take you. Do you need groceries too?' It hadn't escaped her that I hadn't been grocery shopping in over a week. I was in desperate need of milk and cereal. Fortunately, I'd reorganised the neglected vegetable gardens over the past year, and pruned back all the fruit trees, which had come back beautifully, so we always had fresh food.

'Thank you. I really appreciate it.' I didn't blame Marjorie and Doug for being sick of helping me. The caretakers had been friends with Bert's parents and didn't approve of his career as an artist, or of him taking a wife twenty years his junior. But mostly they did their jobs and kept out of our hair. Their cottage was almost half a kilometre away from Hillcrest, on a road that forked off from the driveway where it joined the main road, so I didn't need to see them if I didn't want to. Still, it was nice to know they weren't far away.

'It's fine.' Marjorie pushed open the front door with the basket. Immediately the smell of corned beef wafted outside. 'You should get your licence, though. It's not safe living this far out of town without it, especially with a little one around.'

'Yes, I'm studying for the driving test.' I was too, though I doubted Bert would let me take it. He liked knowing I was at Hillcrest, always at his beck and call. Marjorie struggled with the basket, puffing a little, and it struck me that she was almost seventy. What would happen if Marjorie and Doug retired? How would I get into town then? I'd be trapped.

'What's wrong with Nicola?' Marjorie asked.

'She's very clingy.' My voice broke. 'She cries a lot, doesn't let me out of her sight. It's exhausting.' I gave her a weak smile. 'I'm sure you understand. You had four children, didn't you?'

'Yes, four in four years, though mine were good sleepers. Back in my day children had to do what they were told.' She snorted. 'We didn't put up with any shenanigans.' She makes a show of peering around. 'Where's the little barnacle now then?'

'Oh, she's finally taking a nap.' I held up the baby monitor. 'I'd better head back.'

'She's still having daytime sleeps?' Marjorie walked over to the ironing board, switching on the iron at the wall. 'You'll regret that tonight.'

'Maybe,' I said, giving a nervous laugh. 'I'll come down a bit before two?'

After Marjorie agreed, I walked back up to Hillcrest, my heart lifting as I approached the house. Hillcrest had proved to be every bit as beautiful as Bert had said.

I adored it.

The graceful old homestead was falling apart at the seams, with peeling paint on the ceilings and water damage on some of the walls. Most of my days were spent trying to keep the old girl's head above water. Dusting and polishing the old furniture, cleaning the windows and repairing what I could around the house – from filling holes and painting walls to replacing washers on taps. The time would come when a more substantial renovation would be needed, but for now I patched up the place as best I could.

The doctor ran late that afternoon.

In his late sixties, he was cut from the same cloth as Marjorie, and his advice had amounted to little more than to give Nicola some children's Panadol and let her cry. He said that 'tough love' was good for children.

Afterwards, Marjorie bought her own groceries as I scurried around the shop with Nicola holding one hand while I grabbed snacks, meat and chocolate with the other. The older woman grimaced at my loaded trolley, packaged food overflowing from the bags. An overtired Nicola started crying as we packed the car and I fervently vowed to get my driver's licence, find a new GP and reclaim my autonomy.

By the time we arrived at Hillcrest that afternoon it was dark. Nicola had finally calmed after eating chicken nuggets bought from McDonald's on the way out of town. Marjorie had disapproved, tutting as we negotiated the drive-through. As we approached the turning circle at Hillcrest I swivelled around to my daughter. She was asleep, the empty box on her lap.

Of course she'd fallen asleep right before we got home, that was just my luck.

'It appears Bert made it back after all,' Marjorie said, dryly.

I spun around and saw Bert's motorbike in the turning circle. My heart sank.

'Do you want some help with the groceries?' Marjorie asked. 'Or with the little one?'

'No, no. Bert will help.' He wouldn't. He'd be passed out on the lounge, but Marjorie didn't need to see that. 'I'll unload them from the car then go get him.'

Marjorie paused for a moment.

'Did you know I was raised on this property, Joyce?' I shook my head, not really listening, trying to determine if I could sneak Nicola in and go to bed without waking Bert. 'My mother moved here to marry my father. He was the first caretaker at Hillcrest.' She took a mint from a tin in the glove box, offered me one. I said no and she popped hers in her mouth. 'He was a little man. A mean little man, if I'm honest.' Marjorie's face was impassive as she sucked the mint, her cheeks dimpling. 'Back then, if you were married to a man like my dad, you had to put up with his ways. No such thing as divorce, not for nice girls. Dad's problem was the drink. My mum put up with a lot. One night, a clear night like this, he beat her pretty bad. I told her she should go to the police, but she refused. She was stubborn. She told me he was dying of cancer. That she was glad of it.' She gave me a wry smile that shocked me more than her words. I realised I hadn't seen her smile before. 'Then she told me to check under the very bottom porch step. She said there was a small gap on the right-hand side, to reach in there and see what I could find. I jumped up and went to see. It was a cricket bat. Mum raised it in two hands as if it was a weapon and told me, "This is my back-up plan. If he lasts longer than they say and I'm not here to protect you, or if he hurts you in *any way*, then use the bat."' Marjorie paused, then continued, 'Thankfully, my father taught me all about shitty men. That's why I married Dougie. There's not a bad bone in that man's body.' Her face was soft. Marjorie turned to me then. 'What I'm trying to say is get yourself a back-up plan, Joyce.' She patted my knee. 'Always have a back-up plan.'

My throat was tight as I squeezed her arm in silent thanks, then I got out of the car. Nicola woke as I unbuckled her seatbelt. I left the grocery bags on the ground and watched Marjorie's hatchback speed off down the driveway.

I took a deep breath.

No, life hadn't turned out the way I'd planned. But I was lucky. Luckier than Marjorie's poor mother, at least. I had a beautiful child and a wonderful house. Albeit one was sending me a little bit insane with every sleepless night and the other was falling down around my ears.

My husband might be cheating on me, but he didn't hit me or Nicola. He didn't hurt us. So long as we had each other and Hillcrest, we would pull through.

I put my key in the lock and opened the door.

*

The crunch of gravel alerts me to Cara's arrival.

I peer through the sheer curtain and watch her car come to a halt on the far side of the turning circle, then venture to the front door.

'Cara,' I say, as she approaches. She has come prepared for gardening, wearing jeans and an old jumper.

Clouds have been rolling in for the past hour, and the wind is brisk and cold.

Cara gives me a tentative smile. 'Hi, Joyce.'

I close the door behind me. 'I thought we might start right away in case it rains?'

'Sure,' she says. 'What do you need me to help you with?'

I point at the ruined violets. 'A couple of days ago something destroyed this patch of violets. Feral cats? I'm not sure. When Bert was alive I could get the caretakers, Doug and Marj, to help fix this sort of thing.'

'Who's in the caretaker's cottage now?' She lifts a hand to shade her eyes and peers back down the driveway, though you can't see the cottage from here.

'Oh, a Sydney couple own it. They rent it out, though it's not very popular.' I gesture at the plants from the nursery. 'Anyway, I bought some lovely foxgloves to replace the violets.'

'They're very pretty.' Cara walks over and squats near the foxglove plants. They're delicate flowers, with clusters of bell-shaped petals in pleasing shades of purple.

'Yes, they're my favourites. Some call them fairy bells. I have more in the back garden. Smell them.'

She bends right over and inhales deeply, then frowns. 'They don't smell.'

'Oh? I must be getting them mixed up with snapdragons. Maybe these are the ones that taste good?'

'The petals or the leaves?'

'Both, I think. Maybe try a petal.' Cara tugs a petal loose and nibbles it, then spits. 'Ugh, no! They taste terrible.'

'Must be the snapdragons. Sorry.'

She peers around. 'Where are the gardening gloves?'

'I've misplaced them all, can you believe it?' I give her a rueful smile. 'I gathered them up to clean them and ...'

I make a confused face. 'Well, I put them down somewhere, but I can't for the life of me recall where!'

Cara gives me a sympathetic look. I guess I seem old enough to be losing my marbles.

'Where should I start?'

'Can you free them from the pots and I'll dig the violets out?'

I sit on the stool I'd brought out earlier and pull the violets from the soil. Cara loosens the first foxglove from its pot, shakes some of the soil free from the roots and sets it aside.

'So, my dear, Abby's been telling me some things about you, and I have to say I found them most upsetting.'

'Oh, Joyce, it's nothing. Honestly.' Tears spring to her eyes. 'I didn't do anything wrong.'

She absently strokes the foxglove's petals and I give her a stern look. 'Abby said there's a photograph. Of you and Lee.'

'Um, well. There is, though it wasn't my fault. Can I tell you my side of the story?' Her eyes are wide.

She's good.

I slowly incline my head.

'I've been at home while the trials are on, then last Saturday I came to school to study in the library – for a change of scenery, I suppose. That day my laptop was stolen.' She puts the plant down and stands up. 'I was upset – it had all my notes for the exams on it – and I didn't know what to do, so I called Lee.' She extends her palms towards me, an entreaty that has vaguely religious overtones – almost as if she's supplicating herself – then averts her eyes as she goes on. 'He offered to come and see me to take a statement, but the library closed at five so I told him to meet me in the boarding house, in my room.' She flicks me a tearful glance.

'That's when he … he tried to kiss me. Of course I told him to stop! And he did. I only showed Abby because it was the right thing to do.'

I keep my expression stern, though allow a flicker of uncertainty to creep in.

She really is very good.

'How did you manage to catch that exact moment on camera?'

She casts her eyes down. 'I have a webcam set up. It captures most of my bedroom.'

'I won't ask why,' I mutter grimly, plunging the trowel into the soil. The loamy smell *is* Hillcrest to me. Earthy and rich. 'So you didn't sleep together?'

'Of course not!'

'Abby said you insinuated you did.' I motion to the hole I've dug and she puts the plant in. I smooth soil around it and pat it down.

'Oh, I certainly didn't mean to insinuate that.' Her eyes slide from mine.

'Cara?' I ask, warning in my voice.

'I mean –' she lets a tear run down her cheek '– I might have insinuated that. I was upset because Abby was angry with me!'

'Why was she angry with you?'

She fidgets, bites her lip, then exhales. 'She thought I was interested in Taj, that I was trying to steal him from her.'

I'm silent. My eyebrows lift in a question.

'I wasn't,' she says, hurriedly. 'It was just a little mistake. I apologised! I never meant to hurt Abby. I love her.' I can see in her eyes there's some truth in that. 'I feel terrible. And the thing with Lee … I would never hurt Nicola either. She's been so nice to me. You all have. You're like family to me. You *are* family.'

'Family don't behave this way, Cara. I'm very disappointed in you.' I motion for her to place another plant in the next hole. She comes back over and does what I ask.

For a moment I consider forgiving her. After all, she'll be gone soon. Off to university.

Then I remember the look on Nicola's face when we talked about Sam. She can't go through that again. If I believed Cara, then everything was Lee's fault. I'm sure Lee would say the same about Cara.

We'll never find out the truth.

Hang on, Cara said she filmed the encounter so perhaps I could get hold of the tape ... But she said her laptop had been stolen, so wouldn't that be connected to her webcam? Something in Cara's story doesn't add up.

'You don't know how sorry I am.' She hesitates. 'Joyce, I need to tell you something.' She tilts her head to one side. A clap of thunder startles me and fat drops of rain start to fall. Cara ignores them. 'There's a reason I wanted to get to know Abby. And you and Nicola too.'

'Oh?' Something in her tone makes me wary.

'Yes. You see, when I said you were my family, I was being literal. You *are* family.' My brow furrows. The rain comes heavier, chill against my skin. 'My mother is Donna Ross. Her maiden name was Hopkins. Her mother, my grandmother, was Trish Hopkins.'

My heart starts beating faster at that name. I haven't heard anyone say it out loud in years. Water runs down my face. I struggle to my feet as Cara continues. 'Mum's father was Bert Miller – your husband.'

I turn away, hurrying towards the front steps of Hillcrest, reeling at her words. At the top of the stairs, Cara is right behind me. She smiles at me with hope in her eyes, as I blink through the rain that wets my cheeks like tears.

'Abby is my half-cousin.'

*

Inside it was quiet and dark. The grandfather clock in the hall ticked loudly.

'Is Daddy here?' Nicola whispered, knowing to be quiet without me having to tell her. She loved her father when he was sober and in the mood for her. When he was in a temper, she clung to me, which enraged him.

'He's in bed, sweetheart,' I said. 'Just as you'll be in a minute.'

Please God.

We passed the door to the study. Bert's sleeping form was stretched out on the chesterfield lounge. He was snoring lightly and didn't stir as we hurried past. Upstairs, I put toothpaste on her brush and measured out a careful dose of Phenergan to help her sleep. I hated doing it, but I never knew what Bert would be like when he came home. It was safer that way. That night was a good night, though, and Nicola fell asleep a few pages into *Possum Magic*. I left her nightlight on and tiptoed downstairs, then crept back outside and carried the groceries in, making two trips, quickly putting the cold things in the fridge.

Bert's satchel was spread out on the island bench in the kitchen, papers strewn around it. A bottle of scotch sat next to a glass containing a half inch of brown liquid, lighter in colour thanks to ice that had since melted. He'd drunk almost half the bottle.

The papers seemed official. I picked up the topmost sheet, my pulse thumping in my ears when I figured out what they were.

Bundling the papers up, I took them to the study. Bert lay on his back, his face showing the slackness of alcohol-induced sleep. He'd aged since we met, thanks mostly to scotch and red wine. His cheeks were jowly, reddened with broken capillaries.

'Bert?' I lay a hand on his shoulder, shook it. He opened his eyes. They were bloodshot and unfocused, yet the man I married was still in there. 'We need to talk.' I waved the papers at him.

'Joycie.' He blinked at me. 'You found them.' He pushed himself into a sitting position with a groan.

'You want a *divorce*?'

'Oh,' he said, with a yawn. 'Well. Look, not really. I'm happy enough with how things are.' My heart leapt a little at this, I had to confess, no matter how much it pained me to admit it. 'It's Trish. She's insisting.'

'Trish?' He'd never spoken her name out loud to me before. 'But why?'

'She's pregnant.' He said it bluntly and the air whooshed out of me. 'She wants to settle down. Move in here.' He waved a hand, taking in Hillcrest. 'Now that she's pregnant, she's all about the country life, thinks Byron is too busy.'

My heart thudded in panic. 'You're going to throw us out of Hillcrest? Where will we go? Nicola needs a stable home, Bert. This place is all she's ever known.'

'Not Nicola,' he said it almost sympathetically. 'Just you.'

I blinked in confusion.

'Everyone told me not to marry again. They were right. I'm sorry, Joycie. I'd have you both here if I could.' A small smirk escaped him then, before he stood up and strode around the study. He was remarkably unaffected by the whisky, as his tolerance for alcohol was high. 'A true artist's love nest that would be. You and Trish!' He halted and faced me, his amusement disappearing. 'Unfortunately, pregnancy has made her stubborn. Surprisingly maternal too. She wants to be properly settled in here by the time the baby comes. That's four months. You can have a couple of months to get something sorted. And then you'll have to go.'

Most of what he said didn't register. 'What do you mean you're keeping Nicola?'

'Oh, Joycie,' he said, flashing me the smile I'd once found so charming, 'It's all out of my hands, really. Trish has it in her head that she wants you gone, and that's that. So be a good girl for me, won't you?'

'But Nicola's my baby. I'm her mother.'

Anger glinted in his eyes. Bert didn't like his charm being ignored. And he could never abide my defiance.

'Playing the mother card won't help you, I'm afraid. Not in Arundel. You know how it is. I have money. I'm friends with the local magistrate – James Rogers – he bought my Bulga River painting, the one with the cockatoos taking flight.' I could see him admiring the artwork in his mind, his ego returning to his own genius, even as my life was crumbling around me. 'I drink at the pub with the cops. Arundel will rally around me.' He considered me, not unkindly. 'I can make sure of that, if I have to. Most people don't remember your mother, but all it will take is a few mentions for them to recall what she was. I don't need to spell it out for you, do I?' His voice was soft, almost sorrowful.

My face was hot. Bert had never mentioned my mother before. My adored mother. I didn't realise he knew who – and what – she was.

He understood my look. 'I met her. At the pub many years ago – before you and I met. I admired her. She did what she had to do to keep food on your plate.' He pointed at an imaginary plate, earnestly. 'If that meant sleeping with men for money, then that's what she'd goddamn do. I certainly don't want to bring your mother into this. So let's be adults about it all, hey?'

I wanted to vomit. My mother was a *cleaner*. She had worked hard, scouring and scrubbing the local shopping centre for her boss, a miserly man who hauled her back into work more than once to complete a job deemed not good enough, who never paid her a cent over the bare minimum, no matter that her back gave out, then her knees.

The men who came and went, well, I blocked them out.

They weren't important.

Mum was important.

Gone now, of course. Dead at forty-three, looking like a woman of sixty.

I put thoughts of my mother aside. Right now, Nicola was my priority. She was *my* baby.

'Bert.' My voice was smooth and reasonable, almost wheedling. 'You don't want Nicola here. Trish won't either, not when the new baby comes along. Why not let her stay with me? We don't need money; we'll leave town if that's what you want. Or we could live somewhere – anywhere – you want us to. You can see Nicola whenever you like.' I hedged my bets, throwing everything at him in the hope of keeping my child, despite sensing that he'd already made up his mind. Bert had so much sway with the police, with 'polite society'. Sure, I could go through the courts, though he would make it hard on me. And on Nicola. Plus, I had a horrible feeling that he was right. He'd find a way to keep her.

'Nicola is mine, Joycie,' Bert said, as if that was a given. He sat back on the couch with a sigh. 'I'll have her with me,' he added simply, then saw my devastated expression. 'Come, come. It's going to happen. Accept it.'

Something broke inside me then.

Smashed into a million pieces.

Bert was going to take my child and my home and leave me with nothing. At least my mother had had me by her side. How would I cope without Nicola? I'd have to leave Hillcrest, move back to town and start over. I'd be an outcast. I remembered what that was like. Small towns are only good places to live when you are respected, even feared. At the very least, ignored. I refused to return to a life where I'd be reviled as my mother had been.

No.

I wouldn't do it.

Thoughts jostled inside my head, too many at first. I took several deep breaths, slow breaths, and the ideas solidified. The broken pieces of me started to come back together, like a magnet was drawing them in. But they weren't forming the same Joyce I'd been before. I was creating a new Joyce. A stronger one.

Bert couldn't win.

It was clear what I had to do.

The man I'd married – the man I once thought was my saviour – sat there with his eyes closed, the red flush across his cheeks. Marjorie had been right. I should have had a back-up plan.

But it wasn't too late to come up with one.

Making the biggest effort of my life, I reached out a hand and tucked a lock of Bert's hair behind his ear, then exhaled. 'I understand. Maybe it's best if I make a fresh start, anyway. Perhaps we could sit and talk a little longer? Have a drink for old times' sake?'

I'd only known Bert four years. Still, he bought it.

'Love to, my girl.' Bert seemed relieved that the worst was over. 'That would be wonderful.'

In the kitchen, I selected two wineglasses and opened the best bottle of red we had, one I'd been saving for our next special occasion.

There'll be no need for that, anymore, I thought, grimly.

I poured a generous slug into each glass. Then, listening out for Bert, I opened another cabinet, the one where our medication was kept, selecting a bottle of eye drops I used for my dry eyes. I emptied half the bottle into one of the glasses. Lifting it to my nose I took a sniff – there was no scent. In a newspaper article that Maggie had read to me over fried eggs one morning back in our share house, a woman had poisoned her husband this way.

Was half a bottle enough to kill someone? I wasn't sure. I added another long squirt to the glass, just to be safe.

Bert beamed at me when I entered, holding the wineglasses. 'I'm glad you're being civilised about this, Joycie. It will make everything much more pleasant.'

I lifted the glasses at him in a gesture of surrender, letting tears form in my eyes. 'I'm not happy about it, Bert, but I know you. You always get your way. There's no point fighting.'

'Good girl,' he said with a small laugh, and took the wineglass from me. His acceptance of my acquiescence angered me almost more than anything else he'd done to me that night.

Didn't he realise I was a fighter?

This was my house. Nicola was my daughter. I had no intention of giving either of them up.

Bert took a big mouthful and I held my breath. He swallowed and lifted his glass as if in a toast. If I remembered correctly, the eye drops caused drowsiness and, if one drank enough, a coma and death. I hadn't determined how to deal with Bert's body yet, though I was confident I'd find a way. Hillcrest had many possible burial sites.

'Well, I should be off. Trish expects me back tonight.' Bert sculled the rest of the wine in one swift movement. I almost gasped in surprise.

'You're leaving? Now?' Panic fluttered in my chest. He needed to stay here, where I could control him. Watch him. 'Why not stay? Go see Trish tomorrow.'

'No can do, my darling. I promised her.'

You promised to love and obey me, I wanted to say.

Bert must have seen the apprehension on my face, as he put a hand on my arm. 'Read through the papers. You'll see I've been very fair. It's just a draft, so call me if you have any questions or changes tomorrow before I meet with the lawyer.' He lurched to his feet. His breathing was heavy.

Is that the eye drops? Do they take effect so quickly?

'Seriously, Bert. Stay.' I rose and put a hand on his arm.

He shook me off. 'No, Joycie. I've got to go.' He blinked, confused. 'My motorbike. I'll take my bike.' The words were slurred. He stumbled to the door without taking his wallet or bag, yanking it open and almost falling down the steps.

I could have stopped him.

I didn't.

I let him get on that motorcycle, turn the key in the ignition and give me a cheerful wave as it roared into life.

'Bye, love.' His mouth made the words, but I couldn't hear them.

Gravel flung up behind him as the bike spun away and darted erratically down the driveway.

Then he was gone.

Inside, I finished my wine. Both glasses then went into the dishwasher, which I turned on. I took the divorce papers and the bottle of eye drops out to the forty-four-gallon drum we used as an incinerator and lit the old newspapers that were in the bottom. I warmed myself by the fire until it grew very hot, then added the papers, throwing the bottle in after them. It spluttered before melting into a white blob. The air grew cooler as the flames died out, and the melted plastic was covered by fine grey ash.

The doorbell rang at 5 am. I was waiting, sitting in my room wearing a dressing gown. The uniformed police officers told me Bert had died after veering from the road as he took a notorious bend on the way into town. He'd been seen earlier that day drinking in Byron Bay. No one else was injured. Cause of death was deemed to be drink driving. Nicola appeared at the door as the officers finished and I drew her close. Her warm little body was safe now.

I cried then, and some of those tears were even real.

We would be all right.

*

'You're Trish's granddaughter?' I blink, trying to take it all in.

We've moved into the kitchen now, both of us wet from the rain but neither making any effort to dry off.

'Yes. Mum never wanted much to do with her, so I didn't know Nan well. I only met her a few times.' Cara smiled dreamily. 'She was beautiful, though, even when she was old. Mum hates that I'm like her.' It wallops me over the head now. Cara is so similar to Trish, only short where Trish had been tall and willowy. I'd only met her the one time, though Cara has the same ethereal beauty. That innate sense of style. 'And Mum hated what Grandma was. Bohemian was the polite term. Free-spirited.' She raises her eyebrow. 'She got around.'

'Didn't Trish move to Sydney?' The words float from me, but my brain is still playing catch-up.

'Yes. That's where Mum grew up. She left home when she was still very young, not even sixteen. She met Dad and they were married and pregnant almost immediately. They lived in a few places before they started the Orange Dawn Church in Calder Head.'

'Did Donna tell you about us?'

'Mum tried to ignore you all. She was dead against Dad moving to Calder Head, though she was a good little Christian soldier, and did as he said.'

'How did you find out then?'

'Nan died a few years back. She left me a painting, a Bert Miller original. It was of her, in a not-so-clothed state.'

The image was all too clear in my mind.

'It's why I got this. One of the reasons, anyway.' She lifts her shirt and shows me a tattoo below her ribs, a knife with a droplet of blood. It makes me think of Bert's pocketknife, and the blood it shed. 'Trish had a tattoo just like it. It was clearly visible in the painting, in the same spot as mine.' Her eyes narrow. 'Actually, it's quite a popular little tattoo.'

I frown at her, but she doesn't elaborate. 'A knife dripping blood means transformation, apparently. Overcoming personal trials. It seemed appropriate.' Cara drops her shirt. 'Anyway, it was clear Bert and my grandmother were lovers. I did some research. Found out about the existence of Bert Miller's real family. You can imagine how shocked I was to discover the girl I met at the beach when I was eleven was my *cousin*. Well, half-cousin. Something had drawn us together; I truly believe that. We are family and we are meant to be together. That's why I applied for the scholarship to Arundel Christian College and convinced my parents to let me go.'

'Donna was happy with that?'

'Not happy, no.' Something flits across her face. 'But I can be very persuasive.'

'All that, just to meet us. Why not tell Abby who you were?'

'What's the fun in that?' I frown and she becomes serious. 'I wanted her to love me without *having* to love me.'

'Oh, Cara.' I exhale, thinking of what I had planned for today. I open the cupboard and reach for the vial of distilled foxglove, ready to add to Cara's lemonade or tea, whichever she chose. Foxglove – also known as digitalis, or digitoxin – is found in heart medication and can kill those who eat or drink even a small amount. If questioned, I could honestly say Cara had touched the plant, even ate a little, while she helped me plant the foxgloves. How was I to know foxgloves were deadly?

I'm just a clueless old lady.

My back to Cara, I turn the vial over in my fingers. Now that I realise who she is – *Bert's granddaughter* – I want her dead more than ever. Not because she might know what had happened to Bert back then, as surely Trish wouldn't have suspected I was involved in Bert's death and then told her grandchild. And not even because she might think she has a right to Hillcrest.

No, I want her dead for a reason that's far more primal.

I want her dead because I'm scared.

Cara Ross is clever and beautiful and oh-so-charming.

She befriended Abby.

She kissed Lee.

She fooled me.

What else might Cara Ross do to the Miller women?

For a moment I'm tempted to go through with it. Perhaps it would be for the best?

'Nicola,' Cara's voice breaks, 'is like a mother to me.'

I set the vial back on the shelf, shut the door and face Cara.

Tears have formed in her eyes. I'm not sure I believe her act, but I can't hurt her.

'Wash your hands, Cara. There's potting mix in that garden and it can be dangerous. Then go home. Leave Abby alone for a while. I'll talk to her.'

Ten minutes later, I stand on the stairs and wave the girl off.

'Joyce?' she says, her car keys in her hand.

'Yes?'

'Thank you. You aren't my grandmother, but Nicola and Abby are very lucky.'

She climbs into her car and drives away.

And that's the last time I see Cara Ross.

14 August, 8.03 am

Greg,
*   Still no word?*
*   AC*

14 August, 8.05 am

Hi Andrew,
*   No, not yet. Perhaps we shouldn't have been so quick to transfer the money?*
*   Greg*

14 August, 8.10 am

Greg,
*   The money means nothing. Get me her name and location by close of business today or I'll take my business — all of it — to a PI who can get the job done. And don't question my judgement again.*
*   AC*

14 August, 8.11 am

Hi Andrew,

Sorry, of course, I'm on it. I'll get back to you ASAP.
I won't let you down.

Warm regards,

Greg

PS How do you know it's a woman?

14 August, 2.19 pm

Hi Andrew,

I pulled some strings and traced the money. You were right –
it's a woman. A girl, actually. The money is still in the bank
account she specified. Untouched. The account was opened
the day the email was sent. Cara Albertine Ross. Seventeen
years old. From Calder Head on the north coast of New
South Wales, south of Byron Bay. She's been missing since
Saturday night – the day after you replied to her. The police
are investigating her disappearance, which is being viewed as
suspicious. Missing Persons are providing support. Cara was
attending Arundel Christian College, in Arundel, about forty-
five minutes inland. It's a boarding school, though she was at
home at the time she went missing. What would you like me
to do next?

Warm regards,

Greg

14 August, 2.32 pm

Arundel? Why is that name familiar? Check the files and get back to me.

14 August, 2.40 pm

Hi Andrew,

   Your memory is impeccable as usual :-) One of the suspects in our database is from Arundel. She was investigated by a contact of yours years ago. I've attached the file.

   Also, I found Cara on an interesting website called WatchMe. I'm not sure if you've heard of it? Basically it's one of those subscription-only sites where people post porn. Screenshots attached.

   Let me know what you want me to do.

   Warm regards,

   Greg

14 August, 2.45 pm

See if you can find out if the girl is dead. Perhaps her going missing had to do with her website, not this matter.

14 August, 2.47 pm

Hi Andrew,

That's possible, or perhaps she's been knocked off by your son's killer.

Warm regards,

Greg

14 August, 2.51 pm

Send me a photo and address for the woman in Arundel. Then delete all evidence of these emails. My IT guy will look after the computers at this end.

I'll take care of this myself.

PART IV

AFTER

NICOLA

Eva's words ring in my ears all the way home. It was Abby who'd been at Tom Foley's house? Why?

Had she and Tom been having an affair?

Had they done something to Cara?

Thoughts swirl in my brain. Abby and Cara facing off in the café. The way Abby had looked at the other girl with murder in her eyes.

It's almost lunchtime and the house is silent. Lee's at work and Abby is at school. As I walk inside my phone buzzes. I check the screen, my heart in my throat until I see the name.

Hudson.

I ignore it. I can't deal with him – with anyone – right now.

My phone buzzes again as my keys drop onto the kitchen benchtop. With an exasperated sigh, I read Hudson's text message. *Call me. It's about Lee. It's IMPORTANT.*

My heart thuds.

It's about Lee.

I touch the screen and the phone dials Hudson's number.

'Nic? Thank God. Where have you been?'

'I'm at home.' Hudson doesn't need to know about Eva. About my snooping. 'What's happened to Lee?'

'Nothing. I mean …' Hudson pauses. Now that he's got hold of me, he seems reluctant to continue. It's not like him.

Hudson is usually a straight-to-the-point kind of guy. 'It's …
Jeff told me something this morning. We were watching
breakfast TV and Lee came on.'

'Yes.' I'm impatient. 'He had a press conference.' Lee hates
them, but his boss had insisted.

'It jogged Jeff's memory. A couple of weeks ago, a week
before Cara went missing, Jeff saw …' He hesitates again. 'He
saw Lee going into her bedroom at school.'

'What?' Hudson's hardly making sense. I switch on the
heating, my body going through the motions as my brain
flails. 'Is he sure?'

'Yes. Jeff was called in about a plumbing issue – girls
flushing tampons down the toilet again. They get him in after-
hours sometimes. It's cheaper than calling the professionals.
Anyway, he said it was definitely Lee. Cara went inside first,
and Lee followed her. This was around ten pm on Saturday
night. Then the door shut.'

'He was probably …' And yet there's no reasonable
explanation for Lee to have been there and not to have told
me about it. I think back. He had been working that Saturday
night. He takes weekend night shifts quite regularly, despite
my complaints. I hate him doing night duty.

'I'm sure it was a work thing. I'll ask him about it tonight.'
I try to sound blasé and know I'm failing. Hudson's silence
speaks volumes. 'You've never liked Lee, have you, Hudson?'
I pace the kitchen, my anger growing. 'Telling me this makes
you happy, doesn't it?'

'Of course not, Nicola. He's …' He hesitates. 'A great
guy.'

'Don't give me that.'

'Okay, fine,' he snaps. 'I've never trusted him, I'll admit it.'

'We've been together five years, Hudson. And he's never put a foot wrong.' *Until now.*

Hudson doesn't answer.

'Look, just don't tell anyone else about this, all right?'

'Nic—' he starts, his voice now so kind it makes me even more annoyed. I hang up before he can continue.

I press my hands into the island bench, breathing hard.

What the fuck is going on in this town? In my family?

Abby and *Tom*?

Lee and *Cara*?

No, he wouldn't do that to me.

I spin to the cupboard where we keep our alcohol. Several bottles of wine, a bottle of gin and one of scotch. I grab the scotch, find a tumbler and pour a generous finger. I take a big slug, grimacing at the taste, hoping it will settle my nerves.

Why didn't Lee tell me he'd been to see Cara?

My phone buzzes again, a message from Mike Ross. It's only one word.

Anything?

I almost hurl the phone across the room. I don't care about Mike Ross and his concerns that he's a suspect. I have worries of my own. Abby and her teacher. Lee and a teenager. I type, *No. Nothing*, then hit send.

My phone beeps again.

I thought I made myself clear.

Annoyance flashes through me and I stab at the keys. *I can't do it.*

I'll have to talk to Lee then. Maybe the local paper too.

I pause, deciding to call his bluff. *Fine. Do what you have to do.*

The three dots hover menacingly for what seems an age. *Cara means everything to me, Nicola. I have to find her. How would you feel if your daughter was in danger? I've seen her, at the school. She's a very pretty girl.*

I fire straight back. *Is that a threat, Mike?*

A short pause. *Just check the files, Nicola.*

Would he hurt Abby? Perhaps it's best to do what he says.

Fine, I reply. *I'll get back to you.*

I skol the rest of the scotch, put the glass down and make a beeline for Lee's study. Why the fuck should I worry about betraying Lee anyway? It seems there's no one I can trust anymore.

Lee has his briefcase with him, and his desk is tidy. No folders, no neat piles of paperwork to rifle through. He does have one of those large desk pads to doodle or write notes on, and it's covered with almost illegible scratchings. Lee makes phone calls from here when he's doing paperwork or following things up outside of office hours.

I sit down and stare at the desk pad. When Lee talks to colleagues or witnesses on the phone, he always has a pen in hand, is always scribbling. On the pad there are all sorts of doodles – little faces, or patterns around a shape, or borders around words. He's underlined some words excessively, completely obliterated others. Various phrases leap out at me from the chaos. 'Alibi', 'at home', '10 pm', but in the bottom left corner there is something useful: *TF argument? SZ.*

That must be the exchange I witnessed between Cara and Tom Foley at Sweat Zone two days before she disappeared. Nearby are two more words: *WatchMe?*

Watch who?

I squeeze my eyes shut in frustration, then consider the word again, this time noticing the caps.

WatchMe.

My pulse races. It's an app, or a website. I'm sure I've heard of it before.

I open a browser on my phone. Yep, WatchMe. The home page is simple, with the one-line descriptor reading, 'WatchMe. A site for fans to watch *you*.'

The memory comes to me now. WatchMe had been on the news, controversial for the way it allows celebrities to post explicit content. Fans can subscribe to watch it.

My breath catches in my throat. Surely Abby doesn't have anything to do with this? Or Cara?

Oh God.

No, they're too smart for that.

Aren't they?

My fingers tremble as I search for them both, finding nothing. I release a breath, relieved but disheartened too. It's a dead end.

I'm about to get up and leave when my eyes light upon a password or a username, printed neatly along the very bottom of the desk mat: caramel_69.

I enter the name into the WatchMe search bar.

I have a hit. An account. A number of videos pop up on screen. They are slightly blurred, with a dollar sign icon inviting me to pay to view them. Scrolling down, most have a woman's foot or feet in the centre of the screen, either up on a desk or on the bed behind the desk. Despite the fuzziness all the videos seem to start in the same location. It's a bedroom. A dormitory.

The décor – in navy and grey school colours – is recognisable from brochures and school tours.

It's Arundel Christian College.

Oh, Cara, what have you done?

Then from behind me, echoing my thoughts, comes a man's voice.

'Nicola? What are you doing?'

I swivel around.

Lee stands in the doorway.

*

'What are you doing in here?' Lee asks again, stepping closer so that he blocks the exit.

'I'm sorry. Am I invading your privacy?' My eyes are wide and I speak in mock concern. 'What are *you* doing here?'

'I came home to have lunch.' Lee frowns. 'I thought we might eat together since I've been so busy lately. Are you okay?'

'I don't know. Are *you*?'

He gives a short laugh, and I sense something underneath. He glances at the desk pad and then back to me. 'Have you eaten? Do you want me to make you a sandwich?'

'No, thank you,' I say, then keep watching him.

'What is it? Is something wrong?'

'Is it? Maybe you can tell me?'

He opens his mouth, then shuts it. 'I'll be in the kitchen,' he says, turning his back, unwilling to be drawn into an argument. Lee avoids confrontation, something I usually admire, though I hate it when he tries it on me.

Taking a deep breath, I launch straight into it.

'Why were you in Cara's room at the school the weekend before she went missing?'

There's a fraction of a second's silence before he turns around. 'What?' He's stalling.

'Jeff saw you. Hudson just told me. He said Jeff saw you going into Cara's room late on the Saturday night.'

Lee stares at me, then his shoulders slump. 'Can't they stay out of our business for once?' he mutters.

The breath is sucked out of me.

Lee and Cara.

I can't believe it's true.

He gives a small sigh and comes into the room. 'Fine. Yes, I was there. Look, Nic, I should have told you, I know that. I've wanted to tell you ever since it happened. But you might have jumped to the wrong conclusion and I didn't want that.'

'Spit it out,' I say, though I'm terrified.

'Cara kissed me.'

'I'm sorry? What?' My heart somersaults in my chest.

'She kissed me.' Lee runs a hand over his shorn skull. 'She called me that day. Told me her laptop had been stolen. She was upset, said it had all her HSC study notes on it. I felt bad for the kid. She was a mess, crying. I went over there myself. I mean, I've met her. I thought it would be nicer than telling her to come down to the station late on a Saturday night. All the drunks, druggos.' He rubbed his eyes. 'A mistake, in hindsight. A big one. I told her I'd bring the report and we could fill it out, get the ball rolling.' He pauses. 'She got me inside, seemed pretty upset. A few minutes later she was all over me. I couldn't believe it! As soon as I realised what was going on, I pushed her away.'

'As soon as you *realised*? What the actual fuck, Lee? Why would Cara kiss you?'

'I don't know, Nic.' He sounds frustrated. 'It was strange. She really launched herself at me.'

'Why would she do that?'

He exhales. 'I have no idea.' He gives me a rueful smile. 'I'm not that irresistible.'

I don't smile back.

Lee comes over and kneels in front of me. He takes my hand. Something inside me cracks at the familiar feel of his hands. Soft and rough. He sighs again.

'I should have told you. I didn't because ...'

'Why?'

'I didn't want to hurt you, Nic. I know how hard you found it to trust men after ... Canada.'

My head spins. 'You know?'

He nods.

'For how long?'

'Always.' He rubs my hand, peers into my eyes.

I examine his face. 'And when you say you know, you mean ...'

'That you were raped. That Abby is a product of that rape.' The words are harsh coming from his mouth, and yet a little of the tightness in my shoulders loosens at hearing them.

'How did you find out?'

'There's a ...' His brow furrows as he tries to find the right words. 'It changes a person when they go through something like that. I could see it in your hesitation to let me touch you. The way you flinched at my closeness. It took a long time to get you to trust me and I wasn't going to risk all of that because Cara did a stupid thing. I'm sorry.' He peers up at me. 'Are we good?'

'Is there anything else you need to tell me? Did you have anything to do with Cara's disappearance?'

'How could you think that?'

I look into his eyes. I believe him. 'Does Abby?' I ask, holding his gaze.

'Abby?' Lee seems puzzled. 'No. She's your daughter.'

I raise my eyebrows.

'There is no evidence that Abby is involved.' He says it solemnly.

'What about Tom Foley?'

Lee hesitates.

'Come on, Lee, we're past you keeping things from me now.'

'It doesn't seem that Tom Foley was involved. Actually, he gave us useful information. You can't tell anyone, but Cara was on WatchMe—'

'Yes.' I flash my screen at him. 'I saw.'

'It's a foot fetish site, among other things.' *Oh, Cara.* 'Tom Foley told me about it. He overheard boys at school talking and pulled the girl aside. He was concerned for her. Something like that could ruin her chances with overseas colleges.' He pauses. 'Cara told him she'd been forced into it. She implicated her father. Suggested he made her do it. Tom thought it sounded as if Mike might have been too involved in his daughter's life, if you get my drift.'

'Mike knows about this?'

'Encourages it, apparently.'

I recall Mike's weirdly close relationship with Cara, how he'd bought her those clothes, just for 'Daddy'.

Bile rises in my throat.

Her own father.

I ball my fists, recalling that powerless feeling. How I'd lain in that bed, so alone, the blood sticky on my thighs.

Lee sees the murderous look in my eyes.

'Don't interfere, Nicola. Leave it to the police. That's our job.'

'Absolutely,' I say, as calmly as possible. But I know I won't do that. I can't.

That prick almost convinced me he was innocent.

It's not just that, though. If Mike is capable of pimping out his own daughter, what else is he capable of? He just threatened Abby.

Is my daughter safe?

'We haven't shown Cara's account to him yet,' Lee continues. 'We've been getting our ducks in a row. The plan is to present it to him tomorrow and see how he reacts. We can't risk him finding out beforehand.' I nod, and he changes tack. 'Are we all right, Nic?'

I hold his gaze. 'As long as there aren't any other secrets you're keeping from me?'

'No, nothing.' His eyes slide away from mine.

So, there is something else. Then I think of my own secret, the one I'll never tell Lee. I don't push him.

'I guess we'll be okay.' I pause. 'Abby's not on WatchMe, is she?'

He scrunches his face up and he gives a sharp shake of his head. 'I don't think so. She asked me about the site before Cara went missing. At the time, I thought one of her friends might be going to join to have a look. I certainly never thought they'd actually be the ones posting things. I guess that's when Abby found out about Cara's page.'

Ten minutes later Lee has gone – he never made a sandwich after all – and I'm in the kitchen when my phone beeps.

Find anything?

I bite my lip. This is it. I should leave this to the police.

Yes. I found something, I type in my response. *Can we meet? Today?*

Tonight. 8 pm, he responds almost immediately. *My place.*

*

I can't talk to Lee again before seeing Mike, he'll figure out something's up.

I text him to say Petra has asked me to cover the junior basketball games that night. Not my best excuse, though I believe he'll buy it.

Then I call Abby. I want to ask her about WatchMe but there's a part of me that's scared to. What if she tells me she's involved? Or was she at Tom Foley's house to talk to him about Cara?

Instead, I say, 'Mike Ross hasn't contacted you, has he?'

'Of course not.'

'No weird messages?'

'No.'

'Okay. Can you go straight home after school today?'

'Is this about Cara? Has she been found?'

'No, no. It's probably nothing. Look, I have to work tonight, and I'd feel better if you were at home with Lee.'

There's a short pause, then Abby says, 'Whatever. I've got study to do, anyhow.'

At three I leave for Calder Head. I need time to think everything through and I may as well do it at the beach. I park opposite the wide stretch of sand and take my shoes off, heading down to the shoreline. The sand is cold and sharp, shells dig into my feet as I leap across piles of seaweed left by the last high tide. The water is chilly enough to make me wince.

Last time I was here I'd been keen to write about Cara's disappearance, but now the stupid article is the last thing on my mind. I just want to keep my daughter safe. And find Cara. Mike Ross is involved in this, I can feel it. He needs to confess. And I need to be there to see his face when he sees Cara's website.

I bite my nails. But perhaps I *should* leave Mike to the police. It's only tomorrow, after all. He will be on his guard with them, though. He won't confess. But if I show up at his house and ambush him with her WatchMe page, his defences will be lowered. Perhaps I'll find out the truth.

It's about protecting Abby, but I owe Cara something too.

Justice.

What if Mike has killed her? I picture Cara, so eager to please Mum and me. There's a light inside her. A spark. Some people want to snuff it out, others want to keep it for themselves. She tried to kiss Lee, yes, but her strange relationship with Mike must have affected her in so many ways.

She needs saving.

It's dark by the time I return to my car. I eat an apple and a dried-out sausage roll I bought from the supermarket as I wait for eight o'clock. It's cold, but I don't feel it. Images chase one another through my brain. Donna's bruises. Cara's arched foot, the nails painted a glossy hot pink or bright red or purple, her fine gold anklet. Red blood on stiff white sheets. Abby's face as she argues with Cara.

I bite the inside of my cheek. That last one still worries me.

What were she and Abby fighting about at the hospital? I don't believe it was about Taj. Could it have been about another boy? My mind lands on Lucas. No, surely not. He's far too old for them.

It's 7.55 pm when I arrive at the Ross house.

Their Orange Dawn four-wheel drive is parked on the street, and the house is softly lit. I kill the engine, listening to my car tick as it cools. As I approach the front door a security light comes on. Mike opens the door before I have a chance to knock.

'You found something?' His eyes glitter and he's unshaven, wearing board shorts and a jumper with a large stain over his heart that could be mayo.

'Is Donna here?' I ask, touching the knife I've put in the front pocket of my hoodie. My hands aren't sweating this time, in fact I'm oddly calm.

'No, she's at the hospital. She'll be home around ten.' When I don't speak, Mike says, 'Come in,' and steps back impatiently. He leads me through into an all-white kitchen. To my right there's a timber dining table and a door leading out to the deck and backyard. The Hills Hoist and old concrete path leading to it are lit up, before the yard disappears into darkness. On the dining table are several empty beer bottles, and one that's half full.

'Can I get you a drink?'

'No, I'm good.'

He takes a swig of his beer. 'So, what did you find out?'

I withdraw my phone from my handbag and swipe it open. 'Have you seen this?' I tilt the screen to face him.

'What is it?' Mike is puzzled by the image of the foot on the desk. I examine him closely yet there's no sign he's familiar with what he's seeing.

'It's Cara. She's got an account on WatchMe.' He looks blank then knits his eyebrows together. 'WatchMe is a site where people post intimate videos.' His eyes lift to mine. 'Porn,'

I elaborate. 'Cara has posted videos of herself performing sexual acts. Usually involving her feet. Foot fetish porn is big business on these sites. People pay to watch.'

Mike turns white. 'Porn?' he echoes, dumbly, recoiling from the phone as if it might bite him. 'What are you talking about?'

It's clear he has no clue what his daughter's been up to. Even so, I'm compelled to ask, 'Did you know about this? Encourage it?'

'Sweet Jesus.' His mouth hangs open. 'Porn? Cara? She's my … my baby.'

He stumbles through the kitchen to another room, slamming a door behind him. I hear retching.

'Nicola?' There's a voice from the doorway. I turn my head. It's Donna. She views me with concern, a handbag over her shoulder and her car keys in her hand. 'What are you doing here?'

'I came to see Mike.' I gesture towards the bathroom where we hear the toilet flush.

'What about?'

Mike reappears, his face blotchy. 'Donna! You're home early.'

'Fiona didn't show so we called it a night. What's going on?' She turns from him to me with narrowed eyes.

'It's Cara.' He starts crying, big sobs that jerk through his body.

'Have they found her?' Donna asks, glancing outside as though expecting her daughter to materialise. Now it's her turn to pale.

'No,' Mike says, through his tears. 'There's this website. Cara's on it. She posts …' He struggles to get the words out. '… videos on it. They're sexual. Oh my Lord!'

Donna rushes to him, holds him as he stumbles.

'Nicola thinks I had something to do with it,' he says in a strangled voice.

'What?' Donna rounds on me. Her soft features sharpen, her eyes are bright with anger. 'How dare you come in here and accuse my husband of something so despicable! Mike would never be involved in that filth. He's only ever treated Cara with respect. Not that she deserves it. Sexual videos of feet! Disgusting!'

I freeze.

'I'm sorry, Donna,' I say slowly, 'but Mike didn't mention her feet just then. Did you know about this?'

'I ... I didn't ... I don't ...' she stammers, turning back to Mike.

'Donna?' Mike pulls away from his wife. 'You knew? Why didn't you tell me?'

'I ... couldn't.' She drops the pretence of ignorance, making a face. 'It was disgusting. So *humiliating*. If people at church or at the hospital found out what she'd done ... I couldn't bear it! I demanded she take the videos down. But she wouldn't!' She straightens and speaks forcefully to her husband. 'Our daughter brought shame to our family, Mike. Even more so, she was shamed before God. She needed to be punished.'

'Donna,' Mike whispers. 'What have you done?'

'Me? Nothing.' She averts her eyes, blinks at the floor.

'Did you hurt Cara?' he continues, confused.

She clasps her hands together and lifts her gaze to Mike. The words that follow start quietly, imploring. 'I didn't mean to.' Tears glisten in her eyes. 'She wouldn't take the videos down.' She lifts her chin. 'It was Cara's fault! She grabbed me, Mike!' She holds out her wrist to show the bruises. Now, her words pour out. 'I hadn't been able to confront her privately, not until Saturday night when you were at that church fundraiser. She came home from God knows where and found me out the back, bringing in the washing. I told her I knew about the videos. She didn't care!' Donna's voice rises in her outrage. 'She said she was proud of them. That she'd made so much money from them. I was disgusted. I tried to walk past her and she shoved me! Me! Her own mother!' Her eyes grow wide, her breathing shallow. She visibly controls herself before speaking again. 'I pushed her back and she fell and hit her head on the old concrete path out the back. I didn't mean to hurt her, Mike, I swear!'

My brain reels. Donna killed Cara? Despite my shock, I can't help but notice that at first she'd said Cara needed to be punished, then changed her story.

'You killed our daughter?' Mike's voice is a whisper.

Donna drops her gaze. 'There was so much blood.' She lowers her voice to match his. 'She wasn't breathing.'

'What did you do with her?'

'I didn't know what to do!' Her eyes snap back to his. It's as if I'm not in the room. 'I dragged her body into the shed. Put a tarp over it. Hosed the concrete. Then, the next morning when you went surfing, I dug a hole between the back fence and the shed — the soil is so sandy there — and buried her. I put some old bricks on top. You can't even tell she's there.'

Mike turns, runs for the back door. I see him pass the Hills Hoist until he is enveloped by the darkness outside.

Donna blinks. She's glassy-eyed and far away.

I see now that there's something missing in her. She's empty.

'Why are you even here, Nicola?' She speaks softly, but there's menace in her tone. 'Truthfully?'

I step backwards. 'I came to tell you and Mike about the videos.'

She steps towards me. 'Why?'

'I was worried about Cara. About Abby too. I thought Mike might hurt her.'

'Mike wouldn't hurt a fly. He doesn't have it in him.' She scrutinises my face and I step back further, the curve of my back pressing against the kitchen benchtop. 'You're just like her.'

'Who?'

'Your mother. Joyce Miller.' Her eyes narrow. 'You're the reason Cara was so desperate to go to that school.'

'Me?'

'Yes. You and Abigail. She wanted to meet "the Miller women". You and Abigail and Joyce bloody Miller.'

'But why?'

She tilts her head to the side and something tugs at me, a realisation just out of reach. 'You don't know, do you?'

'What?'

'Ask Joyce. See if she'll tell you the truth.'

My mouth is open to ask her more when Mike stumbles back inside. He has dirty brown sand on his clothes and hands, a smear on a cheek. He lifts one hand. A necklace is draped over it.

'You actually did it. You killed her!' he says, disbelieving. 'Why?'

'She pushed me too far, Mike. She'd fallen too far from God's way. I knew she would never find her way back.'

'She's your daughter.' His voice breaks. 'Our daughter.'

'You always loved her more than you loved me. You and Cara didn't need me. No one needed me. Not even my mother.' She gives me a look here, and I frown, before she focuses back on Mike. 'I saw her tattoo, in her videos. It's just like yours.' She grabs his wrist and jabs at the dagger. 'You think I'm stupid, don't you? You think I didn't know what you did with my mother?'

Mike's mouth falls open, then he blurts out, 'Once, Donna. Once. A very long time ago. It meant nothing.'

'It was important enough for you to get a tattoo to match hers. And then Cara got one as well.' She waves her arm around theatrically. 'Harlots and adulterers, the lot of you. My mother was more interested in men than me. You aren't much better. No one ever loved me just for being me. I had to fight for every scrap of love from all of you. I thought that having a baby would change all that. I thought you'd have to love me because I gave you a child. But you loved Cara more than me and I was back to having nothing.' She pauses, blinks.

'Cara always needed you, Donna. You were everything to her when she was sick.'

'I remember that first time.' A half smile plays on her face, a dreamy look in her eyes. 'She had a fever and we rushed her to hospital. It was an infection, and she was better in, oh, twelve hours, maybe. Those twelve hours were magic. The nurses at the hospital brought me tea, they listened to my worries and patted me on the back. Brave mamma, they called me. They said I was amazing. It was wonderful.' She lifts her gaze to Mike and shrugs. 'And Cara got better. Babies are remarkably resilient.' She blinks. 'Robust, even when they seem so little and fragile. They can pull through almost anything.'

Mike becomes deathly still. He stares at his wife.

'You ... you didn't!' He runs at her, grabs her by the throat, the necklace still in his hands.

I'm frozen for a moment, stunned. 'Mike! Mike, get off her!' I clutch at his arms, but he's possessed. He's much bigger than me and his hands are like iron around his wife's neck. Donna's eyes bulge, but she makes no sound. I grasp my knife and pull it free from my hoodie pocket but Mike jerks to one side and bumps me so it falls from my hand and skitters across the floor, disappearing under the fridge. 'Fuck!' I try again to pull him off Donna, but Mike is unreachable. My eyes rake the room. I dart to the bench, lift the electric kettle and spin around, striding back and whacking Mike across the head. Cold water sloshes over my arms and over him too. It isn't a hard hit, but it's enough to make him let go. Donna falls to the floor and I step around Mike to shield her. He glances at me, his eyes wild. Donna is still.

'Enough, Mike!' I yell, my arms up.

His shoulders slump a little and I repeat, more softly, 'Enough.'

With trembling fingers, I dial triple zero.

*

It's a long night.

Mike and I wait in a strange limbo for the police and paramedics to arrive.

He's grief-stricken, seated at the dining table, Cara's necklace twined around his hands, the chain pulled so tight his fingertips are white. He has a red lump near his right temple and scratches on his hands, but otherwise he seems physically fine.

Donna, on the other hand, hasn't fared so well.

There are red marks on her throat. I've laid her on her side and she's breathing, though it's shallow. The dispatcher assures me an ambulance will come soon, that the Ramsey depot is only ten minutes away. I hover over Donna, hoping she'll hold on till they get here.

'What did she mean?' I ask, lifting my eyes to Mike's.

He doesn't answer, just stares at the necklace in his hands. I've given up thinking he'll answer and am checking the time on my phone when he speaks.

'It was her. Cara's sickness.' His voice is hoarse but the words are devoid of feeling, as if he's numb. 'It was her all along.'

'What?' I put a hand on her forehead. It's moist and too warm. I don't understand what he's saying. 'What do you mean?'

'She must have made Cara sick to get *attention*. To feel loved. To have people pity her.' He jerks in his seat, frowns. 'I remember it now. How the staff at the hospital were so fucking solicitous, so sad for us. *Do you want tea? Here are some flowers. Come to the canteen and eat something, please. You have to take care of yourself.* She was the centre of attention, the poor mother whose baby was sick with an unknown illness, possibly dying. She'd cry for our child, pray for her. Everyone thought she was stoic, such a woman of God. And now I discover that she was the one who was making Cara sick in the first place.' He chokes back a sob. 'Her own mother. God, how could I have been so stupid? I should have protected her. And now she's finally killed her.'

I touch his arm but he ignores me. I open my mouth to speak, but what is there to say? It's horrifying. He sobs, the sound echoing through the quiet house.

I sit beside him and we wait together.

*

The paramedics arrive in a sea of lights and sound, and uniforms suddenly surround us.

Within moments, it seems, Donna is on a stretcher and whisked away. Police take Mike to the lounge room and I'm left with several police officers, including Lee.

A very angry Lee.

He avoids my eyes and forces concern to hide his fury. I explain to the officers that I was giving the beleaguered Rosses moral support in their time of need – mentioning nothing about my questions to Mike about his daughter's online pornography. I tell them I was in the wrong place at the right time – and, fortunately for Mike, who had just discovered his wife's role in the death of their daughter – I was able to stop him from killing Donna.

Lee knows differently.

And he's more than pissed.

Even so, I try to be helpful, guiding the police to Cara's body and telling them what Donna told Mike and me. More police arrive, most of them unfamiliar. Soon after, the forensics team shows up. Finally, hours later, Lee directs a young constable to drive me home in my car, while another officer follows. Lee has called Abby and arranged for Joyce to take her back to Hillcrest, so when I arrive home I shower and fall into bed.

The house is dark and quiet and I'm bone tired.

I sleep.

*

I dream that Mike stands over Donna and me. We're lying shoulder to shoulder in a shallow grave. Donna whispers in my ear, her breath hot and fetid. She croons the same words, over and over. 'You don't know, do you, Nicola? You don't know!'

'Nicola?' I startle awake to find Mum by my bedside, her hand on my shoulder.

'What time is it?' My heart thuds but I'm groggy too; stiff and sore.

'It's eight in the morning.'

'I need more sleep,' I mutter, my mouth dry.

'Abby and I came here as soon as we woke up. I let you sleep but I can't wait any longer. I need to talk to you. How are you feeling, darling?'

I hear Abby's shower clunk on and I sit up, yawning. 'I'm fine. How's Abby going? She knows about Cara?'

'She'll be all right. Tell me everything.'

As I finish, Abby sticks her head around the door, her hair still wet.

'Mum!' She comes over and hugs me and the smell of her coconut shampoo is almost my undoing. She pulls back and frowns at me. 'You look like shit.'

'Thanks,' I say, my voice breaking. A sob escapes me. 'I don't feel so great. Lee told you about Cara?'

As if saying his name has conjured him up, my phone rings. Mum picks it up and holds it towards me. 'It's him. You want to take this? We can give you some privacy,' she says, sensing my ambivalence. 'He called about fifteen minutes ago too. It might be something important?'

'I'll call him back soon.'

Mum puts the phone back on the bedside table.

'I can't believe Cara's *mum* killed her!' Abby says, her eyes wide. 'That's wild. Mrs Ross always seemed so nice.'

'Do you know how she's going?' I ask, raising an eyebrow at my own mother.

'She's not well,' Mum says, shaking her head. 'I called Phyllis Neil. She still works in the ER. Donna is stable though they're worried about hypoxia—' She turns to Abby and explains. 'A lack of oxygen to the brain. She's still unconscious.'

'And Mike?'

'He's in custody, given what he did to her.'

We're silent for a moment. I almost ask Abby about what Eva Foley had said – that she was at Tom Foley's house. Then don't. What's the point?

Donna killed Cara.

Not Abby.

'Mum, I'm going to Lili's. She's going to take me to school.' It dawns on me that Abby is wearing her uniform.

'You want to go to school? Today?'

'I need to be with my friends right now. Is that okay?' She asks it so carefully it breaks my heart.

'Absolutely, hon.' I motion her closer and kiss her forehead. 'Be safe.'

'I can drive you to Lili's,' Mum offers.

'No, it's only a short walk and it'll give me time to think.' A wan smile flits across her face, then she departs.

When the front door slams, I turn my attention to my mother. 'Donna told me that Cara went to school at Arundel because she wanted to meet us. "The Miller women" she called us. She told me to ask you why. What was she talking about?'

Mum opens and closes her mouth. Then she seems to come to a decision. 'Donna's mother was Trish Hopkins. Your father's mistress. You and Donna are half-sisters. Abby and Cara are half-cousins.'

Trish Hopkins. I know that name. Not well. Mum never talked about her, though I heard things growing up. But I never knew she'd had a daughter.

Donna. My mind reels.

Half-sisters. Half-cousins.

And then it hits me. The way Donna tilts her head to the side. Abby does that. Cara too. I exhale.

'How long have you known?'

'I only found out when Cara told me.'

I scowl. '*Cara* told you? When was this? Why didn't you say anything?'

'I don't know.' Mum sighs. 'I'm so used to keeping secrets now,' she says, sadly. My thoughts return to Canada. And Sam. To Abby waiting outside a teacher's house for some unknown reason.

'Perhaps we should fix that,' I say. 'Talk to Abby. Even Lee. Tell them our secrets.'

She lets out a long breath. 'Maybe.' Then she smiles and pats my arm. 'You have another nap. I'll tidy up and then make us some tea. Perhaps we can discuss this a little later?'

'I'd like that.'

Mum bustles off and I lean back against the headboard. I've just closed my eyes when my phone buzzes. I groan, almost letting the call go to voicemail. It's probably Lee again. He'll still be pissed, and he'll probably have ditched his colleagues, meaning I'll be in for an earful. But there's an off-chance it's Abby.

I open my eyes and snatch it up.

Not Lee, Hudson.

Though I want to sleep, I accept the call, knowing he will keep trying, or more likely rock up on my doorstep if I don't talk to him now.

'Nic! Are you okay?'

'I'm fine.'

'Thank God. I've been so worried. Look, I'm sorry about yesterday. I shouldn't have said what I did. You're right. You can trust Lee – of course you can.'

'It's all right, Hudson.' I can't decide if he's a great friend to say this even though he doesn't really believe it, or if he just feels bad for me, given what happened. Either way, I'm too tired to argue. 'You were just worried about me.'

He pauses for a few seconds then asks, 'What went on out there last night? The town grapevine has almost spontaneously combusted! The gossip is next level. They're saying Donna killed Cara. That Mike almost killed Donna. I don't know what to believe.'

'Both those things are true.'

'Holy crap! And Cara was blackmailing her mother? Because Donna was responsible for making her sick all those years. The poor girl! I can hardly believe it.' He pauses. 'What a giant fucking mess.'

'Who told you that?'

'Cassie at the police station. I rang them to ask after you and we chatted until someone told her to put the phone down and get back to work. You know what a blabbermouth she is.'

There's a lump in my throat. Cara never had a chance, not with a mother like Donna. 'Look, Hudson, I desperately need to rest, I didn't get much sleep last night. Can we catch up later? Tomorrow, maybe?'

'Of course, gorgeous. You get some rest. I'll call tomorrow.'

*

I must have rolled over and fallen asleep on my phone, as I'm woken by a buzzing under my arm.

Jerking awake, the previous day's events come crashing into my mind. It feels like a dream – a nightmare. Rolling onto my back, I pick up the phone.

No caller ID.

I frown. The school? Hopefully not the media, not yet. Against my better judgement, I swipe to answer.

'Hello?'

'Good morning, Nicola.' The man's voice is well-modulated, confident. Familiar, somehow. 'I'm sorry to call out of the blue like this, but it's time we met. I understand you were well acquainted with my son, Sam, about, oh, eighteen years ago.'

The man pauses. I feel faint. Light-headed.

'Cat got your tongue? No matter. You'll talk when you hear who my guest is this fine winter's day.' I hear a rushing in the background, as if he's in a car, driving somewhere fast. 'Arundel is cooler than I'm used to,' he continues, conversationally. 'Luckily I packed warmer clothes. I'm good at planning ahead, you see.'

There's the sound of tyres on gravel, then silence, as if the car has pulled over.

'What do you want?' My voice is croaky.

'What do I want?' he muses. A door slams. There's a ripping sound.

'Mum!' The word is a knife to my heart.

My child.

He has Abby.

She drops her voice to a whisper. 'Mum, help me. Please.' There's the sound of a scuffle and Abby screams, but it is abruptly cut off. My heart jumps into my throat.

'We have things to discuss, Nicola,' Andrew Cargill says.

'Abby! Put Abby back on!' I'm out of bed now without even realising I've leapt up.

Mum appears, summoned by my screaming. I make a desperate 'be quiet' motion with my hand, then put the phone on speaker so she can hear.

'Abby will be fine,' Cargill says. 'If you do what I say. Meet me at the caretaker's cottage at your mother's. One hour.'

I open my mouth to ask him something then he adds, 'And don't call Lee. I'll talk to him. I'll tell him to stay away.'

'You know Lee?' My head is filled with Abby, but even through the fog it's obvious this is strange.

Cargill laughs. 'I know Lee very well. Although he was always Riley to me, back in his schooldays.'

Riley.

Where do I know that name from?

Cargill laughs again and I hear Sam in the sound. 'I sent Riley to find you a few years ago. And he did, though he never told me you killed Sam. Apparently he was so enamoured by the very sight of you that he uprooted his life and moved to Arundel. All to meet and woo you. He just never cared enough to tell you the truth.' There's a smile in his voice, but it is gone when he continues. 'If he comes with you to the cottage, I'll kill Abby.'

And then it hits me.

Sam's friends.

The uni friends. Smithy? No, *Jonesy.* That prick *Angus*, of course.

And his school friend. *Riley.*

Lee.

What the hell?

'He went to a public school …' My words peter out.

'No.' Andrew Cargill says in a pleased tone. 'He was a scholarship kid. Rugby.'

Lee lied to me. But my anger at him is swamped by fear for my daughter. 'He'll stay away,' I continue. 'I won't talk to him.' My words are garbled. Mum is pale and very still. 'This is between us. Let Abby go, drop her at the police station. I promise I'll come—'

'Your word is worth nothing. You are a murderer. Be at the cottage. One hour. Oh, and bring your mother. I saw her car at your house, and I don't want her running for help. If I hear police sirens, or helicopters – anything at all that makes me think you've told the police – then Abigail is dead.'

Bring your mother.

He wants to kill all three of us.

Cargill speaks as if he heard me. 'If you do as I say, I might let Abigail live. She is my granddaughter, after all.'

I peer over at Mum and almost recoil at the expression on her face. She looks like a snake ready to strike.

The phone goes dead.

ABBY

'So now we wait,' the man says.

The man, of course, is Andrew Cargill – my grandfather. I recognise him from TV and my Google searches. He grabbed me this morning on my way to Lili's house. Presumably he'd been watching us and took his chance when he could.

I totally freaked out at first, but now that I'm out of the car and at the caretaker's cottage at Hillcrest, which is at least familiar territory, I feel calmer. I might even get out of this alive.

The front porch is home to a table and two wrought-iron chairs draped with spider webs. Cargill gestures to the furthest one and I shuffle over and sit gingerly. He has taped my legs together at the knees but freed my ankles to allow me to walk, albeit awkwardly. I'd made it difficult for him to tie me up, aiming a headbutt at him that almost knocked his front teeth out. Unfortunately, he moved, and the blow glanced off his chin. Instead of being angry at my act of rebellion, Cargill had rubbed his face and watched me with what almost appeared to be admiration.

I stored that piece of information away for later.

He leans back in his seat. 'God, these chairs are uncomfortable,' he mutters. I lean forward as much as possible, silently agreeing with him, though it doesn't help that my hands are secured behind my back with cable ties that cut into my wrists, while my shoulders are stretched uncomfortably apart. I grunt and he looks at me. My eyebrows raise in an entreaty, and I grimace to make it clear I'm in pain.

'Fine,' he says. 'I'll remove the duct tape. Don't scream. No one can hear you anyway, and it will only give me a headache.'

My mouth flexes as he rips the tape free, but I don't let myself cry out.

'Thank you,' I wheeze. 'Could you tie my arms in front of me, please? They've gone to sleep and it's really painful.'

He watches me, his eyes sharp, then speaks. 'Don't even think about trying anything.' He digs around in his backpack for more cable ties, setting them on the table between us, then picks up a pocketknife and prises the blade free. He holds it in his left hand and walks behind me, the gun in his right hand trained on me. He slices through the cable tie and I sigh, rolling my shoulders and hissing in suppressed pain.

'Thank you.'

He walks back around and puts the gun on the table, just out of my reach, then quickly reties my hands, not quite so tightly as before. When he finishes, he sits back down and picks up the gun.

I stare at him. 'So, you're my grandfather?'

'Yes.'

'Andrew Cargill. I didn't suspect until a couple of weeks ago when I saw you on the news. Mum never told me. I can guess why.'

Cargill appraises me. 'You are an intriguing mix of both your parents, and yet nothing like either of them.'

I grunt. 'She and my father. I gather things didn't work out between them?' I hope that talking to him might be the first step in convincing him to let me go.

I can be very convincing when I want to be.

'That's one way of putting it.' Cargill raises the knife, examines the blade, holding it out for me to examine. 'This belonged to your mother.'

'What are the initials?' I ask.

'AJM.'

I think for a moment then say, 'Albert James Miller. That belonged to my grandfather.'

'Your mother used it to stab your father.'

'That's what killed him?'

'No. He died when she pushed him over a balcony into a ravine. She stabbed him with this first.' Cargill lays the knife on the table. 'I'm keen to use it on her.'

A jolt runs through me, but I don't show it. I simply nod. 'I get it. Poetic justice.'

This guy is a lunatic.

'Yes.'

'I understand why you want my mother dead.' I raise my eyebrows. 'But I'm your granddaughter. I can be anything to you. I can be all the things that Sam was.' His eyes widen in surprise. 'I know you, Andrew Cargill. You tell yourself you want to kill my mother in revenge for your son's death. But you know, and I know, that you want to kill for another reason entirely. Something much less noble.' I smile. 'You want to know what it feels like, don't you?'

Cargill is silent for a long moment. Then he smiles.

I continue. 'What does your wife think about all of this?' I'd noticed Cargill's glamorous wife was absent for most of the interviews where he spoke about finding Sam's killer.

'Lorraine?' His voice is raised in surprise. 'She knows nothing about it. Lorraine doesn't have the balls to be a part of this.' He sweeps a hand around to encompass his plan, though it really just highlights the overrun gardens and weed-infested gravel driveway in front of the cottage. 'She says that Sam would want me to move on. Well, I know Sam better than her. He only ever showed his mother his good little boy side. To me, he showed his whole self. He wasn't perfect, my son, I'm under no delusions about that. But he had spirit. He was going to take over my business, provide me with heirs. And now I'm left with nothing.' He pauses. 'Someone has to pay. Obviously. Of course, that someone should be your mother. But is that enough, I ask myself? Is her death enough to atone for Sam's? All these years she's been free. That's not fair. So, perhaps she owes me more.' He watches me. 'Perhaps she needs to pay with what's most valuable to her.'

The sound of a car turning onto the gravel driveway from the highway makes him look away.

I beckon him close with a tilt of my head. 'If you free me, I can help you.'

'You aren't scared?' he asks, examining me curiously.

'A bit. But we share blood. I'm not just Mum's. I'm *yours*.'

'Are you scared for your mother? Your grandmother?'

I can't help the flicker in my eyes. He sees it and I can see straight away I've lost him. He doesn't buy it.

'Yes,' I admit, changing tack. 'Although, if we're going by the odds, I'd put money on the Miller women. We've killed more people than you.'

NICOLA

'What do we do?' I ask Mum.

She's driving because I'm a mess. The paddocks outside Arundel flash past, a blur of khaki and grey. My brain is full of thoughts of Abby, bound and gagged and at the mercy of Sam Cargill's father. A man desperate for revenge, thanks to something I did.

I want to be sick.

My thoughts flick to Lee – *Riley*. I recall what Andrew Cargill said, that Lee knew about Sam before we even met. Lee and I had the same tastes in music, we loved jogging. Had he made all that up just to woo me? What else had he lied about?

Was our whole relationship a lie?

I can't think about Lee right now. It's too much.

Abby is what matters.

'We'll kill him, of course.' Mum says it so conversationally, I turn to gape at her. She glances at me. 'Cargill. Before he hurts Abby. We have no choice.'

'How?'

'Just follow my lead, darling.'

We turn off the highway onto the driveway leading to both Hillcrest and the caretaker's cottage. I grew up here. I'd fallen off my pushbike at the corner right over there, grazing my knee. I'd caught butterflies with a net down that gully. I know this place. I love it.

Will it be the place I take my last breath?

If it means Abby will live, I'll happily take my last breath here today.

I reach over and grip my mother's arm. Her skin is sun-damaged, freckled and dry. She's not a young woman anymore. That doesn't matter. I know her. I trust her. 'Focus on keeping Abby alive, Mum. Don't worry about me. The most important thing is to save Abby.'

She takes the bend with the practised ease of someone who's done this a million times. The cottage is straight ahead. I haven't been here in years, though I'm unsurprised to find it hasn't changed. A simple structure, it has a front porch with five steps. There's no railing on either the stairs or the porch, which wouldn't be to code now, though no one from the council would have been out here in decades. On the porch Andrew Cargill sits nearest the door, Abby on the other side of him. In Cargill's hand is a gun, trained on Abby.

My mouth feels as dry as the gravel road. I take a deep breath, trying to stay calm.

He stands up and steps forward as Mum kills the engine. He seems rattled. I run my eyes over Abby. She's composed.

What's she been saying to him?

I'm not sure if I'm proud of her or terrified for her.

Or terrified *of* her.

'What do we do?' I whisper to Mum. 'Do you have a plan?'

'I'm not exactly an expert, Nicola.' Does she sound *amused*? 'Though I'm confident we'll think of something. It's three to one, after all.'

'But he has a gun.'

'Yes, he does,' Mum says, thoughtfully. 'We'll have to fix that.'

ABBY

Cargill stands up and points the gun at Mum and Grandma.

'Welcome, ladies.'

They get out of the car, their hands in the air. Standing beside one another like that, they appear ordinary. Two smaller-than-average-sized women.

So *normal*.

I swallow. We have to survive this.

Cargill motions for Mum to walk around so that she is on the same side of the vehicle as Grandma.

I move and he glances my way, but I'm motionless again by then. Something rushes through me. Not fear. *Elation*. I wink at him, and he is taken aback.

'Welcome, Nicola. And Joyce.' He glances briefly at Grandma, then turns to examine Mum, his face cold. 'We finally meet. In my head you've been larger than life. For years I pictured you as a man. I thought perhaps Sam had slept with someone's wife or blackmailed an unsavoury type. Or that he'd simply wronged someone he couldn't charm. Briefly, I thought you might have been a burglar, that his death was accidental, but no, his murder was planned, or at least a decent attempt had been made to cover it up. Even though that hillbilly waitress from the café mentioned that Sam had been with a woman the morning he went missing, I never seriously suspected a female might have killed him. It turned out I was wrong.' He gives Mum a bitter smile. 'And now I see that you're just an ordinary woman.' He sneers. 'You've told your mother what you did?'

'Not in detail.' Mum's voice wavers, her fear palpable. 'But she knows.'

'You never thought you should report what your daughter did to the authorities?' he asks Grandma, looking her up and down.

The tilt of Grandma's chin is defiant, which doesn't surprise me. 'No.' She expels a puff of air through her lips. 'Would you have done that to your son?'

'He didn't kill anyone.'

'He raped my daughter,' she spits at him. Cargill doesn't respond. 'So, what's your plan? You'll shoot us.' She motions to the gun. 'Then what?'

'The clean-up will be my problem.'

'He'll get his goons in,' I offer. 'That's what his kind of people do. Rich people.'

'I'm here myself, aren't I?' Cargill can't help rising to my bait. He's ridiculously proud he's done all this without relying on his staff. 'I haven't needed any assistance. No one knows I'm here. I want to finish this myself.' He indicates for them both to come up the stairs. 'I'll shoot you up here, then burn the house down. It's all ready to go in there.' He waves the gun at the house. 'I just need to slosh some petrol around and strike a match.'

He pulls me to my feet and steps to the right, dragging me with him. 'Come on. Nicola first.'

Mum gives me a look of pure love. Cargill sees it and smiles. He's happy at our pain.

I won't let him win.

NICOLA

'Get a move on!' He shoves the gun against Abby's temple.

'No! Please! I'm coming.' I start up the steps. Mum follows more slowly, very slowly, as if it's difficult for her. I almost tell her to hurry up, fearing for Abby's life, but something stops me. I reach the porch and stand with my hands raised, facing him.

Mum treads on the first step, then stumbles. 'My knee!'

Cargill points the gun at her but he's watching Abby and me too.

Mum falters again, falling a little to one side. Cargill glances at me to make sure I'm not about to lunge at him, but I'm as surprised by Mum's feebleness as he is.

'My knee!' Mum says again, pain in her voice.

Cargill's attention is on her when Abby moves.

He spins, but before he can swing the gun around, Abby is at him and he cries out in pain.

He steps back and then I see it. The pocketknife – my dad's pocketknife, the one I'd left behind in Edmonton all those years ago – is sticking out of his side.

Abby has stabbed him.

Cargill is blinking at her, confused.

'You got distracted,' Abby says with a shake of her head. 'A rookie mistake.' Her hands are still bound in front of her, and she shuffles back a little, breathing heavily.

Cargill touches the knife, watches blood bloom around the protruding handle. He stumbles but remains upright.

'You should have kept my hands tied behind my back,' Abby says. Then she peers beyond him.

Cargill pivots. Too late. Mum steps forward, a bat in her hand. A cricket bat. I can't help but think how odd that is. She swings it, all signs of frailty gone, and Cargill drops to the porch with a grunt, the gun spinning across the wooden floor as he stops his fall with his hands. He pushes himself up so he's kneeling in front of Mum.

He almost looks like he's praying.

Abby's eyes are wide, but not with fear. She moves closer to him. 'This, right here, this is how it feels,' she tells him, in not much more than a whisper.

He hisses in anger or fear, I can't decipher it.

'You'll never know this feeling.' She walks over and picks up his gun. 'Remember our chat about poetic justice, Grandad? Can I call you Grandad?' She raises her eyebrows and Cargill sways but stays on his knees. 'You should have paid more attention. Also, you've got to keep track of your weapons.' She shrugs. 'It's murder 101.' Abby turns to me.

'Mum?' She beckons and I go to her. We hug. Standing beside her, I peer down at Cargill. Mum joins me, her shoulder touching mine.

Cargill looks at us. 'The Miller women.' He wheezes the words, then coughs and blood speckles his hand.

'Do you want to finish this?' Abby holds the gun out to me. I glance from Mum to my daughter, then take it and aim it at Cargill, who stares down the barrel.

I pull the trigger.

JOYCE

One of Cargill's legs is at an awkward angle and the top of his head is missing. To my left, Nicola still holds the gun, the barrel pointing to where the man had knelt a moment earlier. My ears ring. Nicola's hair is wild, her face slick with perspiration, the underarms of her shirt damp with sweat.

I look down at my hands and heft the cricket bat. I can hardly believe it was still there.

Thank you, Marjorie.

On my other side, Abby is inspecting what's left of Cargill, her lips parted. In contrast to her mother, she is calm, with a light in her eyes that makes her glow. She turns to me, holding the knife out to me from her bound hands. I take it, sawing through the cable ties to free her arms and then the duct tape around her knees. Abby did well to palm the knife when Cargill was distracted. She stretches and shakes her head. Her ears must be ringing too.

'Nicola,' I tell my motionless daughter, using a gentle voice. 'Call Lee. We're going to need his help.'

*

We stand by the foxgloves in the front garden.

The ground has been disturbed again, though it's nothing that can't be explained away by a little light gardening. I regard Nicola and Abby, both of them filthy with blood and soil.

'Poetic justice,' Abby whispers.

I sense Nicola's eyes on me. She's worried about Abby's part in this; I'm not. I don't turn to my daughter. I don't reassure her. Nicola needs to accept her daughter for what she is.

'Yes.' I agree with my granddaughter. 'Good fertiliser too.'

'The cottage is ready to go.' Lee's voice comes from behind us. He is speaking into his phone. 'Thanks, mate. I owe you one. We all do.' He puts his phone away.

'Hudson's on board,' he says.

'What did you tell him?'

'Not everything. Enough. He's going to be your alibi. He's been cooking all day – making a stew – cassoulet, he called it. It was going to be a fancy dinner for him and Jeff, though now it's for all of you. He says there'll be enough, certainly for our purposes at any rate. You've been there enjoying drinks all afternoon, and soon you'll have dinner there too.' He studies his stepdaughter. 'Abby, you'll need to do a dessert like you would usually do. Hudson says he's got most things – eggs, milk, cream, flour, chocolate. You can't go to the shop. Can you come up with something?'

'Yes.' Abby thinks. 'Flan pâtissier.' She sees our incomprehension. 'It's a fancy French custard tart. I've been meaning to cook it for ages. It'll work.'

'Perfect.'

Lee takes in our bedraggled state. 'Shower here first. Then go straight to Hudson's house. Try not to be seen,' he says to Nicola, unable to meet her eyes. 'Stay together. Create an airtight alibi. I'll finish this off.'

'You've planted the evidence?' Abby asks and Lee flinches.

He wasn't keen on this, but we didn't give him a lot of choice.

'Yes. It's done.'

'So, when questioned I'll tell the police there have been lots of visitors to and from the cottage, especially at night, as well as a strange chemical smell.' I try to calm his nerves. 'Anything else?'

'No, that should do it. The place is really going to burn. Cargill had a lot of petrol inside and I've used it all. Thankfully, there was already word out on the street that there's a new dealer in town. With that, and the stuff I took from Seth's place, well, it'll be enough.'

Breaking into the drug dealer's place was a risk, one Lee thought was worth it. The man was hardly going to report his missing drug-making supplies to the police. It was a good point. I was impressed with how well Lee was handling our peculiar dilemma.

'Won't the drug-making evidence burn up?' Nicola asks.

'I've placed it strategically. It'll burn but there are enough plastics and glass to give forensics something.' He sighs. 'Now go. Leave the rest to me.'

'I'll have first shower,' Abby says. 'I've still got spare clothes upstairs, don't I?'

'Yes. They're in the tallboy.'

She gives me a curt nod, then goes inside.

'I'll check in your wardrobe, Mum,' Nicola says. 'See what I can find to borrow.'

Lee keeps his eyes averted from Nicola as she passes him. I'm not sure their relationship will survive this. Maybe it shouldn't.

The main thing to worry about right now is how to keep us all out of prison.

I take one last look at the pretty foxgloves and then at Nicola as she approaches me. 'It's done now, darling. It's over.'

She halts. 'Those secrets we said we were going to tell Lee and Abby? Maybe we should reconsider.' She tilts her head and for a moment all of them are in her. Abby. Cara. Donna.

And Bert, of course.

'Abby can't know that Cara was her half-cousin. Ever.'

Nicola is right. 'I agree. What's one more secret?'

26 August

Police have requested anyone with information about missing Sydney property developer Andrew Cargill to please come forward to assist with the investigation into his disappearance.

Cargill was reported missing by his wife, Lorraine, two days ago after failing to return from a reported business trip to Brisbane. There are no records of flights or other travel documents in his name.

Police remain baffled by the case, refusing to rule out the possibility that Cargill attempted to fake his own death. Grave concerns are held for the multi-millionaire's welfare and Lorraine Cargill is offering a substantial reward – one million dollars – for information leading to his whereabouts.

Anyone with information is urged to contact Crime Stoppers.

27 August

In local news, a suspicious house fire that gutted a cottage outside of Arundel earlier this week has been now linked to drug use. The Airbnb, once the caretaker's cottage for well-known homestead Hillcrest, went up in smoke on Thursday night.

A police statement says drug paraphernalia was found among the remnants of the fire, which burned so brightly that fire crews were forced to keep back at the height of the blaze.

According to Detective Sergeant Lee Cook, of the Arundel Police, the male who had rented the property for the period in question had given a false name to the website.

No evidence of human remains was found by the fire department.

EPILOGUE
Six months later

ABBY

'Hey, Mr Foley, what can I get you?'

My History teacher is next in line. He's with his cute daughter, who examines the display cabinet with awe. Intricately decorated mini cupcakes, generous slices of dense mud cakes and light sponges with passionfruit icing, macarons in five colours – I've been busy this week.

Killer Cakes has taken Arundel by storm. I've been run off my feet for the past month. I make everything from scratch, from those delicious, delicate macarons right up to three-tiered wedding cakes to order. One of our best sellers is the white chocolate and macadamia slice I call the Cara. Mum and Grandma gave me a sideways look when I added that to the chalkboard out the front. The rest of the town assumed it was a tribute to a friend taken too soon.

It turns out I didn't need to leave Arundel. Everything I wanted was right here.

I took Grandma up on her offer of the patisserie, but I study psychology part-time too. It's fascinating to learn about the science behind our actions. To delve into why people behave the way they do.

The shop is exquisite, decorated like a traditional patisserie with pastel pink walls, an old-fashioned awning along the front window and shelves lined with expensive baking supplies. It smells of sugar and spice and … well, you get the drift.

'Two slices of cheesecake, one cupcake and two vanilla slices, thanks Abby. Oh, and a couple of pistachio macarons for your mum, eh, Josie? They're her favourite.' The little girl nods, her eyes still on the cupcakes. 'Takeaway please.'

'Coming right up.'

Mr Foley seems happy, and I'm pleased. That Friday, the last time I saw Cara outside his house, I knew then that she had to go. In fact, I'd already set it in motion. It wasn't luck that I ran into her there. Cara had neglected to delete herself from the location settings on the app our group used. I'd been brooding since our fight and when I saw she'd returned to school to study in the library, I spied on her from a distance. When she drove off in her mum's car I followed her to Mr Foley's, then watched her scurry outside when his wife and kids arrived home. I confronted her on the footpath.

'Abby!' Cara had said when she saw me, sounding delighted. I found it unreasonably annoying that she hadn't been put out. 'Are you following me?'

'Is he one of your clients?' I asked, motioning to the house. I'd always respected Mr Foley.

'Mr Foley?' She'd laughed. 'A foot-fetishist? No. He's a do-gooder sticking his nose into my business. I've handled him. Left a little surprise for his wife to find. What are you doing here?'

'Did you contact Andrew Cargill?'

'What's it to you? We aren't friends anymore.'

'Don't do this, Cara. Mum doesn't deserve it.'

I reached out and touched her arm and I felt that same zing I'd felt when I'd touched her that very first day. She'd been a sickly little thing, but she had a spark I couldn't resist.

I hadn't imagined it. There *was* something between us. I didn't know what it was, only that it was big. Important.

For a second I wondered if I should stop everything I'd put into motion. ⁂

When Cara told me she'd slept with Lee, I'd made a decision. I saw Mrs Ross at the hospital as I left with Mum and I followed her. I told her about her daughter's foot-fetish website, which horrified her. I didn't expect her to confront Cara and kill her, though I have to admit I wasn't too disappointed.

That day outside Mr Foley's house, I could have told Cara that I'd exposed her to her mother, but I didn't. I thought about it. I mean, a tiny part of me almost felt sorry for her. *Almost.* After all, her own mother had been poisoning her for years. I'd overheard Dr Patrick and Dr Grange talking about it in the hospital café.

'We should have done more to protect that child,' Dr Grange had grumbled, his eyes on Cara's retreating back. 'That woman brought her in too many times, with too many unexplained illnesses.'

'You think it was Munchausen by proxy?'

'Don't you?'

'Maybe. But you couldn't prove it. And she got better, so at least it worked out in the end.'

That day outside Mr Foley's, I told her I knew what Mrs Ross had done to her when she was a kid, and I asked why she'd never gone to the police. She'd laughed, a bitter sound. 'Why? So they can throw her in jail? No. I get my own back. How do you think I got her to let me come to your school?'

'Why'd you want to do that, anyway?' I asked, genuinely curious. I always figured Cara had some ulterior motive, but I could never work out what it was.

She'd stared at me, then shrugged and spoke lightly, 'A spur of the moment thing. A whim.'

I didn't believe her.

Her phone had buzzed. She smiled widely when she saw the message. 'Gotta go.' She gave me a calculating look, then added, 'I need my beauty sleep before I collect my cash.'

She left me without a backwards glance, her blonde hair swishing across her back. I turned towards the house. A woman stood at the window, Mr Foley's wife, presumably. I walked away.

'Here you go, Mr Foley,' I say now. 'On the house. For my favourite teacher.' I'm pleased he and his wife have managed to sort things out.

'Abby! You don't have to do that.'

'I insist.'

It was outside Mr Foley's house that I first realised something.

Sometimes it was *necessary* for a person to die. Now that Cara is gone, my heart is lighter. Every time someone orders the Cara I feel a jolt of joy.

The bell dings as Mr Foley leaves. My grandmother enters and smiles at me from the doorway.

'Emily, can you handle the counter for a minute?' I've hired a year ten student from Arundel to help out on busy weekends. Mandy now works for me too, she's our barista.

I walk around the counter and meet Grandma near the door. 'Need some macarons for the CWA?' I tease.

'This whole enterprise has ruined that little scam. They're onto me now!' She laughs. 'No, I wanted to tell you that the coroner's report for Donna Ross's death came in today.'

Mrs Ross lasted a week in hospital, dying in her hospital room, alone.

'Her death was attributed to an arrhythmia of the heart,' Grandma says, 'thought to possibly be due to the trauma of being strangled by Mike.'

We share a look.

'Foxglove has much the same effect on the heart,' she says.

Grandma and I share a look of understanding.

She knows what I am.

Right from the start, the day I told her how happy it had made me feel to see Isabella on the floor, the life leaching from her body. I admitted to her that watching Isabella almost die was the most exhilarating thing I'd ever seen.

Grandma knows me.

I glance up and see Mum and Lee enter. They're arm in arm and smile when they see us.

'Busy as usual, hon?' Mum asks after giving me a hug.

'Yes. I'll have to get back in the kitchen later.'

'Do you have time for a quick coffee break?' Lee asks.

'Sure.'

'You ladies sit. I'll fetch the drinks. I'm going to choose something sweet too.' He grins. 'I wonder if the management took note of the request for doughnuts I put in the suggestion box.'

'We don't have a suggestion box, and I told you I'm not making doughnuts especially for the police.' I poke my tongue out at him.

He points a finger at me. 'I'll remember that, young lady.' He smiles and walks over to the counter, while the three of us sit at a nearby table.

I think about telling Mum and Grandma about my new tattoo – a knife with a drop of blood on it, high up on my rib cage – but I decide against it. Perhaps the fact that I've had a reminder of all that's happened lately inked onto my body is not something I should share with them.

That's okay, I'm very good at keeping secrets.

'Have you heard from Hudson yet? I've been so busy I haven't had a chance to call him.' Hudson and Jeff moved to Perth last week, deciding it was time they made a new start, just the two of them.

'They're loving it over there,' Mum says. 'Lee and I might visit at Easter.'

'Lee's happy to go?'

'It's weird – he and Hudson get along better than ever now.'

We are quiet for a moment. I suppose the others are remembering that day too. Washing the metallic blood and the dark earth from our bodies, driving back to town, the car smelling of soap and shampoo. I can still taste Hudson's cassoulet with its creamy beans, meaty pork belly and rich duck leg, the bone slipping free at the first touch of my fork, followed by the vanilla egginess of my flan pâtissier with its flaky, buttery pastry. The pleasure of that dinner returns to my mind, how we'd eaten every last crumb, not left a drop of custard.

We'd savoured that meal as if it was our last.

'Did you apply for that job, Mum?'

'Not yet.' Mum scrunches up her face. 'I'm not sure it's right for me.'

'A freelance role for a real newspaper? You'd get to write the sort of articles you love to write,' Grandma says. Her brows knit together. 'It's not Lee, is it? I thought he was fine with it.'

'Oh, he is.' Mum smiles. Lee and Mum seem to have got past the secrets they'd kept from one another. Apparently, covering up a crime can occasionally bring a couple closer together. 'It's just that there's something else I might like to do.' She hesitates. 'I thought I might try my hand at fiction. Maybe a thriller. Nothing that has any basis in fact, naturally,' she hurriedly adds. 'I want to write something that makes the reader's heart race. Does that make sense?'

What happened out at Hillcrest appears to have offered Mum some sort of closure. She's brighter now, her movements lighter. She's cut back on her boxing and taken up yoga. She might have been the most reluctant of the Miller women, but murder seems to suit her best of all.

Grandma regards her for a long moment, then smiles. 'I can't wait to read it.'

I nod my agreement, then Mum glances at Lee before speaking. 'I saw on the news last night that Angus –' his name catches in her throat, but she continues '– Fraser has taken over as the CEO of the Sam Cargill Group.'

'Angus?' Grandma asks, leaning back. 'Sam's friend ... from Banff?'

'The one who ...' I add, letting the words peter out. Mum had told us the whole story as we drove from Hillcrest to Hudson's house six months ago. How Sam was ready to 'share' her with his friends. Later that night, Lee had explained that he'd never seen either Angus or Jonesy after Canada. Said they were as despicable as they sounded.

'Yes, him,' Mum says, but her voice is tentative. Wary. Seeing her like that after her newfound confidence of just a moment before fills my lungs, my brain — my dark, magnificent *soul* — with sudden rage. I glance at Grandma. The set of her jaw tells me all I need to know.

'So, Angus has made a big success of himself, has he?' she replies mildly. 'That's not right, is it? That's not ... *just.*'

'No, it isn't,' I reply.

Mum turns from me to Grandma, then back again.

We all sit quietly for a moment.

Then I say, slowly, 'Perhaps there's something we can do about that.'

Acknowledgements

This is the fourth novel I've published with HarperCollins, and I count myself incredibly lucky to work with such an amazing team. *The Miller Women* was such a joy to write. I adore Abby, Nicola and Joyce and it was so much fun slipping into the skins of those very different women, each from a different generation.

Thanks to everyone at HarperCollins, particularly my brilliant and kind publisher, Anna Valdinger. To my editors, Madeleine James and Deonie Fiford, for picking up my errors and not making me feel bad about writing them in the first place, and to Pam Dunne for her thorough proofreading. Thanks also to the HarperCollins publicity team for their insightful marketing advice and support. A big shout out to HarperCollins Design Studio, particularly Louisa Maggio, for another gorgeous cover. I love how each one just gets creepier and creepier (please don't judge me)!

And of course, thank you to my family, especially my kids, for putting up with my 'writer's brain' gibberish and the post-it notes that litter the house with odd, confusing or sometimes downright disturbing messages scribbled on them, such as 'Give Abby a tattoo?', 'add in bit at end' and 'stabbed or poisoned?'

Huge thanks must also go to my readers, who are so loyal and lovely. I am very grateful to all those who read and review my books on social media. Your support is invaluable, not just to me but to so many Australian writers.

Finally, thanks as always must particularly go to my agent, Melanie Ostell, for all her ongoing support.

KELLI HAWKINS

THE PERFECT HOUSE.
THE PERFECT FAMILY.
TOO GOOD TO BE TRUE

OTHER
PEOPLE'S
HOUSES

The perfect family. Too good to be true.

Kate Webb still grieves over the loss of her young son. Ten years
on, she spends her weekends hungover, attending open houses on
Sydney's wealthy north shore and imagining the lives of the people
who live there.

Then Kate visits the Harding house – the perfect house with,
it seems, the perfect family. A photograph captures a kind-looking
man, a beautiful woman she knew at university, and a boy – a boy
that for one heartbreaking moment she believes is her own son.

When her curiosity turns to obsession, she uncovers the cracks
that lie beneath a glossy facade of perfection, sordid truths she
could never have imagined.

But is it her imagination? As events start to spiral dangerously
out of control, could the real threat come from Kate herself?

'An intriguing psychological thriller with a brilliant
twist at the end' *Australian Women's Weekly*

Ask no questions. Tell no lies.

Lindsay just wants to be a mother. And when she discovers her partner is leaving her for another woman, her dreams are left in tatters. He was her last chance at a family ... or was he?

Then she meets Jack; they fall hard for each other, and suddenly everything seems perfect. But why is his sister, Natalie, so strangely protective of him, yet eager to pass the responsibility to Lindsay? Who are these siblings, why did they really leave the UK, and what terrifying secrets lie in their past?

And does Lindsay really want to know?

'Intricately crafted, twisty and unputdownable, *All She Wants* is
a gripping domestic thriller, perfect for readers of Gillian Flynn'
Better Reading

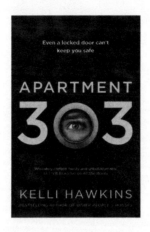

Even a locked door can't keep you safe.

Twenty-six-year-old Rory rarely leaves her apartment, though her little dog, Buster, keeps her company. Days are spent working for her aunt's PI business, and watching and imagining histories for the homeless men, the Dossers, across the road. At night she walks Buster on the roof, gazes at the stars and wonders.

The night before New Year's Eve, one of the Dossers is murdered, an incident which brings the world – police, new neighbours, her dark past and new possibilities – crashing through Rory's front door.

She thought she was keeping her fears at bay. But has her sanctuary turned into her prison? Or is it safer for everyone if Rory stays locked away?

'Hawkins continues to show her expertise in the psychological thriller genre through her fantastic and layered exploration of a troubled narrator in a sinister plot. Rory is an utterly intriguing protagonist ... Each line resonates with a building sense of danger that will keep readers guessing ... [and] on the edge of their seats with every chapter. It's a perfect, simmering slow burn that gets your heart pounding ... I couldn't put it down!' *Better Reading*